His Chance

by

Sheila Kell

HIS Series, Book Four

Cover Art by *Lea Schizas*

The Wild Rose Press, Inc.
PO Box 708
Adams Basin, NY 14410-0708
Visit us at www.thewildrosepress.com

Publishing History
First Edition, 2024
Trade Paperback ISBN 978-1-5092-5722-5
Digital ISBN 978-1-5092-5723-2

HIS Series, Book Four
Previously Published by Cunningham Publishing 2017
Published in the United States of America

Dedication

To Christine Ardigo
The best book wifey

A Note from Sheila

Thank you for taking the time to read *His Chance*! If you enjoy Devon and Rylee's story, I would be grateful if you could help spread the word and recommend it to your friends, readers' groups, and discussion boards. It would mean a great deal to me if you could write an honest review and share your thoughts on my story. Your reviews can bring my work to the attention of other readers. The good news is that you only need to write a few words. Thank you again for your support!

Prologue

Fogginess attempted to lift itself from her thoughts but failed miserably. Rylee's head throbbed and her stomach roiled. Her eyes fought to open, then after the success of only a small slit, the blinding light of the day urged them closed. Her waking mind attempted to process what her eyes weren't seeing. Not an easy task when it was ready to explode from pain.

Lying on her right side in a soft bed, Rylee Hawkins tried again and blinked slowly, opening her eyes a fraction more with each painful blink. The wall in front of her was actually a wall of glass supporting a set of patio doors with golden handles in the middle. Long, thick, navy blue curtains with thin cream inserts hung aside to display a balcony that housed a small wrought-iron table, two chairs, and two empty wine glasses. Tall buildings stood in view with the sun shining behind them, which increased the beating tempo in her head. Beside the comfortable bed, a solitary lamp sat upon a light-colored wood nightstand.

Nothing was familiar. Her gut told her it was a hotel room. She just had no idea which or where. Rylee was mildly aware that this was the point when most would panic. Instead, she could barely muster confusion. She squinted and ignored the shot of agony behind her eyes to read a sign flashing in the distance. The Las Vegas strip.

Closing her eyes, Rylee groaned. She and her FBI teammates had taken a long weekend break after closing a major case and thought this would be a great place to visit since Sara and Zack, two fellow agents, wanted to marry right away.

She searched her mind and came up mostly blank of the prior evening's events. They'd made it to the chapel, and an Elvis impersonator had married the two. While it wasn't how she'd want to be married, to each his own. Zack was a huge Elvis fan and Sara loved Zack. So, Elvis it was.

Thinking back, she remembered them going to a casino bar to celebrate. Then…nothing. With the monster hangover she had, she must've had way, and she meant *way* too much to drink. That wasn't like her.

Rylee considered it pretty fucked up she couldn't remember most of the night. She hoped she hadn't made a sloppy mess of herself. That type of embarrassment she didn't need with the other agents.

Swallowing past what felt like a wad of cotton lodged in her throat, she decided it was too early to deal with anything. Her flight wasn't until close to noon. First, she'd get up, relieve her full bladder, take several aspirin and close the damn drapes. Then she'd set her alarm and slip back into la-la-land. Maybe she'd wake refreshed and remember the evening. She just couldn't believe she'd been stupid enough to drink to excess like that.

"Good morning, beautiful," a gravelly, male voice said from behind her.

Her eyes flew open and she stiffened. Holy shit! A man was in her bed. How had she not realized that? Panic and shame flushed through her, washing away any discomfort from her hangover. What the hell had she done?

Without moving her head, she glanced around for a weapon and noticed the white lamp. *Fuck. Fuck. Fuck.* She wasn't even in her room. The bedside lamps in her room were baby blue.

Rylee squeezed her eyes shut. She couldn't face what she'd done. Getting out of this room and away from this man was imperative.

She spotted clothing tossed haphazardly in front of the patio doors, like the owners had been unable to get them off fast enough when they'd come in from the balcony. She couldn't get to them without exposing herself to her bed partner. That she didn't want to do. At least not again... knowingly.

Since she never had a one-night stand before, she didn't know how to properly extricate herself. Did he expect her to roll over and continue what had obviously occurred the night before? Sexy as that voice sounded, it wouldn't happen.

When a hand touched her arm, she reacted and launched herself from the bed and to her clothing. Screw him seeing her naked body again. "I... need to... go-o," she stammered as she pulled her blue dress over her head. Fuck it. She'd carry her undergarments. She'd just have to experience the walk of shame.

Rustling sheets and a slight squeak of the mattress alerted her to his exiting the bed. "Rylee, what's the matter?"

Crap. He knew her name, and she had no idea who he was. She couldn't even bring herself to look at him. "Look, last night was fun and all"—she snagged her black stilettos—"but that's all it was. I'll see you around." Or at least she assumed it had been. Her memory was still misbehaving.

He stood behind her. His close presence had her breathing heavily and trembling with need. Christ, had he slipped her a roofie or something? That could be why everything was blank. She hadn't had a drunken blackout since one stupid night when she'd been eighteen. After that, she'd learned to limit the amount of alcohol she consumed. She liked being in control too much.

She reached the desk to grab her purse, and he touched her arm again. Her heart hammering, she reacted in a flight-or-fight mode. Actually, she did both. She snatched the only weapon she saw—the large ceramic desk lamp—and swung it at the man's head.

He staggered a moment, then collapsed to the floor.

She picked up her purse and rushed to the door, only to stop for a moment as her conscience pricked her. Shit. Quickly, she moved back to the man, knelt and checked his pulse. Steady. Good. No blood. Good. *Now, get the hell out of here, Rylee*, she told herself.

Yet, she had to take a good look at him. She didn't want to walk up to him one day and find out later he happened to be the man she'd been so drunk she forgot she'd fucked.

Handsome. Sexy. Dark hair, albeit a bit longer than she'd usually choose. Toned body. She hadn't chosen a slouch, that was for sure. His face would not easily be forgotten. His strong jaw teased her memory. It seemed familiar, yet she couldn't recall ever seeing this man before. Maybe it was just teasing her memory from the evening before. Or, he could just look similar to someone she knew. She told herself to leave before he woke because he might want to kick the shit out of her for hitting him.

A niggling feeling told her that he wouldn't be that way, but she didn't plan to stick around and find out if her instincts were on target or not. Standing, she saw his wallet on the desk and reached for it. She wanted to know who he was. When he moaned, she snatched her empty hand back.

Her blood gushed through her veins, and her pulse skipped erratically. She had to escape. Back at the door, she opened it and peeked outside. Seeing no one in the hallway, she slipped through the opening and a sense of panic hit her full force, almost knocking her back into the room. *Please, God, let this at least be my hotel.* She peeked at the room number and exhaled loudly to see it was in the same design as hers. Shoulders sagging, she turned to the elevator.

Back in her room, four floors up, she stripped the dress over her head on her walk to the shower. She had to get clean. She'd fucking had a one-night stand with a stranger and didn't remember a moment of it. How did she wash away the dirt and disgust she felt worming their way around her insides?

The thought of his waking right away and seeking her out pushed her into action. He knew her name. At least her first name. She didn't plan to see if he knew more.

After a hot shower, she glanced at the time and rushed to pack her bag. Not realizing it had been so late in the morning, she'd taken a leisurely shower. If she took a taxi rather than relying on the courtesy transport, she hoped to make her flight check-in time.

She wanted nothing else to do with this city and

doubted she'd ever return. Rylee just hoped she hadn't told the man in the bed too much about herself because she didn't wish for him to just show up out of the blue wanting more of whatever she'd given him.

With that thought, Rylee wanted to smack herself on the forehead and shout, "Stupid. Stupid. Stupid." But her head still hurt too much for that abuse.

Once in the cab on the way to the airport, she remained rankled that the desk agent at the hotel hadn't given her the stranger's name, even after she'd flashed her badge. Admittedly, she knew they were following protocol, but she was hardly in the right mind for sane decisions, as made evident from the previous night. She sighed as she stared out of the vehicle's window. It had been her last chance to find out who he was without asking him directly, and since she'd knocked him unconscious, she couldn't do that.

Before long, she'd made it to the airport, in just enough time to check in and grab herself a coffee. Settling into her seat on the flight back to Baltimore, she took a deep breath and heaved a sigh of relief for being rid of the city. Finally, her body began to settle. The reaction to what she'd done—sleeping with the stranger and hitting him on the head for no reason—had sent an adrenaline rush spiraling through her to get the hell out of Vegas. Her trembling hands on her lap grabbed her attention. *Oh shit.* She couldn't get away fast enough.

Chapter One

Ten months later

Rylee Hawkins jumped at the sound of her name and looked around to the door. Dammit. She'd been thinking of her Vegas trip again. Most days she tried to pretend it was only a dream. Only, it'd been real as hell, and she couldn't forget it…or him.

Eight months later, when she'd returned home from one of the worst ops in her life, she'd finally read his messages. He'd attempted to reach out to her a month after Vegas, and tried consecutively for a few months before he'd finally given up. The kicker was, she wasn't quite sure how she'd felt about that at the time. The fact he'd attempted to pursue her had done all sorts of things to her heart and libido, but so much time had passed since Vegas, she'd had no intention of reaching out to him. Plus, she had still been embarrassed about her drunken behavior.

Yet, Devon Hamilton—a man she'd never met before Vegas—discovered she was back on the grid and had managed to make one last attempt at contacting her. It was a call that she pushed fiercely to the back of her mind and buried as deeply as possible.

Every memory and association with Vegas was marked by anger, confusion, and disappointment. It was best off forgotten and left in the past.

"Rylee," an insistent voice called, breaching the bubble of her wayward thoughts.

She looked at the man attempting to gain her attention.

God, she was exhausted. It had been a shitty night. No longer an FBI agent, as co-owner and acting manager of Pynk Nightclub, she dealt with women who liked to let loose. That evening it'd been a woman who kept groping a waiter, a jealous customer's fiancé who just knew she was having an affair with the bartender, said bartender who made a pass at a different bride-to-be, and two women who passed out in the bathroom. She hated bachelorette party nights. They drew a crowd, but the headache wasn't necessarily worth the revenue. She'd have to speak with her stepsister and business partner, Madison Maxwell, about it when they saw each other next.

Who knew when that would be? As a supermodel, Madison traveled extensively. She'd purchased the club a year ago and had convinced Rylee to buy in with her so they'd have something to rely on after they were done with their current careers. It had only taken Rylee a few months and her growing frustration with the restraints enforced by the FBI to convince her to make the change sooner rather than later. While a club was a far cry from her experience and knowledge, she had known staying in the FBI would have eventually broken her. That had been about the time the club manager they'd hired had walked away without a word—with one of the bartenders. Now, to keep herself busy, and paid, she ran the business. At least she'd finally been able to put her business degree to use.

The male voice repeated her name.

She smiled at him. Brent Fuller. Not the man in her dream, but a damn fine guy. He'd stayed over from a get-together with his buddies to walk her to her car. He was a blond, fun-loving Immigration and Customs Agent she'd met while they were both undercover on her last job with the bureau, and he'd clung to her ever since. Yet, he'd never been pushy. In fact, she wasn't sure if he truly wanted her, or if it was just fun play for him to try to win the one who wouldn't drool at his feet.

She stood from the leather chair in the manager's office and walked around the wooden desk to where he'd been waiting to escort her out of the building.

"Are you sure you won't marry me?" A glint of humor laced Brent's voice.

She smiled at his persistence. "Yes, I'm sure. You know as well as I do that it wouldn't last. We'd end up hating each other." Without a spark, and there was none, which she admitted was a shame because he was handsome and kind and would be a great Prince Charming, she couldn't do it without something holding them together. Besides—

He placed a hand on her arm, then lifted his other hand to lightly stroke her face.

A ripple of unease infiltrated her body.

"You know that won't happen to us. I won't allow it to happen." His mouth turned up into a sweet, yet determined smile.

She shook her head. Had he stopped joking? "Brent, we don't love each other. I told you I'd only marry for love."

"Ah, that's where you're wrong. I love you, Rylee."

Stunned, she swallowed hard, and with her heart

pounding, she could only stare. Could that be true? Good grief. What had she done to lead him on so? She'd never even allowed him to kiss or hold her. Well, he had held her when she'd cried over losing track of the girls during their joint mission. But that hadn't been intimate. At least, not to her. She had to stop this now because she couldn't tell if he was still having fun or being dead serious.

Brent placed his index finger over her lips, effectively silencing her. "Don't say anything now. Just think about it. I mean it. I want to marry you because I love you."

Without giving her a chance to respond, he swooped down and kissed her, a mere touch of the lips. He pulled back before she could push him away. "Now, let's get you home to that ice cream you've been craving."

Rylee frowned, bewildered at this change of atmosphere for them.

He laughed and reached his hand out for the keys to lock the front door of the club. Pynk had been a refuge of sorts after she'd left the FBI. While she'd come out of her last op without injury, they'd lost track of some of the young girls Keith Westbrook had sold into sexual slavery. Her gut clenched at what the girls must be enduring.

Hired as a maid for that creep Westbrook, she'd kept a close eye on the girls he had kidnapped. When the time finally came, as a housekeeper, she'd snuck into their room to prepare the girls for their rescue by the bureau that evening. They had been so scared, and she couldn't blame them for their fear. The fear of knowing something was going to happen…but not knowing what, had to be turmoil. But Rylee knew the plan for the girls. That night, the girls were scheduled to be sold to the highest bidder. The FBI would get both sides of the sick equation and save the girls in the process.

Only, two of the seven girls had not been there that morning. According to the remaining victims, the two had been taken during the night. They hadn't seen who had snatched them since their room was kept dark.

The FBI made the raid as planned and saved the remaining five girls, plus they arrested the sickos who'd sought to purchase them. But they couldn't find anything about where the missing two girls were located. Misty and Mandy—identical twins—had vanished.

She'd failed them. Sure, she wasn't the only person who'd worked the case, but she'd held a certain personal responsibility for them since it'd been her job to keep an eye on the girls.

"Rylee?"

Placing a smile on her face, she willed the memory to vanish and brought herself back to answering Brent. "I'll think about it." She hated giving him hope, but after the night she'd had…the daydream of Devon…and thinking of how she'd failed the girls, this discussion was the last thing she wanted to deal with.

In a synchronous manner that suggested they'd done this quite frequently together, he switched the lights off while she set the alarm. Amidst the beeps of the security system, they exited through the heavy wooden door. As Brent locked it, Rylee glanced around the parking lot with only their two cars in attendance.

Pynk was an exclusive nightclub. She'd originally

scoffed at the idea of her managing a bar. How would she handle the rowdiness that was always there—even if exclusive clientele? Thankfully, the bouncers kept everyone in check. And they had plenty of the burly men watching over the place because partying women could definitely be a handful. Especially when they were drunk.

She snorted. She knew what could happen when one drank too much. Her Vegas experience was a prime example.

Brent turned and raised his eyebrows with a big smile on his face. "What's so funny?"

She hadn't told him about what had occurred on that trip. She couldn't. She didn't need anyone else to know about her shame at not remembering. Sometimes she wished she could remember her night with Devon. From what she'd learned, he was a good man. And he was damn fine to boot. It didn't matter how close they were as friends, she wouldn't speak the words to Brent. "Just thinking of the Lawson bachelorette party tonight. I think the bride may feel worse than the groom tomorrow."

He laughed and shook his head a fraction. "You may be right. I saw the women leave. Her friends tried to support her, but they all fell. The bouncer helped them into the limo. It's a smart idea to have car service as part of those packages."

"That was Madison's idea." She turned with Brent in the direction of their vehicles. Several lights were broken in the parking lot, so she picked up her step, hurrying to her car. Even with Brent, a little apprehension hit her with the near darkness. "She's been a stickler about the rules for the club. Number one was no drinking and driving." Club membership, or party packages, included a ride home by taxi or car service for anyone who had any alcoholic beverage. Oddly enough, most were always agreeable on that front.

A noise reached her ears and she looked around nervously, stepping closer to Brent.

"Lookie who we have here." A deep voice reached out from the shadows as a tall man stepped into the dim light.

Rylee froze, trying her hardest to calm her pounding heart. She'd stepped away from the agency, having had enough of dealing with thugs. Wanting out of the situation as quickly as possible, she surreptitiously looked around for the best way to escape.

Brent stiffened beside her.

She turned her head and almost cried out at the sight of a second man, with arms the size of tree trunks, holding a gun to Brent's temple. *Holy fuck!* These men had slipped up on them almost noiselessly.

Adrenaline and fear struck their way through her bloodstream, the mixture confusing her system.

"You can have my wallet. It's in my right back pocket." Brent's calm voice surprised her. Trained agent or not, a gun to one's head could change one's reaction. Yet, his demeanor ratcheted down her nerves, enough to think clearly. To work out how they could get out of this mess.

"I don't give a shit about your wallet, pretty boy." The thug who'd first spoken pulled back his jacket to display his weapon in a shoulder holster.

Shock reverberated in her mind at learning this

wasn't a robbery. She had to do something but had no idea what. Fear held her immobile. While it hadn't been long since she'd left the agency, her reactions were no longer the same since she didn't carry a weapon. She wished she knew how to read Brent's thoughts.

"Rylee, run," the man who'd just poured his heart out, and admitted loving her, whispered.

No way in hell would she leave him to deal with this alone. Unfortunately, she and Brent were without weapons. At least she was. As a civilian, she didn't carry anymore, and she cursed herself for not doing so. Brent, a federal agent, should be armed, but she couldn't quite reach inside his jacket without notice.

The sound of an engine pulled her gaze from the men. A black limousine stopped beside them. Her eyes darted from it to the figure who'd spoken as he strode into the light, walking to the car. With each step, a crunch echoed around the dimly lit lot. Following the man's progress, she assumed it was broken glass from the security bulb under his feet. Immediately, her thoughts went to the camera. She hoped it wasn't broken and was recording.

"What do you want?" She forced anger into her words, pleased that no syllable quivered.

Her stomach soured when the man holding the weapon to Brent laughed.

Brent's voice stood strong in his demand. "Rylee, when we're out of this, we'll sit down to peach cobbler."

She stiffened. That was a code for them that things were not going to go their way, and he wanted her to leave him. He thought he might die. *Bullshit! She wouldn't leave him to that fate. They'd find a way to escape.*

A grunt sounded from the goon holding the limo door open. "Get in the car, bitch, and we leave him alone. Our boss wants to talk with you."

"Boss? Who the hell are you people?" she questioned.

"Rylee, honey, come here and see me." The voice that drifted from the vehicle sent a chill scraping its way up her spine. *No. Not him.*

Dave Westbrook was Keith Westbrook's son. He'd been cleared in the investigation of his father's sex slave business since he'd been clueless of what Keith had been involved in, or so it had seemed. His presence sent her senses reeling more than she thought possible.

What could he want? He'd been ecstatic when they'd arrested his father. There'd been no love lost between them. Yet, it was Dave's father. His meal ticket. Did he blame her for it all? She'd only been one of many agents involved. Shit. Brent had been another.

"I have information for you on those two missing girls."

Dave's admission from the vehicle's interior darkness caught her attention. Misty and Mandy. Would he really help them? She had been searching for the two girls since she'd left the FBI, but she'd hit nothing but dead ends. According to her FBI friends, she was doing more than the bureau to find them.

Her heartbeat raced at the thought of finally finding the twins. She had to know what the man knew, but she wouldn't leave Brent to these men. "I'll go, but only if Brent is released."

"Get in the damn car." Tall, dark, and menacing, the guy by the car door made his order and frustration clear.

Brent bit out through clenched teeth, "Rylee, they're going to kill me no matter what you do. You run and save yourself." He no longer held back by talking in code, and there was no way she would be able to outrun a gun.

The man holding the weapon laughed again. *Fucking asshole. I'll remember that snub-nosed face after this is over.*

She turned back to the man holding the limo door open since he appeared to be the leader of the two thugs and narrowed her eyes. "I promise to come quietly if you let him go."

"Or," the man replied in a slow, calculating voice, "I can kill him now and toss your ass in the car."

"Just put them both in the damn car, Chuck," Dave snapped.

Chuck—thug by the car door—shrugged at her. "Sure, whatever. Just get the fuck in the car, or I'll put you in it."

"Rylee, save yourself," Brent pleaded, his eyes sincere and desperate.

She touched his forearm like he'd touched hers earlier, tender and loving. "It's the only option. I won't chance them shooting you." She dropped her voice so only he could hear. "Besides, we're stronger together, and he might know where the girls are."

The man holding the weapon to Brent's head laughed again, letting her know she hadn't been quiet enough.

It was that possibility that had her turning and entering the limo, keeping as far away from Dave as possible. His smile sickened her, but for the moment, she had to trust him. When Brent slid in beside her, she breathed a short sigh of relief.

Dave, sitting on the side bench seat, poured himself a drink as the limo moved forward. "I'm starting Dad's business over again."

That statement and the determination resounding behind it stunned her to silence. He'd always turned a blind eye to how his father made money. He just went about his playboy life, spending like he had a bottomless pit of funds at his disposal. She'd always wondered if he secretly knew what was happening. Now, he wanted to start the disgusting business again? She couldn't picture Dave being that ruthless. It must boil down to money. Since they'd taken his father's funds, he'd been left broke and in need of an income source.

"I thought you had no idea what your father was doing?" She studied his reaction to see if they'd got it all wrong when they'd cleared him.

His laugh set her nerves on edge. "I knew. I didn't participate, but I knew. And, he didn't let me forget that I was a disappointment for not being part of his enterprise." He gave an insolent shrug. "Do you think he'd turn in his own son? The one he asked to keep the good name going?"

"So, you have no problem doing this? Kidnapping and selling young girls?" Anger boiled in Brent's words.

Settling back in his seat, Dave tossed his arm across the top of the seat and crossed a leg over a thigh. "I have a partner who knows exactly what to do." He sipped his drink, but his eyes didn't leave Rylee's.

She wanted to slap the smugness from his voice.

"If they know what to do, what do they need you for?" Rylee clasped and squeezed Brent's hand before releasing it. They would find out what they needed to save the girls, but they had to think of how to get out of this mess. Why would Dave tell them and then release them? She cursed her delayed instincts. Something definitely wasn't right.

"Because, I have my dad's contacts, the ones the FBI never found. And, since my dad didn't turn the buyers in, I have the family name to trade on." He shot her a menacing smile. "And, the twins will be the first to go."

"What—" She cleared her throat and started again, "What do you mean?" It appeared that the information he had for her about the girls hadn't been to help her find them, but to brag that he had them and planned to profit from them. Her muscles tightened as she restrained herself from leaping across the car's interior and punching the bastard in the nose.

"They'll be glad to see you again. I'm tired of hearing their whining and crying all the time."

Her spine stiffened and she sat straighter. See each other? Why would he take her to them? *Oh no. Brent. This shit just got worse. What will they do with him?* She took a deep breath and held it. *Settle down and think. There must be a way to get out of this...for all of us. Keep him talking until you figure it out or Brent acts.* "How did you find the girls?"

"Don't you know?" He laughed at her apparent bewilderment. "Good ole Dad gave me the twins in hopes that my tastes would change," he spat out with bitterness.

Dave liked men, and it rankled his father to no end,

especially considering his father's line of business.

"Where are they?" Her pulse pounded, awaiting his slow response. They'd find out this information, then prepare to escape.

"I have a friend keeping them safe for me." He saluted them with the glass in his hand. "Untouched."

She released the breath she'd been holding. Her temper flared at the thought of how afraid they must be. "Why are you taking me to see them?" *Which means I won't be allowed to leave, nor will Brent.* She prayed Brent had figured out what they would need to do to remain alive because she couldn't.

"Two reasons, really. I need someone to take care of them and the ones we add. Plus"—he drilled his stare into her as her heart plummeted—"you will pay for sending my father away and making me have to work. I have a client Dad lined up who wants *you*. Consider it his revenge from behind bars."

"Like hell—" Brent's angry words were cut off by a jolt.

A loud crunching sound of metal against metal from a car hitting them preceded the jar from behind that sent Rylee flying forward into the barrier that separated the passengers from the driver before she slid to the floor. Pain radiated through her head, and she could do nothing more than lie there, cradling it between her palms. A warm liquid slid over her hands. It hurt so much that she couldn't bring herself to open her eyes. But she had to move. She and Brent needed to escape. She'd try something else to find the girls.

A heavy weight of a full body pinned her to the spot. Her vision began to tunnel, zooming in and out of focus as she fought hard to remain conscious. She couldn't pass out. She had to be in control. It was their only chance.

The sound of fabric swishing across leather alerted her that one of the men had returned to a seat. The body on top of her groaned but didn't move.

"Rylee?" Brent whispered. His voice was close to her ear.

He was the man who covered her, and thank God he was alive. For her, at least nothing hurt severe enough to prevent her from escaping. "I can't breathe. You're too heavy."

He grunted and shifted, and then she felt his arm move between them. A sigh escaped her at the sound of a gun being slipped from its holster.

As he began lifting his body from hers, the car door flew open. Rylee's view, still blocked by Brent, meant she wasn't able to see who'd opened it. She assumed it was whoever had hit them.

"No!" The panic lacing Dave's words sent fear pulsing through her.

Before she had time to speak, three shots rang out. She cringed at the loudness and then barely bit back her scream as Brent slumped back on her. Holding her breath, the sobs threatening to escape, Rylee then heard the door being slammed closed.

Fuck! She opened her eyes, not wanting to turn and look at Brent. But she had to know. Angling her head, her gaze connected with Brent's lifeless eyes. *God, no!*

Trying to keep it together, if only for a few more moments, she peeked around him as best as she could without moving. She saw Dave. Bile rose in her throat when she zoned in on his blood and brain matter on the seat.

Trying to get her brain to work before her emotions took over, she realized two things. Brent hadn't gotten off a shot and the person who had killed both men was still out there.

Rylee looked back to Brent and squeezed her eyes shut as a tear rolled down her cheek, followed by another. He'd blocked her from the shooter's vision. If he hadn't, she knew she'd also be dead. It was her fault he'd been here instead of back at the club. And he'd paid with his life.

She fought the racking sob welling inside her at the painful loss of her friend and attempted a few calming breaths. She couldn't lose it; she had to move. Closing her eyes, ignoring the tears and what she assumed was blood staining her cheeks, she knew moving put her at risk. It might shift the limo and alert the killer to her presence. They'd left an unexpected witness. It didn't matter that she hadn't actually witnessed anything.

More gunshots broke the silence. She had a sinking feeling that the driver had been murdered too. What happened to Dave's goons? They must not have followed. Unless that had been them. No, it couldn't be because they knew she was here. So where were they?

What the hell did she do now? Obviously, no one was riding to their rescue. She had no idea who had killed the men, and she'd be damned if she even attempted to chase them. She was a civilian, alone, and with a bleeding head. She released a deep, shuddering sigh. Without Dave, she had nothing to give the FBI about the girls except hearsay. Hell, they wouldn't believe her that he was involved. Not after they'd cleared him.

The squeal of tires, a vehicle racing away, broke

the silence, yet she waited. With all quiet for minutes, she knew it was time. Rylee pushed aside the agonizing pain and crawled from beneath her friend. She said a short prayer and kissed Brent on the forehead before closing his eyes. Then, she emptied both men's pockets.

When she found what she needed, Rylee ran.

Chapter Two

Devon Hamilton stared at the document in his hands and called himself every form of fool possible. All he had to do was sign his name. It wasn't a difficult task. It was just a damn signature. He'd done it hundreds of times in his life. Yet, he couldn't bring himself to pick up a pen. He wasn't a quitter and signing this document would shout, "I quit."

The whole situation didn't seem real. How could it? To him, it truly wasn't. Yet, here in black and white, it was about as real as it got.

Fuck. He'd thought once he'd stepped back and waited, that things would've turned in his favor. But life had a way of surprising the hell out of you.

If only he could remember….

The sound of shuffling feet and men's voices entering the room interrupted his thoughts. He slid the paper into his desk in the HIS war room for safekeeping. This document contained his problem…his decision…his secret. He'd have to deal with it later. Right now, he had a job to do.

The room filled and he confirmed all necessary personnel was in attendance. Well, all except Trent McKenzie, their half brother. Trent had another skin graft surgery two days prior. His physical healing was progressing well, but he'd forever be scarred. His emotional healing was another story. He'd sacrificed a lot to save Amber, their niece's life from a terrorist bomber.

Dealing with his near fatal injury, and learning he was a Hamilton, the family had agreed to give Trent the time and space he'd requested to figure out what he planned to do with his life. No way, though, would Devon allow him to slip away and disappear like he feared the man planned.

The eldest Hamilton brother, Jesse, brought the meeting to order. Hamilton Investigation & Security, or HIS, had been Jesse's idea. He'd wanted a family business that utilized each member of the family's skills. Jesse had built his as a U.S. Army Ranger and FBI agent. After Devon, the second eldest, left the CIA, his brother approached him with the idea, but he'd scoffed at it thinking his brothers would never leave their alphabet agencies, even to work with family. His younger brothers had wanted those jobs since they were boys. That was his thought…until Matt left the Navy SEALs. The three banded together and created HIS and waited patiently for the rest of the family to join them.

Devon smiled. After a while, each family member had left his or her employ, and it became the business Jesse had planned with only one holdout for partnership—Trent. He'd been happy as a team member even after being shot to protect Megan, AJ's wife, and almost killed saving Amber, Em and Jake's daughter. But he wouldn't commit to joining the family-owned company. Hell, he'd been a surprise addition to the family and dealing with it had been hard on Trent.

A busy business it was. They had a team of eleven men, mostly from law enforcement and government agencies, and two K-9s, but they needed to add talented people to the team. He didn't care as long as the brilliant men and women added value in the field. Value he couldn't add.

He glanced at the pile of requests for their immediate services. These potential clients were damn lucky the planned assignment canceled at the last moment. Otherwise, HIS wouldn't be available. Why the hell couldn't people plan ahead? Most knew their boss's travel schedule and knew he or she wanted a protection detail.

Devon worked hard to schedule jobs for the team to ensure each member had time to work, with time to relax and play. Hell, it seemed that lately, half of the slotted time off had been used to protect his brothers' new wives. He wasn't complaining about that. He was glad they'd taken those steps or Jesse, AJ, and Jake wouldn't be married to great women…and happy. Christ, Jake might not even be home.

He wanted to slam his hand on the desk and shout in anger. It had almost taken too long to find their foster brother. And the FBI delay in retrieving Jake had cut it down to the wire. By not finding him until he did, Devon had almost failed the family in the worst way possible.

"Dev?" Jesse questioned.

Catching the raised eyebrows of his older brother, Devon put an abrupt halt to that train of thought and joined in the conversation. He recounted the information the family needed to make their decisions. "As for priority, I suggest we accept the top two jobs. They're both simple security details and won't screw with future job timelines." He shrugged and shook his head in exasperation at the potential clients' piss-poor planning. "Last-minute travel plans for each. Taking these options would leave the team with a short break before we send them on their next scheduled assignment. We know the investigation requests could take longer than we have open on the schedule." He waited to speak again until after the group looked over the material. "Now, the third job is interesting."

Em perked up. "That one is mine while you're away."

As one of the newest partners, their baby sister, Emily Hamilton, or more recently Emily Cavanaugh, hadn't allowed her brothers to dictate to her. And they wouldn't in this case either. As an accountant, it was right up her alley. A possible embezzling of funds.

She rolled her chair closer to him and elbowed him in the ribs. "Dev already agreed we could do it."

Quite a few eyebrows were raised at him in question. Damn her impatience. He'd told her that he'd get the group to agree to allow her to run the case, but it would be done his way. He'd managed them long enough to know what would sway their minds to his way of thinking. Turning his attention to Jesse, he smiled. "Well, it makes sense if the team takes the top two jobs. Em and I won't really be needed."

"You could come with us this time," Jesse suggested with a pointed look at Devon.

Panic clawed at him. Go out in the field? He hadn't held a weapon other than at the range in what, four years? He almost snorted aloud in disgust. Like he didn't remember the date Greg Donovan, a fellow CIA agent, had been killed.

"Nah." Matt shook his head while he spoke, saving Devon from blundering through a response. "He might mess up those pretty hands." His playful wink scoffed at Devon's pride. "And then where would we be when we need that computer magic shit?"

Jesse narrowed his eyes at Devon.

The assessment by his brother ripped into him. Sometimes he wondered if his brothers knew what had happened…why Devon had left the CIA. Yet, they'd never asked him to go out in the field with them…before today.

He'd made a deal with Jesse when they'd started the business that he would be the logistics behind the operation, but he wouldn't brandish a weapon with them. Sure, he'd ensure they had the latest in weaponry and security, but he participated from behind his computer. It made sense. They needed someone to take care of the administrative junk and find any information they could to be successful in each case. He'd been doing just that, and he knew he was damn good at it. The CIA had taught him well.

But he'd also given in and still went to the shooting range with them regularly. It had been important to his brothers that he at least knew how to use any new weapon he procured.

Jesse eventually shrugged. "Okay. Let's talk through these two jobs and get on the move."

Devon released a sigh of relief. The burden he carried became heavier every time the team went out on assignment, and he stayed back. He worked hard on his end to overcome it, but it always remained in the background.

Kate, Jesse's wife and a former FBI agent, cleared her throat from beside her husband.

Devon didn't know why he'd purchased chairs for

their war room. No one except he and Em sat and that was because they were in front of computers. The group stood, crowded close around an oval oak meeting table in the middle of the room. They left an opening to be able to view where he and his sister sat. No one appeared to notice the smart boards and screens on the walls. They wouldn't look at them until their mission planning began. They preferred to review the potential jobs on paper. He went to a great deal of work to make the room interactive. He'd bring them to the twenty-first century if it killed him. Hell, wait until they saw the new meeting table he'd ordered with a touch-screen in it. Giddiness bubbled inside him just thinking about it.

When no one acknowledged her, Kate cleared her throat again. "I want us to take a case. It's not in the pile. It's for an old FBI friend of mine."

"What type of case is it?" Matt, the peacemaker brother, glanced up from the papers in his hand. "Do we have time?"

"I'm not quite sure."

Heads bobbed up from reading and turned to her in curiosity.

"Thing is," —she paused and bit her bottom lip— "she hasn't said she needs help."

Matt shook his head. "Then why are you asking?"

"Yeah. I remember how it went when another FBI agent I know didn't feel she needed help." Jesse waggled his eyebrows at his wife suggestively, obviously reminding her of their time together.

Devon smiled at the two of them, remembering the hell of a ride Kate had given his older brother when her life had been in danger, and Jesse had felt the need to step in as her protector when she'd told him she didn't need it. That'd been right after Devon had returned from Las Vegas. His smile faltered, and he closed his eyes for a moment. *Vegas. It's been eleven months. You need to fix this, Devon.* He had to push that away for the time being. He needed to focus on this meeting and getting the team squared away. They counted on him for that. Then, he could deal with that issue. "What's going on that you think she needs our help?"

"Well, she called to tell me she was going off the grid but wanted someone to know where she was…just in case. I couldn't get her to tell me why." She shuddered a bit too dramatically. "It kind of freaked me out."

"Maybe she just wanted to be alone." Matt shrugged. "Doesn't mean we need to ride to her rescue."

The men wouldn't brush off Kate. "Well, there's more. About a month ago, an ICE agent—someone people thought she might be dating—was shot and killed." She glanced around the group. "*With* someone linked to her last FBI case. She's no longer in the bureau and is wanted for questioning. She and her stepsister, Madison, own a nightclub in Baltimore. Even Madison pleads not knowing where she is. This is the first time anyone has heard from her since the incident."

Devon's blood pressure began to spike. *It can't be.* The notion of this woman, a former FBI agent at that, and her sister, Madison, owning a club rang serious alarm bells in his mind. He wanted to whirl around and pound on his keyboard to find out everything the cyber-world had on the case. The urge almost overpowered him. *And what the hell was this dating?*

Tamping down that urge, he attempted to act nonchalant, as if it were just another potential client case. "Do you think she killed him and is on the run?"

Kate shook her head. "Not possible." Looking to her husband, her voice turned pleading. "I really think she's in trouble."

Devon wanted to ask more, but his tongue was tied. If she was really in trouble....

"I get that you have that feeling, sweetheart, but these people"—Jesse waved the printouts in his hand to emphasize his point—"are definitely in need of us and have requested our services."

"I know that, but I want to go see her. I need to see for myself that she's okay. Something doesn't feel right to me. She's not someone who runs and hides."

Jesse, the final decision maker of the group, dropped the papers on the table and placed his hands on her arms. "I'll tell you what. These are short, simple jobs that won't require everyone. While we're on assignment, you can stay behind and visit her to set your mind at ease, and Dev and Em can investigate the murders. It shouldn't keep them away from the third assignment." He turned and smirked at Em, but love and pride showed in his eyes. Focusing again on his wife, he continued, "Will that work?" He cocked his head questioningly. "By the way, which friend is it? Do I know her?"

"Of course you do."

Devon's heart beat double-time in anticipation.

"Her name is Rylee Hawkins. She's—"

Devon surged from his chair. "I'll go with you," he blurted, stunning the room's occupants to silence.

****

"Jesse will have your ass for booking us into first class for this trip," Kate told Devon as he drove them in a rental car through the mountains of Colorado.

He glanced her way then turned his attention back to the road. "You wanted to get here fast, didn't you?" He didn't wait for an answer before continuing, "There weren't any economy seats until later in the day, and it's a hell of a lot cheaper than grabbing a private jet like he tends to do. Besides, it was this or wait, and I had the feeling that wouldn't have worked for you." Truth be told, he'd already checked into a private jet when he'd had trouble finding a quick flight for the two of them. In his mind, there'd been no question on their immediate response, even if Rylee hadn't asked for help. He'd done some quick research before they'd departed. Whether Rylee knew it or not, she was in a damn pickle. The FBI wanted her for questioning in the murder of the government agent and one scum of society's offspring. Disappearing screamed she had something to hide.

He couldn't figure out why she hadn't asked for help, though. Did she plan to just hide out until it all blew over? She had to know that wouldn't happen, especially as she knew how the bureau worked. Even if she wasn't involved, she knew both victims too well in the minds of the investigators. They'd assume she knew something.

Devon kicked himself repeatedly for not checking on what she'd been doing lately. When he'd received the papers, he'd been so taken aback, that his need to keep track of her had died out.

"You're right," Kate said. "Thank you."

They slowed as a family of deer hopped across the

road ahead. The large buck stopped and looked their way, almost menacingly, until the others were safely on the other side, sliding into the woods.

"So," Kate dragged the word out, "tell me why you're here."

Too many reasons to count. Mostly, he had a nagging suspicion Rylee wasn't hiding from the FBI but from who killed Brent and Dave. It appeared to be a professional kill. He assumed a hit. Had she witnessed it? If so, she should've asked for help. Then again, he didn't really believe she'd ask him for anything. "What do you mean?"

"You know what I mean, Devon Michael Hamilton."

Out of the corner of his eye, he caught her crossing her arms over her chest. He knew she'd tossed in his middle name to rile him. He'd seen her do it with her husband often enough. The woman had a stubborn streak that rivaled any he'd seen from his sister.

"I understand you don't do anything unless it's behind a computer. And, as far as I know, you've never met her. So, my question is why now?"

Hell, she'd find out soon enough. He was damn surprised she didn't already know. Once he'd found out the two women were close, he'd expected a confrontation from Kate long ago. But it'd never happened.

He may as well unburden his soul while she couldn't inflict damage on him without running the risk of him crashing the car and maybe killing her in the process. "Right before you and I met, I'd taken a trip to Vegas for a tech conference."

"Rylee went to Vegas about that time also."

He waited for her to process those two statements together.

"Wait. Are you saying you do know her?"

Devon glanced at her and hesitated before speaking. "Apparently, I do."

"Apparently? What kind of bullshit is that?"

"Something happened while I was there, and I lost most of my memory of the weekend. All I know is that I'd been prepared to drop a boatload of money on new equipment, and then I woke up in the hospital not knowing what had happened the prior twenty-four hours."

She relaxed her arms. "Is that when you met her? During the time you lost your memory? Has your memory returned then?"

"Yes and no. Jesse arrived shortly thereafter. The doctor said I'd either been hit on the head or had fallen and hit it hard enough to knock me out. By the time we'd returned to the hotel, maid service had cleaned the room. Jesse found out about a broken lamp the maid had disposed of. The question was still whether I'd been hit on the head or knocked it off the desk when I fell."

"I'm surprised Jesse didn't take the lamp pieces and have them dusted for prints."

Devon chuckled in remembrance of his brother's high-handedness at the hotel. "He'd wanted to do just that, but I finally convinced him that we'd have hundreds of people to speak with since we knew maid service wasn't always that efficient. Hell, there was no telling the last time the lamp had been wiped down." He'd fought digging the pieces out of the garbage, but he'd known it would set up a ton of wild goose chases and probably no answers.

"Nothing had been stolen from my room, so I couldn't imagine someone just coming in and hitting me over the head." He flashed her a smile that he'd learned women appreciated. "I'm real likable."

She playfully swatted at him and laughed. "The most likable of the bunch. Now, get on with it."

He sobered again. "We checked with security to see if someone had left my room. Some idiot on their tech team had placed the security tapes in a view-only status, and no one had known they hadn't been recording until we asked to see them."

"Humph. I hope they fired that moron."

"They didn't have to." He shook his head. "Jesse dressed the kid down so much, he resigned. Probably to get away from your husband."

A proud smile split her face. "That sounds like the Jesse I met."

"We're glad you were able to squash that part of our brother who had become almost unbearable. However, sometimes, when that Jesse reemerges, it's a sight to behold."

The car's navigation directed them to turn onto a dirt road. He and Kate turned to each other and raised their eyebrows in unison. Rylee definitely wanted to be out of the way.

"It's a vacation cabin she's rented. Now, quit changing the subject. What else happened?"

"All right, pushy." He chuckled at his sister-in-law. She was about to hate him, but he loved that she was a part of their family. He liked Jesse's first wife, *God rest her soul*, but Kate brought out the best in his brother. He wanted something like that and hoped the woman they sought might be the one to be his better half.

"Enough of that. What about Rylee? How does she fit into this?"

"Christ, woman, I'm trying to tell you."

Kate waved her hand in a circle motion to encourage him to get on with his story.

"At the hotel, the maid whispered to me about condoms in the garbage. I've had one-night stands before—"

Kate's snort of disgust reached his ears.

He inwardly chuckled at her prudish censure but kept on telling his tale as if she hadn't interrupted. "But this freaked me out for some reason. So, I rushed me and Jesse out of town and didn't want to look back."

He slowed as the car dipped into a washed-out hole in the road. "Jesse pushed me to investigate it, but I kept putting it off because I didn't want to know if I'd done something unforgivable. I might've hired a hooker or something, and I didn't think I could handle that if I had."

"Devon, you wouldn't have hired a hooker. Enough women fall at your feet for you to even need to do so."

"Yeah, well, after a while, I couldn't stand the suspense. I mean, did she hit me on the head? If so, why? No money was missing. Had I hurt her in some way? So, I started sneaking into some of the businesses on the strip's security footage that was still available. It wasn't easy considering it'd taken almost a month to get up the nerve and most places don't keep their security tapes very long—no matter the law." He took a deep breath, held it for a moment, and released it in a long, loud sigh. "It took a while, but I found footage of me walking with a woman down the sidewalk. I did facial recognition and got a hit."

"Rylee."

He nodded and tightened his lips. "Yes, Rylee." He'd been laughing and holding the hand of a dark auburn-haired beauty. They'd only had eyes for each other and had bumped into enough people to unwittingly prove their distraction from the world around them.

Devon couldn't find enough footage to piece together their entire evening. Not even to show that she'd been in the hotel with him. He knew that she'd been there though.

Once he'd learned her name, he'd checked the registry—with some difficulty—and there she'd been. Rylee Hawkins had checked out of the hotel before the maid had discovered him and he'd been taken to the hospital.

He'd called her a cold-hearted bitch for possibly leaving him like that. Yet, he couldn't hang onto that anger because maybe he'd deserved her need to run from him. Maybe she hadn't hit him. What had happened that night had consumed him. He'd had to find out so he'd reached out to her.

Kate's mood flashed to anger. "What the hell did you do to her, Devon? She never would've hit you if you hadn't done something."

"I tried to find her...to apologize...." For what exactly he hadn't known, but he'd known it was necessary. It was always necessary for a man to apologize. "I couldn't contact her though as she'd left on an undercover assignment."

"I remember the night she left my house for it.

36

Actually," she said and brightened, "you came later that evening. You two didn't miss each other by much. Did you know about her then?"

He shook his head. "No. I was still acting like a pussy about finding out. It was while we searched for that maniac after you that I couldn't stand it any longer and began to seek out the truth."

She huffed out a breath. "I knew something had gone wrong on her trip. She wouldn't talk about it. I kind of figured it involved a man. Hang on, if she knew who you were, she would've surely said something to me."

He'd thought the same thing when he'd found out who she was. "Maybe. Maybe not. You'd just met us when Arthur sent her undercover. Maybe she found out I was Jesse and AJ's brother and didn't feel comfortable telling you." He shrugged. "Anyhow, she's back."

"Did you know that before I said something to the team?"

"I've kept tabs." Seeing Rylee and how happy they'd been on tape, he couldn't just let her go without knowing what had changed. Hell, he'd wanted to know how they'd met. The chemistry between them could've melted the surveillance tapes he'd watched. And he'd watched them repeatedly until each movement had been ingrained in his memory.

"Have you tried to contact her since she's returned?"

"Yes."

The Australian male voice that Kate had programmed into the navigation system announced the final turn. His pulse rate increased in anticipation. He'd see her in only a few more minutes. What would her reaction be? Hell, he didn't even know how he'd react. He still hadn't decided how to play things with her. No approach seemed to be foolproof, considering he didn't know everything.

"And I take it she didn't respond. What if things didn't go well between you two? Maybe this isn't such a good idea to have you along."

"You're wrong, Kate. She did respond." He slowed to a stop on the one-lane dirt road and looked at Kate to gauge her reaction before continuing to their destination. "You see, we got married that night in Vegas."

She gasped as her eyes widened, and her hand flew to her mouth. "What did she say? Wait! I thought you didn't remember what happened."

"I don't." He turned back to the front of the car and eased his foot back on the accelerator. "The hotel later mailed me something that had slid under the bed and hadn't been found until a refurbishment." He released a sigh. "Our marriage certificate. I double-checked and it's legit."

Kate swore. "Why didn't you tell anyone? Why aren't you two together?"

"And tell everyone what? Oh, hey, I apparently got smashed, got married, and don't remember it. And, by the way, she hit me on the head and wants nothing to do with me so I must've been one hell of an asshole."

Kate cringed. "You've got a point. Jesse would want to fix it, and the rest of the group would kick your ass." She shifted in the seat. "Hang on. I thought you didn't drink."

He swallowed hard. "I haven't since that night."

"But why stop drinking?"

His reasoning sounded stupid, even to his own ears, but it worked for him. "Because, in the videos I found of us, I had a drink in my hand quite a few times, which means if I did something stupid, I figure alcohol must've pushed me to do it."

"But you could've truly fallen in your room, and Rylee had nothing to do with it."

Kate had a point that he'd tossed around several times, but someone had been in his bed, and he'd put down everything he owned that it was Rylee. "It's possible."

"So, what are you going to do? You still haven't told me what she said, and something tells me she's not going to be happy you're with me."

The small log cabin came into view. The getaway embodied the rustic look nestled in the woods like a traditional hunting or fishing cabin. The sun glinted off something in the front window. His senses went on instant alert, raising the adrenaline level in his system.

"Shit," Kate breathed out.

"Did you call to let her know we were coming?"

"No cell service and the landline isn't active."

He tightened his jaw. Something was definitely wrong. He slowed the car to a crawl and stopped short of the cabin. Unfortunately, they were within firing range if she decided to welcome them that way. "Grab the binoculars from my bag in the back and see if that's what I think it is."

Kate unbuckled her seat belt and angled herself in the back to shuffle through a black duffle bag. She turned and looked through the field glasses to the cabin. "It's Rylee, and she's got a rifle pointed straight at us."

"Son of a bitch!" He snatched the binoculars from her and looked in the same direction as Kate had. "I hope to Christ she doesn't shoot us."

Kate snorted. "Sounds like she might shoot you, but I doubt she'd shoot me, even though I brought you along." She reached for the door handle. "I'm going to step out of the vehicle so she can see me."

Devon reached over to stop her. "Are you fucking crazy?"

"It's Rylee. Don't worry. Just stay right here until I tell you to move the car."

Although he didn't want to, he agreed that once Rylee knew who she was, they'd be safe. He sat helpless while his sister-in-law stepped from the vehicle into a potential line of fire. He prayed Rylee didn't shoot first and ask questions later.

Kate reached the front of the cabin and her friend stepped into view with a medium-sized black dog at her side. The women embraced, then Kate turned and waved him forward.

He pulled the vehicle closer and stopped. Once he'd turned off the engine, he sat for a moment and drank in the sight of her. The live version was much better than the tapes he'd watched so many times. He'd seen how she stood about six inches shorter than his six-one with a body that told him she kept fit—lean and strong.

The image of her standing there in form-fitting jeans, a cream sweater, and hiking boots, with her hair flowing freely around her shoulders, stirred intense lust inside him. It made him nervous as hell, and he couldn't say why. Hell, he prayed he hadn't done anything terrible to make her run from him. He wouldn't be able to stand himself if he had.

He'd put it off long enough. Taking a deep breath, he took the first step to confronting his lacking memory…and the woman he'd forgotten. He exited the car and faced her.

Rylee's eyes widened when she recognized him. "Devon?"

Was that shock or fear in her voice? Maybe a bit of both. He'd have to figure it out as he went along.

The dog bared her teeth and growled. *Shit.* He hoped she hadn't taught the dog to attack. He might be fucked.

Attempting to keep things light, he raised his eyebrows and said, "Did you think I'd sign those annulment papers without even speaking with you?"

Chapter Three

"Annulment?" Kate screeched.

Rylee ignored her friend's outburst and appraised the dark-haired man walking toward her. She swallowed past the nervous lump in her throat. He'd cut his hair, and it appeared to have a problem with gravity in places, but she'd recognize him anywhere. Devon Hamilton dressed in jeans and a long-sleeved T-shirt looked rough and sexy. *Dammit.*

When she'd told Kate where she'd be staying, she had an inkling to expect her friend at some point if she didn't contact her again. Not this quickly, though. She hadn't considered Kate would bring *him*. Since Kate hadn't mentioned knowing that Rylee and Devon were married, she'd guessed he'd kept it a secret also and hoped to avoid him until the annulment finalized. No such luck.

Locked in his gaze, she could drown in those warm, golden-brown eyes. Maybe she had and that had been why they'd married right away. It had to be something because knowing him and marrying him in less than twenty-four hours, by an Elvis impersonator no less—she shuddered when she'd found out that bit of information in her research—was not the type of woman she was. Then again, she'd been dead-ass drunk. Or drugged, her mind reminded her.

She'd worked with two of his brothers, and

because of them, she couldn't believe Devon would've drugged her. However, she didn't believe she'd allowed herself to get smashed. Either way, she'd woken by his side with no memory of him or the night prior, so she'd done what she did best—she'd fled. She hadn't realized how bad things were until she'd settled herself on the airplane and caught sight of the thin, gold wedding band on the ring finger of her left hand. Something she'd avoided thinking about until this moment.

"Why the shotgun welcome?" He nodded to the weapon in her hand and a slow, sensual smile played on his lips. "Is that special for me?"

Stiffening her spine, she silently cursed that her insides warmed and her stomach fluttered. She wouldn't allow herself to fall for the charm that oozed from him. "It's a rifle, not a shotgun." Her reply ended up terser than she'd planned, but he deserved it. Somehow. Maybe. Possibly. Heck, she was too confused, if only by the idea of him and spending too many months thinking about what could have happened that night.

Devon shrugged his strong shoulders. "Figure of speech." He narrowed his eyes at her. "You didn't answer me."

She'd love to put a shot in his ass for marrying her when she hadn't known what she'd been doing. And for taking her to bed when she couldn't have been in any condition to remember. But she thought better, knowing she didn't want to upset Kate, who had only come to check on her.

Instead, Rylee peered around him and searched the area. When she'd seen him, she'd allowed herself to lose awareness of her surroundings. That couldn't happen again. She didn't expect anyone to find her, but it didn't hurt to be wary and on guard. "I wasn't expecting anyone." She forced a smile and turned into the cabin with the dog at her heels. "Come inside."

"I'm sorry we dropped in unannounced, but without cell service...." Kate's voice drifted off.

Closing the door behind her unexpected, and somewhat unwelcome guests, Rylee placed her weapon by the front entrance and turned back to them. "Kate, Devon,"—she placed her hand on the mixed-breed dog—"this is Angel." As the two became acquainted with the pet, she glanced around the room. She'd rushed to put her notes away. Satisfied her secrets were safe, she turned to play hostess.

In the open living-dining-kitchen combo, Rylee settled on a comfortable red-clothed couch beside Kate. Sipping water, she eyed Devon, who lounged in an armchair full of a crayon box of color splatters. His presence placed her off-balance. What was it about him that had made her lose her wits that night? Sure, he was devilishly handsome, but so were plenty of men. She hadn't married them.

"What's this about the two of you being married? And getting an annulment?"

Kate's questions grabbed her attention, and she bristled a bit. She'd hoped she could get away from all this without truly dealing with anyone except a lawyer. Obviously not when Kate Hamilton became involved. Which is why she hadn't told her friend when she'd found out the truth.

Actually, Rylee had almost told Kate that final night she'd visited for their monthly dinner, but had chickened out because Jesse had been there. The two of them had been cozy and she feared Kate would tell Jesse and then it'd be more than she'd wanted to deal with since Devon hadn't sought her out at that point. So, Rylee had kept quiet and had been thankful when she'd received a call from her boss and had to leave early after they'd found her a spot at the Westbrook household.

Unsure how to respond to her friend's question, Rylee turned to Devon and they gazed at each other intently, seeking an answer that would satisfy Kate. The tension in the room weighed down on her like a heavy blanket bearing down on her shoulders. He was a Hamilton, but she couldn't trust him until she knew the truth of how she'd come to be his wife. She had no expectation that she'd ever retrieve her memory of their time together.

When no one spoke, Kate kept up her quest for answers. "So...this is the Vegas trip you wouldn't talk about?"

Rylee looked at her and nodded slightly in resignation.

"And, you, Devon," Kate said, pausing long enough to point her index finger at him, "this is the trip you don't remember?"

What? Her head snapped to him. Not remember? That didn't sound right. He'd called her by name the next morning. Why would he lie about it? Sure, it had taken a while for him to search her out after the trip, but since she'd been undercover when he had, Rylee hadn't thought much about it. She'd actually been relieved to have missed him. Then, she'd conveniently ignored his attempts to contact her after she'd returned and finally contacted an attorney. Rylee closed her eyes. This was so screwed up.

"Kate, I think this is something Rylee and I should talk about later...alone."

Her stomach clenched at the thought of being alone with him. The last time that had happened, she'd assaulted him. She doubted he appreciated that too much—no matter what else had happened between the sheets. Or, at the wedding chapel.

Kate looked shrewdly between the two and huffed. "I'll let it go for now. I do expect the two of you to talk before you go through with this annulment nonsense. You two are perfect for each other. If you give it a chance, you'll realize it soon enough."

The whole thing was too much of a mess for her to even consider at that point, their past too murky. She needed to get him out of here. The court would grant their annulment, and the embarrassment of her actions would be behind her. Although she doubted she'd ever be able to visit Kate again. Which reminded her..."Kate, why are you here?"

"Why do you think? What's going on? Why are you squirreled away up here?"

"I told you. I just needed to get away." It had been a moment of weakness when she'd called Kate. A sudden fear that everything would go wrong. She wished she hadn't phoned her now. Especially since she brought...*her husband*. That word burned her tongue.

"You were hiding out here until after I signed the papers." A muscle twitched in Devon's jaw. "Weren't you?"

She sucked in a breath at the smooth, accusing voice. Is that what he thought? It wasn't the reason, but it fit right into her plans. "Is that a problem?"

Her flippant reply appeared to anger him more judging by the rigidity of his jaw. He tightened his hands into fists. "Hell, yes, it is. I want to get to the bottom of this marriage business."

Confused, she squinted her eyes and cocked her head, yet sarcasm was woven in her voice. "That's right, you don't remember." What game was he playing? Anger wormed its way through her veins.

"A bump on my head took care of that memory. Any idea how that might've happened?" He raised his eyebrows and cocked his head in question.

Oh God. The lamp. Had she really hurt him enough to make him lose his memory? That was ludicrous. She hadn't hit him that hard. Had she? A shard of regret crept into her conscience.

He waved his hand as if pushing away any answers she might have for him. "No matter your reason, you made the mistake of giving Kate a cryptic message about hiding out. She tried to bring the entire HIS team here."

Rylee's eyes widened in panic. "Kate. I didn't mean to make you think I was in trouble. I just—" She couldn't think of a lie fast enough to tell her friend. She'd been thrown off by Devon's appearance and the fact she'd have to deal with him about their so-called marriage. "I just didn't want to get hurt hiking or something and no one looked for me until it was too late. Nothing more."

Her body tensed at the awareness of Devon's eyes on her. Not in a sexual way, but in an "I don't believe that crap" way. She brought her gaze to his and knew she'd nailed his emotion. She braced herself for his response.

"So this trip has nothing to do with the FBI wishing to speak with you?" He posed it as a question, but his tone countered it as a statement he knew to be correct.

Her heart pounded against her ribcage, seeking release from its confines. She'd resigned from the FBI and wanted nothing more to do with them after the way they'd abandoned the girls as "casualties of war." Her boss had said the bureau would keep an open investigation to find them, but she knew that meant the case would be lost to dust. She owed those girls and wouldn't let it go. Did they know she'd been looking? Or, did this have to do with Brent and Dave? Had they found out she'd been there when they'd been killed? Uncertain she wanted an answer to any of those questions, but knowing she had to ask, she spoke up, "Why do they want to speak with me?"

Kate cocked her head to the side and raised her eyebrows, disbelief written on her face. "Rylee, you know why."

She took a stab at it and hoped she didn't give away anything she didn't want. "Brent," she whispered.

"Why did you disappear after he'd been killed? It looks mighty suspicious since he was with the son of a man you helped indict." Devon's accusing voice hit home. It would've been suspicious to her too had she looked from the outside in, especially considering the fact it started in her club's parking lot. Not that they seemed to know that.

"I didn't kill him!" Rage surged through her like a tidal wave.

Kate put her right hand up, palm toward Rylee. "Whoa. We didn't say you did. I don't think the FBI believe that either, but they have questions since you knew them both. And"—Kate stretched out the word—"you disappeared right after they were murdered. It's quite obvious to them that you know something. Our relationship with Arthur is strained, but he did come to me about you being missing. He's worried also."

Arthur Hall, Deputy Director of the FBI, was a well-respected man. She wondered what had happened to strain his relationship with the Hamilton family. They'd been close family friends since the men were young boys.

Devon cleared his throat. "What do you know about their murders?"

She wanted to tell the truth. Maybe they could intervene on her behalf somehow. Rylee didn't want her name involved. If the killers didn't know she'd been in the limo already, she didn't want to give them any ammunition by blabbing. Especially when she really didn't know anything. She dropped her head to her chest and sighed in defeat.

Falling into her old role as an FBI agent, she pulled herself together and briefly recited the events of that horrible evening, skipping over the few details she wasn't ready to share. Rylee's lips tightened, and her eyes watered. "They killed Brent while he was saving my life, Kate."

"Oh, Rylee." Kate scooted closer to Rylee and opened her arms. Rylee slid into them and couldn't hold back the tears.

After a few desperate moments of grief, she pulled back and swiped at her tear-stained face. "Thanks. Anyhow, I knew they hadn't seen me, but I had to leave. After I escaped, I made my way back to the club and took cash from the safe, called the assistant manager to take over for a time, stopped at my place to grab a couple of things, then went to Brent's to retrieve his dog." She looked down at the sleeping mutt. "He'd rescued Angel from a shelter and wouldn't have wanted her to go back."

At the mention of her name, the dog lifted her head to them and cocked it to the side.

Rylee smiled at Angel's expression. "After that, I just drove."

Kate scooted over and gave them a little space. "I don't understand why you got in the car in the first place."

"I didn't have a choice. They had a gun to Brent's head."

"Okay. I get that." Kate nodded. "But what did Dave want with you?"

Rylee had left out the part about his keeping her for a client or his knowing the whereabouts of the two girls. She guessed without those details, it didn't make much sense. But she couldn't share those. If she did, Kate would insist Rylee go to the FBI and that she get protection. She was too disillusioned with the FBI to know this wasn't an option for her. As long as no one knew, she was safe. She shrugged. "We didn't get a chance to talk other than him saying he wanted to start the family business again."

Kate wouldn't let it go. "But why did he, for lack of a better term, *kidnap* you and Brent? I just don't get it."

Rylee dropped her shoulders and hoped her acting skills were strong enough to get her friend to leave this alone. She'd ask for help when she needed it. "I don't either. Maybe he just wanted to brag. Now that he's dead, I won't ever find out."

Devon had watched her with shrewd eyes and when he spoke, she wondered where his train of thought had been during her and Kate's exchange. "Why didn't you at least tell Madison where you were going?"

"Maybe I was wrong not to tell my sister where I was staying. I knew if I told her I wanted to get away, she'd try to convince me to visit her. I didn't want that. I wanted to be alone." *I needed mobility and no one looking over my shoulder.*

"I don't know about all of this, Rylee. I really think you should talk with the FBI. You didn't do anything wrong."

She sighed. "Kate, you know as well as I do if no one knows I was there, I'm safe. If I open my mouth, even to the FBI, all I'll do is let the killer know there is a potential witness and my life won't be worth shit. I don't know anything, but that won't matter. There are always leaks."

"We can protect you." Kate glanced at her brother-in-law before turning back to Rylee. "HIS can protect you."

She looked directly at Devon and was firm in her response. "No." She couldn't have him, or them, around. At least, not yet. "I appreciate it, but I'm fine. There's nothing to protect me from." Unless Dave's partner planned to kidnap her for the client who wanted her. "I just need the space right now."

Whether it was friendly concern or her newfound mothering skills, Kate didn't mind stating her opinion. "I don't like you being out here without any form of communication. The cell service is spotty coming up here into the mountains, and nil here at the cabin."

"If it'll make you feel better, I'll pick up a SAT phone in town." She should've done that in the first place. She'd do anything to placate them so they'd leave.

"Kate can leave. But I'm not going anywhere until we straighten out things between us." Devon's voice brooked no argument.

No matter the situation Rylee found herself in when she'd come to this cabin, fear clouded her knowing she'd be alone with a man who'd married her without her sober consent. Worse, he might find out her true reason for being there.

Chapter Four

Kate surprised Devon by surging from her seat and announcing that she would return to Baltimore right away since Rylee obviously didn't need her. He'd expected her to at least stay the night. She wanted to leave the two of them to figure things out *after* they went into town to purchase Rylee a SAT phone for emergencies.

That spiked his curiosity as they'd brought an extra SAT phone for this purpose. Kate knew that. Plus, he doubted she believed Rylee any more than he did. She was hiding something. Knowing his sister-in-law, she had to be dying to find out more, to dig into what had happened. The woman was too inquisitive to just let it go as it was. That made him wonder what she was scheming.

Rylee jumped up and turned to him with panic in her eyes, and his heart sank. What the hell had he done to her that she feared being alone with him? He couldn't have been such a bastard. He prayed he hadn't hurt her. His insides tightened at the possibility. He'd never hurt a woman before, but he'd done something to spook her and not remembering was killing him.

She appeared to regain her composure and took control. "It'll get dark soon. Why don't you both stay the night, and then you can leave in the morning? I'll follow you into town and pick up a SAT phone."

He wanted to roll his eyes at the women. One was blatantly trying to push him and Rylee together, while the other was trying to pull them apart. He didn't like being put in this position. Maybe he should've stayed behind his computer that was devoid of emotion and drama.

Devon had to step in and grab control back from his wife. *His wife.* When that popped into his head, it sounded right. "That's a great idea for Kate to stay the night with us. The winding roads don't look inviting for night driving. As for the SAT phone, I have one, and, since I'm staying," he said and raised his eyebrow, begging for Rylee to disagree, "there is no need to purchase another one. In fact," —he paused and glanced at Kate, still unsure of her motive on the phone issue and the trip to town— "I believe I have an extra one in my bag." If she didn't want Rylee to have it, she'd have to speak up so he could get on board with whatever cockamamie plan she had brewed. He knew there had to be one with Kate.

Rylee swiveled her head back and forth between him and Kate several times. "I—" She broke off and swallowed as if fighting for the right words. "I—"

Kate flounced back down on the couch, ignoring Rylee. "Perfect idea, Devon." She beamed like she'd won the lottery. "That was smart of you to consider bringing one for Rylee."

Ah. She wanted him to appear as if he'd been looking out for Rylee. He doubted his wife would see him as any kind of hero.

Dropping back in the spot she'd vacated, Rylee sighed in defeat. Yet, he had the distinct impression her attempts to get rid of him hadn't ended. That rankled him to no end. He was a nice guy. Or, at least, he'd always been told that. She had no reason to be afraid of being with him. He'd have to show her that... after Kate departed.

"You know, Rylee, you've missed our monthly dinners." His sister-in-law hosted a dinner with her friends, and now some of the Hamilton men, once a month. She cooked a themed dinner and had the bravery to try out new recipes on them. In August, they'd been in Mississippi and even though her friends couldn't be there, she'd refused to miss playing hostess. She'd sent some of the HIS men down to the Gulf Coast for fresh seafood. She made a feast for them, attempting a new recipe for Crab Stuffed Peppers. They'd enjoyed the hell out of the meal. "I'll cook us up something tonight. We stopped at the grocery store along the way and picked up a few things."

Shit. He'd forgotten. Devon hopped up like he'd been stung on the ass by a bee. "I'd best get the bags from the car." He'd get his personal items installed in a bedroom, or the loft, to strengthen his commitment to stay.

"For September, I'm having Italian night, so we brought stuff to make pizza dough and sauce from scratch...."

Kate's voice trailed off as he walked outside and halted on the porch. He already knew her plans concerning food. Pizzas on the grill. He'd never heard of such a thing, but Kate loved a challenge. He asked her what she'd do if Rylee didn't have a grill out here. She told him not to be so ridiculous.

He inhaled deeply and enjoyed the crisp, clean air passing through his lungs. Although not an outdoorsy guy, the woodsy scent relaxed him. Maybe the lack of city noise set him at ease. A quick movement to his right caught his eye. He tensed and scanned the area. The woods surrounding the cabin were thin enough to see through for a fair distance, but gave the illusion of privacy. A rabbit bounced across the clearing where they'd parked the vehicles, stopping once to look his way and then hopping to the woods on the other side.

Devon shook his head and allowed his muscles to relax again. Nature. The animals, while harmless, could scare the crap out of a person when they decided to show themselves. He hoped he didn't embarrass himself in front of Rylee by jumping when one of them surprised him.

He shoved his hands in the front pockets of his jeans, stretched one leg down the front step and followed it with his other to the dirt, mixed with gravel, area where he'd parked the car. A sudden eagerness overcame him when he thought about being alone with Rylee. He wouldn't deny a strong attraction existed. All the talk from Kate about her friend only intrigued him more. He had to be doing the right thing to keep them married.

Annulment, my ass. He imagined she would be pretty pissed off when she found out he'd shredded those damn papers before he'd left Baltimore. They might not know each other, but he wouldn't quit without trying. There had to be some reason they'd married. He didn't believe in love at first sight. His actions, however, told him he might subconsciously believe differently. Or, he'd been too drunk to know the difference between love and lust.

She wouldn't have married a sloppy drunk and

then tried to rid herself of him right away. Would she? It's not like he was wealthy and she was trying to get his money. So, what had driven them to stand in front of a preacher and say their vows?

He'd only found a few videos of them together as they passed by a business or two on the strip. The chapel typically recorded their ceremonies and posted them online. But the two of them had opted out of it for some unknown reason. Maybe to keep her face safe in case she went undercover again? That was the only reason he could see agreeing to it.

That was how the preacher and his wife had described them when he'd spoken with them on the telephone. He and Rylee had been "so much in love." Devon wanted to throw something. He needed to know what had happened, and he'd only find out from her. Yet, she wanted to avoid it all and wash her hands of them.

The same question kept coming back—why did she marry him only to turn away?

If that wasn't enough to deal with, this situation with the murdered ICE agent bothered him. The fact that they were with Westbrook to begin with was suspicious. His mind even considered that Brent had been in cahoots with Dave and they'd planned to kidnap Rylee. But it sounded like the man had tried to protect her instead. It had been obvious she cared for Brent. She'd shed enough tears for him.

Had he been the reason she'd asked for the annulment? That thought burned through him.

Devon pulled the hands he'd fisted from his pockets and relaxed them. The situation didn't make sense. And her running way....

Not for a moment did he believe she just wanted to be alone. Based on her reaction to him, he didn't doubt she wanted to avoid him until he'd signed the papers, but there was more to it.

He had some serious digging to do. Thank God, he'd brought his laptop with him. He snorted. Like he'd go anywhere without it. Damned inconvenient—the local landline wasn't connected. That, however, wouldn't stop him but it would slow him down somewhat since he couldn't tap into anything but his SAT phone.

He felt it in his bones that Rylee had jumped in feet first into a potential wildfire. Maybe helping her with whatever she'd involved herself with would provide an opportunity to get to know each other. He only hoped her life wasn't in danger because he wouldn't be the right man for that job. But he wouldn't hesitate to recall his family from their assignments. She was his wife, after all…whether she wanted to be or not.

Emptying the items he needed from the car, Devon bumped the door closed with his hip. Laptop bag on his shoulder, overnight bags tossed over the other one and grocery bags hanging from his fingers, he returned to the cabin. Through his convoluted thinking, he had a plan. Kind of. Basically, he'd help her with whatever was going on. First, he had to gain her trust so she'd share. That might be a challenge since she looked scared to death of him one moment and ready to rip out his throat the next. Okay, his plan needed a bit more thought.

Kate lifted the grocery sacks from him and placed them on the kitchen counter.

"Kate, you can stay in there." Rylee pointed to one

of the two rooms off the living area. "Devon, you can sleep in the loft. While it's not a large cabin, there's plenty of room up there. Just watch your head. The ceiling slants." She hastened to the exit. "I'm going outside to rustle up Angel."

He nodded and turned to the guest room, with Kate fast on his heels. He dropped her bag at the foot of a bed covered with a country quilt with hand-sewn squares by the look of it.

She closed the door behind them. "I'm glad you're staying. She's lying to us. Or at least leaving something out," she suggested in a hushed tone.

He couldn't argue with her on that issue; he already planned to get to the bottom of it. "Why aren't you staying past tonight? I have a hard time believing you're just walking away from this." He kept his voice low to match hers.

"It's tough to do, but I expect you to keep me updated. I know there's a reason she's here, and she doesn't want to share it with me. I'm hoping she'll open up to you."

"Have you thought that maybe she really just wanted to hide from me and won't say a word? She did ask for an annulment, after all." That word kept lodging itself in his throat. He'd probably heard it only a handful of times growing up. Since receiving the paperwork a month ago, it had rung in his mind hundreds of times and each time the word repeated in his thoughts, it became more bitter and harder to swallow.

Kate shook her head. "Maybe that's part of it, but not the real reason. Dave's goons know she was in the car. Of course, I'm sure they won't mention knowing anything about it either. If you find out something is wrong, you get in touch with me right away. I'll bring all the men here. Rylee is too important to me. And, I believe she might be to you also."

He narrowed his eyes at her. "I—"

"Don't worry. I'll keep my mouth shut. You fix whatever there is between you two. In the meantime, this is mine." She reached for her bag and withdrew a Beretta. "Take it." She smiled weakly. "Just in case."

His body lurched in surprise. "Christ, Kate. How the hell did you get that through airport security?"

She shrugged, confirmed the safety was engaged, slipped the clip out to check it, slapped it back in and handed it to him with the grip facing him and the barrel pointed down.

A damn handgun. His job was to give them to the team, not accept them for his own use. He knew how to operate one, but that wasn't the point. "Fuck. Please tell me you didn't ask Arthur for a favor."

Indignation shined on her face. "No. Of course not. I put it in a locked case in the bag I checked."

He'd wondered why she'd checked a bag for the anticipated short trip. "Dammit. You could've pulled an alert that Arthur would've found. He'll have someone up here to grab Rylee to question. You and I both know that will be hairy for her with Westbrook's son being involved. Even if she says she wasn't there, her disappearance about the same time tells a different tale of her knowledge that something occurred."

"Look, Arthur feels like shit after what happened with Jake. He loves Rylee, and I think he wants us to watch out for her. Otherwise, he wouldn't have called me."

"Fuck. He called you? You know we aren't working with him. Why the hell didn't you tell us he was who you'd spoken with about the shooting? Jesse is going to be pissed."

Placing a hand on her hip, she sighed. "Don't worry. He doesn't know we left to search for her. I told him that we had no idea where she was located. He won't push me."

Devon grunted in disbelief. The man did love Kate, but Arthur had fucked the family by keeping them in the dark about Jake's location all those years and then the delay in allowing them to rescue him. A shoestring held together a once tight family relationship with the man. Putting his trust in Arthur again was too much to ask, especially with Rylee's life.

"I don't think he'll send anyone unless I say something to him."

He narrowed his eyes at her. "I don't know. Maybe we should get her out of here if she really wants to avoid the FBI."

Kate shook her head. "No. You stay here and find out what the hell is going on. If you find different, then we'll act." She pushed the handgun closer to him. "Now, take this, just in case."

He accepted the weapon and weighed it for comfort. Kate had a point. If Rylee was in trouble, which he didn't doubt, he might need it. Holding the weapon, he hoped that this time he had the courage to pull the trigger in time so no one died.

Chapter Five

Rylee assisted Kate in the kitchen, preparing dinner. To her relief, Devon offered to take Angel outside, leaving her alone with his sister-in-law. She laid the knife she'd been using to cut fresh oregano on the counter beside the cutting board and turned to her friend. "Kate, I can't do this."

Kate didn't even so much as glance her way. She continued stirring the ingredients in a large pot of slowly forming fragrant pizza sauce. "Do what? Make sauce? Sure you can. It's easy enough."

Rylee shook her head, frustrated, since she had no doubt that Kate knew what she meant but acted innocent. "Devon. You can't leave me here alone with him." Her insides fluttered in a weird way at the thought, and it confused her. Maybe she'd picked up a bug. That could explain why her body went hot and cold and all crazy inside. Only, it hadn't started until Devon had arrived. "I don't trust him."

Wiping her hands on a towel, Kate looked at Rylee and shook her head. "Nonsense. Devon is probably the most trustworthy of the Hamilton men." A slight chuckle escaped her lips. "Don't tell Jesse I said that."

"But he took advantage of my being drunk while we were in Vegas."

Kate raised a questioning brow. "How's that? Last I checked, it takes both parties to say, 'I do.'"

Rylee's stomach lurched at the thought. If she could only make Kate understand, she wouldn't allow Devon to stay there with her. "I had a—" She broke off in an almost choked voice and took a deep breath before beginning again. She hated to admit this weakness, but it couldn't be helped if she wanted him gone. "I had a blackout. I don't remember anything except waking up next to him. I had to have been drunk as all get out or hell, something was put in my drink. Either way, he married me when I wasn't in my right mind."

Her friend's expression hardened, and Rylee knew she'd said something wrong. Damn, she hadn't wanted Kate to judge her for possibly drinking herself into oblivion like an over-the-hill alcoholic.

"First," Kate said, and tapped on a finger to emphasize the number, "I'm not happy with you. You should've come to me right away with this. Second"— she ticked off a second finger—"Devon would never, and I repeat *never*, have drugged or taken advantage of you. And finally"—the third finger received a tap— "how can you be sure you didn't take advantage of him since you can't remember? Or, to my way of thinking, be sure of the distinct possibility you two fell in love?"

In love? Was Kate crazy? Ever since Kate had married, she'd become a romantic, believing in fairy tales. Hell, even she and Jesse hadn't fallen in love right away. Two people didn't meet and fall head over heels in love instantly. This wasn't a romantic novel or movie. Things like that didn't happen in real life. Other people might think so, but she wasn't a fool.

Lust. That was what it had to have been. She couldn't deny being attracted to Devon, and she could tell it was reciprocated in the way he looked at her—as if he planned to gobble her up for dinner. But lust wasn't enough to build a marriage upon, especially if it started when neither party could remember.

The whole idea of it was just fucked up. "Does he really not remember?" Rylee wasn't sure why she asked because she doubted she'd believe the answer no matter what it happened to be.

Kate shook her head and frowned. "Did you hit him on the head with the lamp? They say he could've pulled it down when he fell, but I wonder…."

Rylee scrunched up her face and nodded. "Yes." Her voice projected like that of a petulant child who'd been caught doing something they shouldn't have been doing.

Tossing back her head, her friend belted out a laugh that brought Devon rushing back into the cabin with a look of concern etched on his face. How could she think this funny? Nothing about this entire situation was even remotely humorous.

Devon halted, hand resting on the doorknob and eyes fastened on Rylee. His lips twitched and his gaze slid to Kate, and then back to her, and finally, he quirked an eyebrow. "What's going on?"

Kate's laughter died down, and she wiped tears from her eyes. "You two are made for each other."

Rylee and Devon's gaze intensified and a need for something intimate zipped between them.

"Okay, I'm going to say this and then the topic is closed for dinner. Neither of you remember what happened in Vegas, so you need to do a lot of talking."

Devon's surprised expression caught her off guard. "Is that true?" The uncertainty in his voice tugged at her heart.

She flattened her lips and nodded in reluctance. "Yes." She stiffened when she realized her mouth spoke before her brain caught up to it. "I mean, I don't remember the night, only waking up beside you." Could he see the tremble quaking her body at the admission? She worked to gain control of the tremors and failed miserably.

"Something happened that night that pushed the two of you to get married. Like it or not, you *are* married. I think you need to talk this out before you do something stupid, like"—she threw her hands up—"I don't know, get an annulment. Try to remember what brought you two together."

"Kate—" Rylee started, but Kate immediately cut her off.

"No. That's all for now. When I'm gone, figure it out. I don't want two of my good friends tossing away what might be the best thing to happen to them. Now, where's that chopped oregano?"

Rooted to the spot, Rylee's eyes still locked with Devon's, she took a moment to comprehend that she'd lost control of her own guests. She didn't fight it because she didn't want to talk about the topic any longer. Nor did she want to discuss it after Kate left. It didn't seem the time to try to change her friend's mind about leaving her and Devon alone again. She'd try later tonight or in the morning before Kate left.

"The oregano?" Kate's question prodded her back to her task.

Rylee jumped. "Oh!" She scooped the chopped herb from the cutting board, sprinkled it into the pot and watched Kate stir, wishing she could swirl away her problems as easily as the sauce mixed.

Before she realized it, Devon scooted around the kitchen island and appeared beside them near the stove. He reached over and stuck a finger in the pot of sauce and then licked it. "Needs more salt." A mischievous smile fought to break out on his face and failed. He stepped back as if expecting his sister-in-law to hit him for his mocking insult.

"Stick your finger in there again and I'll give you something to complain about," Kate threatened, her voice light, shaking the spoon at him with red liquid dripping from it. "All right, let's make these babies up and get them on the grill. Is it ready?" She looked to Devon for an answer.

He nodded and reached for the pizza crust she handed him. "Sure is."

They picked up the sauce, mushrooms, green peppers, pepperoni, and cheese to carry outside with the dough and then filed out to the back deck and the grill.

Out of habit, Rylee scanned the area, but she couldn't see much with the shadows and darkness forming around the cabin from where the sun had dipped behind the mountains for its evening descent and blocked out most of the light.

"Let's hope this works. I read using a pizza grilling stone is preferred, but this is doable. We'll see." Kate placed her pizza dough on a circular pan with holes made for the grill. "We put everything on them once we flip it."

Devon groaned. "You didn't say you hadn't tried this before."

Kate shrugged and rubbed her hands together, as if dusting them off. "You didn't ask."

"Rylee, please tell me you've got more food here." Devon shook his head with a chuckle. "Something tells me pizza delivery isn't a backup option."

Rylee bit back her laugh. "Have I missed something? My experience with Kate's cooking has always been superb."

He plunked down in a deck chair. "Lucky you."

"Don't listen to him." Kate sat at the table and turned her chair so her back was to Devon. "He didn't care for one of my recipes a couple of months ago."

Devon snorted. "Me? Try everyone."

Kate huffed. "Okay, it won't make my cookbook, but—"

"What?" Rylee almost shouted. "You're writing a cookbook?"

Her friend flushed with embarrassment. "I've talked to someone to put together something for friends and family. Nothing big."

"Thank goodness," Devon mumbled in the background.

Angel slinked over and dropped down on the deck beside him. His attention diverted to the dog, and he slid his hand over and ruffled the pet's ears.

Kate spun around to him. "Oh, hush. You like my cooking and you know it."

Devon stood in one swift motion, sparking Angel to jump up and bark in excitement, rushed to Kate and plucked her out of the chair, gripping her in a bear hug. "You know I do. You're an amazing cook." He kissed her on the cheek and set her on her feet. "You should sell the book. It'd do well. As long as you don't put in that one recipe."

Giggling, Kate swatted at his arm in jest and

smiled. "Quit screwing around and check the food."

With a twinge of jealousy at their closeness, Rylee laughed at the camaraderie between the two.

As the evening progressed, she relaxed. The air chilled enough to drive them inside to eat their almost scorched pizzas. They'd begun talking and had forgotten about the first round they'd had to toss, and Angel chasing a squirrel had almost distracted them too long on the second round.

"I'm sorry I don't have more drink offerings." Rylee handed them bottled water.

"Don't be," Devon said. "This is perfect."

Rylee's skin tingled where he clasped her hand to accept the beverage, not only holding it longer than necessary but also giving her hand a small caress. That threw her relaxation straight out the window and replaced it with worry. She'd been able to push aside the fact that she and Devon would be by themselves soon. With his playfulness, and that damn sensuality that radiated from him without effort, she didn't believe she could handle it.

Unsure how to respond, Rylee instead took a bite from her pizza. Exquisite flavor exploded across her taste buds from the sauce and the entire concoction. She closed her eyes and inwardly moaned at the deliciousness. After she swallowed, she looked at Kate and caught her surprised stare and then Devon's devilish smile. *Crap. Did I moan aloud?* Rylee set the piece of pizza back on her plate and self-consciously put her hand in front of her mouth, lest she have something in her teeth now that everyone watched her so intently. "You've outdone yourself this time, Kate."

"I think we've got a keeper," Devon boasted. Yet,

he hadn't touched his food and his eyes were riveted on Rylee.

She wanted to slide under the table. Did he mean her? He couldn't, not if he couldn't remember the night either.

"What are you going to do about the dog?" Kate asked, breaking into what might've turned into an awkward moment. "I had thought you might want one of Dottie's puppies, but now…."

Regaining her wits, Rylee pulled her attention from the man across the table and turned it back to her friend. "She had puppies? Wow. I've missed too much. As for Angel, I think I'll keep her. She's been great company."

After that, Kate thankfully kept up a steady stream of prattle about Reagan, Jesse's daughter, and Jason, their adopted son, throughout dinner. Rylee and Devon had remained quiet for the most part. The only blessing had been that the two hadn't asked her more about why she was there of all places.

After a team effort to clean up the dinner mess, Kate excused herself to the guest room, and a nervous air ignited in the room. Devon stepped closer to her. "Rylee—" he began in a hushed voice.

Panicked and overwhelmed, she fled. Putting her hand to her temple, she stopped his words. "I'm sorry, but I have a terrible headache coming on. Angel and I are going to bed." Then, she smiled with what she prayed was a pleasant, hostess smile. "Make yourselves at home. I'll see you in the morning."

His crestfallen expression sent her stomach tumbling and a small part of her wanted to stay. Facing what was between them wasn't something she could handle. Of course, she was being a damn coward, but her own self-preservation was vital.

****

Rylee woke suddenly with every muscle in her body tense and on alert. Her hand instinctively moved beneath her pillow to grip the handgun she kept there. What the hell had disturbed her? She'd only been asleep for what seemed like a few minutes. Most of the night she'd tossed and turned, her mind on Devon who slept in the loft. The same damn man she'd attempted to rid from her life without setting eyes on.

She'd set him straight today. No if, ands, or buts about it, he would leave today. Last night had been her last time fleeing from troubles in her personal life. A quick chat with Kate and she'd have her friend backing her to send Devon packing. Having that support couldn't hurt when dealing with a stubborn Hamilton brother.

She sighed. Hell, chasing him away was just another form of fleeing.

There it was again. Rylee tilted her head. Muffled voices came through the window. Throwing back the sheet, in her flannel pajamas, she sprang from the bed and rushed to the window. A shiver rippled through her when her bare feet left the area rug for the chilled wood flooring. She bounced on the balls of her feet the remaining distance, considering what she might find. Moving the curtains aside just enough to barely peek out, she held her breath and willed down the increasing volume of her pulse pounding in her ears. One of two things had happened—she'd been found by whoever worked with Dave, or her houseguests were trying to be secretive. Only, she didn't understand why they'd do that. No matter who it was, they shouldn't have chosen to have their discussion in the front of the cabin where her bedroom happened to be located if they didn't want to get caught.

In the dim lighting of dawn, her eyes focused on a small sparkle of the sun's rays breaking over the mountains. She cursed. A small dust cloud followed the departing rental car, with Kate presumably behind the wheel since Devon stood in the now vacant spot watching it disappear.

Damn Kate! I can't believe she abandoned me like this.

The curtain slid from her fingers, and the room once again plunged into near darkness. How did she get rid of him now? She glanced at the weapon in her hand and shook her head before she placed it back under her pillow.

Thinking of his firm statement before dinner that he'd be staying brought out a sliver of admiration. He definitely had balls since she hadn't invited him to hang around. Working with two of his brothers gave her an inkling that she knew the Hamilton mindset fairly well. If he was like AJ and Jesse and wanted to stay, he'd damn well stay no matter what she said to the contrary. A slow smile crept across her face. Luckily, that same stubbornness lived in her.

She harrumphed in frustration. Then something else occurred to her. What if he wanted to play house or something intimate like that? He didn't seem to be as eager to get the annulment as she did. Her heart sank to her belly. They couldn't be intimate. Then it would be a real marriage and no annulment would be allowed. Calming her jangling nerves, she bit her lip in thought and then shrugged in satisfaction at her plan. She'd take him to the airport herself. Then her mood soured at the thought of the long drive alone, but it had to be done. He'd interfere if he stayed.

Angel whined, and Rylee reached into the closet for clothes. She quietly changed into jeans and a sweater, listening for Devon's activity in the outer room. Plopping her behind down on the bed, she lifted her foot to put on her hiking boots. Angel whined again. "One more second, girl. It may be September, but it's too cold in these mountains to go barefoot, even if I'm just on the porch while you do your thing."

The dog cocked his head at her. The pose was damn cute, but it didn't give Rylee confidence the pet understood.

"We're also going to tell Devon that we're taking him to the airport. I know last night Kate said there was no way he'd have taken advantage of me if he'd been sober, so I'm guessing he must've been drunk also. That doesn't build up my picture of the perfect man any better." She dropped her foot and proceeded to put her boot on the other foot. Once done, she slapped it down on the rug and looked at the dog. "You couldn't care less, could you? You were all over him last night. Like a bitch in heat." She stood, shook her head and chuckled. "Apparently, I must've been at one time as well. It just goes to prove that neither of us can be trusted near him."

Angel raced to the bedroom door with her tail wagging fast enough to generate wind power.

Rylee shook her head, snatched a hair clip from the dresser, and opened the door, prepared to take back control of her haven.

She didn't have to turn in his direction to know that

Devon sat at the kitchen bar with a cup of coffee and an open laptop. She caught a glimpse of him out of the corner of her eye. Besides, her body gave a frustrating, light tingle to his presence. Muttering a quick, "Good morning," she didn't stop on her way to let Angel outside so the dog could relieve herself. No matter how bold and strong she told herself she was, being alone with Devon frightened her deep inside. His presence challenged her resolve.

A chilly gust of wind slapped her in the face when she closed the front door of the cabin behind her, causing her to involuntarily shiver. Angel bolted to the tree line and sniffed around until she found a spot worthy of squatting. After the dog completed that task, she raced back to the door, eager to return inside.

Rylee took a deep breath to settle her nerves, and they entered the cabin with Angel rushing in to confront Devon.

"We need to talk." Devon quirked one side of his mouth as if fighting a smile. "*Mrs. Hamilton.*"

Her heart lurched at the name. Damn him! Why couldn't he have just signed the damn papers and been done with it? What did he want? She sighed, knowing there was only one way to find out and it wasn't to flee. She had to sit with him and talk. Then, she'd take him to the airport.

Resigned, she walked to the counter and poured herself a cup of coffee in an "I don't do fashion. I AM fashion" mug to allow herself more time to bolster her confidence. She reached into the refrigerator and withdrew her French vanilla creamer, doctored her coffee with it, and then blew on the coffee before taking a sip of the warm, strong liquid. "Okay."

His gaze slid over her from head to toe, leaving a warm awakening in its path. "I wish I remembered you, Rylee."

"Yeah, well, I don't remember everything either, so we're even," she retorted.

He cocked his head in question. "If you didn't remember the night, how did you know we're married? I have the license."

She unintentionally looked down at her bare left hand. "I didn't know until I settled on the airplane and saw the wedding band on my finger. Somehow I'd missed it before then." Probably because she'd been in a rush to escape.

In for a nickel, in for a pound. Whatever the hell that phrase meant. She looked back at him and continued, "I didn't know who you were at the time. I had to do a little digging to find out since you didn't come around right away searching for me."

An unsettling silence hovered in the air. Too much had been lost between them. Actually, all that was between them had been lost.

"I guess you didn't give me a ring to remember you by." His eyes gleamed with humor as he scooted his chair back and gracefully stood. "I can assure you of this," he said and stepped closer to her, "had I remembered, I'd have been there without delay."

An ache formed deep in the center of her chest, and she almost whimpered at what could've been. Resolved to regain her life, she took a stand. "Look, it appears neither of us remembers what happened that night or why we lost our heads and got married. Even more reason to get the annulment. We were unaware of our actions. Why can't you just sign the papers and end this farce? Then I can take you to the airport, and we can get on with our lives."

He halted and allowed a wicked smile to spread across his face. The damn man was enjoying this. How had it come to that? Didn't he see they'd made a mistake and there was only one easy way to rectify it? People didn't meet, immediately marry, and live happily ever after. Surely, any idiot knew that.

"There's still the matter of you hitting me on the head with a lamp."

"How?" she croaked out in a nervous voice. Realizing her inadvertent admission, she cleared her throat and pressed on. No reason to lie since Kate might've told him the truth. "How did you know I did that? I thought you didn't remember."

He quirked an eyebrow in an all-knowing gesture that pissed her off.

"I didn't know for certain—until just now."

"What do you want? It can't be me. You don't even know me," she stated, and her forgotten coffee sloshed over the top of the cup and scalded her thumb and the area surrounding it. She turned away, set the mug down, and ran cold water over her hand. His light touch on her hand had her almost jumping out of her skin.

"Let me see." He turned her hand so he could survey the burn under the running water.

She froze, her breath catching in her throat, and her pulse took on a frantic race through her veins. He was too damn close. Her mind screamed, "Flee," and she couldn't fight it even though she'd sworn she wouldn't do it again. She yanked her hand from him. "It's fine." Then she sprinted to the doorway. Taking him to the airport or talking things out flew from her mind. "I'm going for a hike. You can come or not." *What the hell is wrong with me? The last thing I want is him following me around.*

Angel appeared and pushed out the entry with Rylee. She closed it behind her, trying not to care if Devon followed or not. When she made it to the tree line, the slamming of the cabin door reverberated through the clearing behind her. A few moments later, she heard him enter the trail on her heels. His persistence made her smile to herself, and then it quickly vanished when she realized she still didn't know what he wanted. She also didn't know if she should continue this trek with him behind her. She just needed to see if the girls were there.

A hand grabbed her upper arm, halting her forward movement. She spun around and Devon's concerned gaze hit her in the gut. "Rylee, stop for a moment. Tell me what the hell is going on? Why are you really hiding out here?"

She swallowed hard past the lump in her throat. She didn't want to trust him, but since he refused to leave her alone, maybe he could help her. He did work at HIS. Then again, maybe he'd decide to bring in the FBI. All at once, the burden she'd been carrying became too heavy to bear alone. A niggling sensation told her that she needed someone, whether she wished to admit it or not. Kate said to trust him so she would give it a try and pray she hadn't made another bad choice with him.

The only drawback was that they'd have to spend more time together. She'd have to risk whatever happened because she needed someone to have her back. "What do you do with HIS?"

He narrowed his eyes at her, and his intense focus reached to her soul. "I'm the computer guy. If they need it, I find it—whether it's equipment or information. What does that have to do with anything?"

Just the backup she needed. Research was her weak spot. She had to take this leap, for the sake of the girls. "Follow me." She pulled her arm from his grasp and led him in silence for a couple of miles and through several trails until they broke out onto a ledge.

His appreciative whistle matched her regard of the area. "The view is breathtaking."

Her mind couldn't focus on the splendor of color bursting through the forests along the mountain ridges. Only the dwelling below held her attention. She pointed a finger to a house in the middle of the canyon. "They're there."

He squinted to view where Rylee had directed his gaze. "Who's there?"

"Misty and Mandy."

"And they are?"

"Two girls about to be sold into sex slavery who I'm going to rescue."

Emotions washed over his face, and it concerned her that she couldn't grasp any particular one, except for the brief flash of anger. "How sure are you about this?" he asked in a slow, measured voice, and she wondered how hard it had been to control it.

She bit down on the left side of her lip and hated she had to admit the truth. "I've not had time to check the house to ensure they're there. But I've gone through Dave Westbrook's phone and have checked out the other addresses he's traveled to. This one has to be it."

"Dave Westbrook? The guy who was killed with the ICE agent?"

When she nodded, he continued in a near rant, "Goddammit, Rylee! How the hell did you end up with his phone? And"—his voice rose with each word—"what do you mean you've checked out the other addresses?"

The mild, sensual man who'd arrived had disappeared. This man appeared ready to rip someone's head off, and she was in his direct path. "I'll tell you all about it if you agree to help me."

Devon took his time scanning the area from the woods, trails, and mountains surrounding them to the canyon with a large ranch house on it below, and, presumably, two girls in need of their help. When he finally spoke, Rylee had almost given up hope he'd agree. "All right." He turned to her and waited until she looked him in the eye. The angry man had vanished and a calm, calculating one replaced him. "On one condition. We'll get to know each other and see if we can salvage our marriage."

With a ton of disparaging words on her tongue, she surprised herself with the question that left her mouth. "Why do you want to stay married to me so badly?"

His eyes raked over her face as if attempting to read her thoughts. "Because there had to be a reason I married you. I intend to find out." He raised his eyebrows in question. "Now, are we agreed?"

She considered her choice of doing this alone, and maybe failing again, or doing this with help, even though he was the last person she wanted to be near. Her shoulders sagged, knowing what she had to do. The girls' lives trumped her happiness in every way. She'd use Devon to help her and then, after he realized she had no intention of remaining married to someone who would extort her like he was, she'd be able to send him packing.

That begrudgingly decided, she nodded and released a long, suffering sigh. "Fine. You help me rescue the girls, and I'll give our marriage a chance. *But,*" she emphasized the word while balling her hands into fists, "no one else is involved in our search until I say so." The last thing she wanted was for this area to be crawling with people and scaring off the girls' captor. Besides, after two failed home searches, she preferred not to look like an idiot if the girls weren't there. And, if they were, she wouldn't argue about bringing in help to rescue them. She wasn't stupid enough to think she could do it alone. "Oh," she said as an afterthought as she turned back to the trail, "there will be no sex."

Chapter Six

If the situation hadn't been so serious, Devon would've bust out laughing loud enough to scare away woodland creatures for miles at Rylee's stubborn, parting words. *But,* he thought as he turned from watching her luscious backside stalk away from him, then his humor faded and he tightened his lips, *the situation was dead serious. Damn! I need my ass kicked for demanding such an exchange when someone needed help.*

The moment she mentioned the possibility of girls being held captive, he knew he'd help find them, no matter the cost. He couldn't abide by such cruelty as selling girls into slavery of any sort. Any man who walked away from this type of situation needed his balls cut off.

So why had he pushed her to agree to his plan? Hell, even he knew it wasn't the way to win her heart. Yet, there was the crux of it all—he wanted her heart. He'd hate to live his life with someone who didn't love him. Maybe he hadn't had her heart when they'd married. He didn't know if she'd had his either.

This entire scenario read like a bad dream that only got worse with the introduction of the girls.

Devon turned back to the breathtaking view of the mountains and took in the land, home, and barn in the small valley before him in a new, critical light. If, and that was a big if because Rylee didn't appear completely confident, there were girls in trouble down there, he wouldn't even attempt to rescue them without his brothers. They were the muscle of HIS. Her not wanting help bothered him. Something wasn't right and he had to find out as quickly as possible.

The thought of the girls being sold sent bile climbing up the back of his throat, and he swallowed in an attempt to keep it down. He had to find a way to change Rylee's mind about accepting help, which would put a big damper on his plans to remain alone with her and get to know each other. Without a doubt, though, this came first. His love life, or lack thereof, could wait.

One thing that did lighten his spirits was that she chose to tell him why she was here, include him and ask for his help. Either she was considerably desperate or she trusted him, at least somewhat. He smiled to himself. He could work with that.

Turning back, he followed the path she'd left while planning his next moves. Information was golden and he wanted it now. Who owned the home? What about the homeowners? How did they fit with the Westbrooks? He needed aerial views. He needed stuff from his office.

A movement a foot in front of him startled Devon, and he stopped dead in his tracks. A black snake, maybe three feet long, slithered across his path, weaving its long body back and forth with the leaves softly rustling underneath its movement. He'd never been the outdoorsy type and didn't care to come face-to-face with creatures that could kill. He had no idea what type of snake it was and that could be a problem in the future. After the snake cleared his vision, he looked around the area. Did they have bears up here? He had to know what else inhabited these woods if they would be hiking through them. He didn't need more threats to protect her from.

His shoulders slumped, and he dropped his head in defeat. There he was again with the desire to protect Rylee and his knowledge that he was unable to do so. He'd have to convince her to bring in the family.

Arriving back at the cabin with a plan in mind, Devon slid through the doorway, ready to rest his weary body as the several hour hike had kicked his butt. Rylee waited patiently at the wooden dining table with a bottle of water nestled in her hands as if she hadn't exerted herself as he had.

He needed to tell her that he wouldn't hold her to his requirement for help and that he needed the family behind them. After this was over, he'd find a way to see if they belong together.

Her eyes, dull and emotionless, rose and met his. "I'm sure you have questions." She stood and turned to the refrigerator, her back stiff. "Sit. I'll get you some water and we can talk. Fresh coffee is brewing."

Angel whined, and he looked down and smiled at the dog. He petted her and trudged to the table, feeling every bit the heel he'd been. He'd driven her to be like this...this unfeeling, robotic woman.

The chair legs screeched against the wood flooring as he pulled it from the table. Accepting the plastic bottle, he slid down into the seat across from where she returned to her seat. "Rylee—" He took a deep, fortifying breath, ready to tackle the toughest issue first. "I'm sorry. I want to help you."

She narrowed her eyes a fraction and held his gaze. A tiny light flickered in her eyes. Hope?

He was about to smash it. Damn, this sucked. "However, I think we need help."

She jumped from her chair and any semblance of what he'd thought he'd seen in her eyes changed to fear. What the hell was going on? "No!"

"Rylee," he said with as much patience as he could muster, "what's the problem with getting help?"

The heaving of her chest told him of her fear. He couldn't imagine why she didn't want more help though. Not if the girls were truly at that house. That thought twisted in his mind that maybe she'd lied and there was another reason for this that she didn't want to share.

"Look, if others get involved, the FBI will surely find out I'm here and want to speak with me."

He saw no need to inform her that the FBI, at least their deputy director, probably already knew her location. He wouldn't be surprised if the man hadn't tracked their movements. Thankfully, Kate kept him at bay. "This isn't about you though. Why not get them involved in finding these girls?"

She shrunk before his eyes, and it made him want to surge from his chair and carry her somewhere and hold her on his lap and comfort her. Instead, he watched her sit and gather her strength. This went much deeper than girls being held captive.

Devon listened to Rylee share the story of her undercover assignment, how she'd taken the girls' protection personally, and how they had disappeared. The FBI hadn't seemed to care and she didn't believe they'd care now. Not until she had proof. That was what she was seeking.

"And just how did you plan to go about getting this proof?" He wasn't sure he wanted to know her answer.

She stiffened as if he'd slapped her. "The same way I proved the other houses were clean."

He placed his elbows on the table, connected his hands and leaned his forehead on it. Closing his eyes, he took a moment to calm himself. She'd obviously been putting herself in danger, and it wrenched at him that she could've been killed if she'd been dealing with such unsavory elements. "What other houses?" He didn't look up at her, just stared blankly at the wooden table. His thoughts whirled with all she'd told him before about the situation. He fought to remain calm because he knew he wouldn't like her answer. When she didn't respond, he looked up at her and realized she'd been waiting for his attention.

She spread her palms on the table and studied them intently. "Okay, remember what I told you about the car accident?"

He raised his eyebrows in response. He knew she'd been hiding something. "Yes."

"Well, I got into the limo because Dave told me he knew where the girls were. Then, when we were riding, he said that he had them hidden with a partner."

"Son of a bitch. And, he had you in that car?" Holy hell. Fear slid its nasty way through him, leaving a cold shiver in its wake. They'd planned to kill her. He'd thought it bad enough the bastard had told her he planned to restart his father's business. There would've been no other reason for the man to tell her about the girls unless he had no intention of releasing her.

"That's not important."

"Hell yes, it is!" At her shocked expression, he took a deep breath and ran his hands through his hair in frustration. He missed the longer length in cases like this. Running his fingers through it had soothed him. By God, he would do it now with the shorter length. "Go ahead," he directed with a nod.

Taking a moment to respond, he thought he'd pushed her to silence. Then, she huffed and spoke. "I've been looking for the girls since the day they disappeared. I won't give up on them."

"After you left the FBI, you still searched for them? How?"

"Brent and I followed up on any lead he heard about that was being overlooked. There had only been two...and they both led nowhere, but it was something more than the FBI, or ICE, was doing."

He'd bet his paycheck someone had found out what Brent was doing and it got to the wrong person. Otherwise, why would Dave grab him also? Kidnapping one agent trained to protect themselves was bad enough, but to add a second one? Like most of this, that made no sense to him. Maybe Dave was just an idiot. "I guess I still don't understand why this guy picked you up and bragged about what he planned to do." The man took one hell of a risk by doing that, no matter if he planned to kill her later. There had to be a reason why.

"I think he wanted to rub it in about the girls because he knew how frantic I'd been when they couldn't be found."

"And he planned to tell you this and just drop you at the next corner?" He chuckled, but no humor escaped within it.

Her mouth dropped open and her face reddened. Now he wanted to truly laugh because he had an inkling her change of demeanor was in anger at him and not embarrassment.

"No," she asserted. "At that time, Dave wasn't a threat."

"They held a fucking gun to your friend's head to get you in the car!"

She shifted her gaze away before she responded. "I thought Brent and I would be safe together with only Dave. It would've been two against one. If we'd stayed, there were two of his men there." She looked back at him with a look begging him to understand. "Plus, Dave wanted to tell me about the girls, so I couldn't just walk away."

He wanted to scream at her, but he knew if someone held a gun to her head and told him to get in the car or they'd kill her, he'd get in the damn car, but not without her. Like she'd done with Brent. Then the information she'd been seeking for months was available to her. No, he'd probably have done the same thing. He inwardly scoffed at himself. He'd never admit it to her. "All right. You thought your safest route was with Dave. Then this sicko tells you all."

"Yeah."

"What if Brent was actually one of them? Have you considered that? He might not have kept you safe."

She surged to her feet, almost knocking the chair to the floor. "No!"

The force of emotion behind her statement told him that she cared deeply about the dead man. Well, hell. The Colorado Mountains weren't the only ones he'd have to climb. He waved his hand for her to sit. "Calm down and sit. You sound so certain. How do you know?"

"I—" she sputtered. "He—" she tried again. "He loved me. He wouldn't have put me in that situation. Besides, they had a gun to his head."

His gut churned at her admission, but a swig of hope sprang free. She hadn't said that she loved the man, only that he loved her. "Yet, they didn't kill him." He realized his mistake at the sharp look of pain on her face. "Not at first." He reached across the table and touched her small, warm hand. "I'm sorry for your loss, Rylee." It pained him to say it, but he didn't like to see her hurting.

She sniffed, swiped at her damp eyes, and nodded. "He wasn't bad. I just know it," she said in a low, yet determined voice.

He removed his hand and immediately hated the loss of her touch. Damned oddest thing. He sat back in his chair to focus and hide his jealousy over a dead man. "Okay. He wasn't bad."

She looked up from her hand, the one he'd touched, and nodded again. She assumed the demeanor he'd seen many times on the HIS men—cold, distant but alert. She may have left the FBI, but the training hadn't left her.

He cleared his throat. They needed to get back to the main topic. "You've given me a lot so let me see if I've got this all down right. Two girls were taken while on your op. You got so upset the FBI wouldn't chase them, you quit your job with the bureau and looked on your own while managing the club." He raised his eyebrows. "A club, by the way, that generates its own set of problems."

Devon held up his hands when she started to interrupt. "Okay. Okay. Back to the problem at hand. Dave Westbrook, a man the bureau cleared of all wrongdoing during your undercover op, drags you and an ICE agent—" He couldn't bring himself to say the man's name. Dammit. He cleared his throat again. "Drags you both into a car—at gunpoint—and brags about stealing two girls and planning to sell them into sex slavery. But then the car was in an accident. An intentional one, it sounds like. Everyone, but you, because you believe they couldn't see you, was killed."

He took a deep breath. "You grabbed phones and weapons from the victims and then disappeared. You don't know who killed Dave and Brent. Yet, you refuse to speak with the FBI so it doesn't become common knowledge you were there and could've witnessed who the killer was. Even though the two goons know you were there. With all that, you're still searching for the girls, and you believe they're here."

Rylee nodded again.

"Hell, Rylee. Can you do anything but nod? This is serious shit." He wanted to reach over and shake her out of this business-like stance.

She huffed, and he silently cheered that he'd elicited some emotion that riled her to life. He didn't care if he pissed her off, as long as she participated.

"That about sums it up," she finally said.

That wasn't even close to summing it up. Too many things were missing, and he intended to find out everything. He'd tackle one thing at a time though. He believed she knew why that asshole picked her up and told her everything. The possibility of what it was scared the hell out of him. His dismal thought was interrupted when she continued to speak.

"Before I powered down Dave's phone so no one could locate it and me, I copied down his most recent phone calls with the person's information. I also pulled the e-mail folder he kept of travel. I figured he would've been to see the girls at some point."

Good girl, he wanted to tell her as a spike of pride welled in him. "What about Brent's phone? It sounds like you had both?"

She twisted her mouth into a grimace. "It was locked."

With what he was learning about Dave Westbrook, he wasn't surprised the man didn't lock his phone. Incompetent sprang to mind. But a government agent knew better. "I'll check it out."

Her eyes sparkled and awe floated through them. "You can get into it?"

He lifted his shoulders and held them a moment before he dropped them from a shrug. He hoped his delight at her barely masked excitement of his possible abilities didn't come through in his expression. "Probably."

Her chair creaked as she made to move from her seat. "I'll get it."

Devon reached out and clasped her hand to hold her in place. "Wait. There's still plenty I want to know before we can move forward."

"You're right. Ask away." She straightened and clasped her hands together on the table in front of her.

"Let's start with the house you're watching. Who owns it?" He'd confirm whatever information she'd obtained, but he'd like to hear all she knew. He thought of her joining HIS for a moment then pushed it to the back of his mind. He had to stick with the current problem...or, at least one of them. "What do you already know about his relationship with Dave?" His hands itched to get hold of Dave's phone and find out all he could. He'd need to retrieve some equipment from the office to assist them. Getting it without raising an alarm would be difficult since he knew Em wouldn't keep it from her husband and Jake wouldn't keep it from Jesse, but he'd find a way.

He also had to figure out what he'd tell Kate for the time being about the situation. He wouldn't lie to her, but he'd concede to Rylee's request not to share. If the girls were actually in the house, all bets were off, and he'd deal with Rylee's reaction.

"A man named Robert Carver."

Jagged ice sliced through Devon's veins and the cold made a strong attempt to paralyze him. He took a long drink of water to settle himself. "Robert Carver?" he asked with care to keep the question light so she had no idea the name wasn't welcome. There was more than one man by that name, but his gut churned anyway.

She nodded. "I don't know anything about him except Dave flew here several times last month."

If it was the Robert Carver Devon knew, she wouldn't have found out much and digging would alert him. That Robert Carver had been Devon's CIA boss and had convinced him to keep quiet about the circumstances of CIA operative Greg Donovan's death and Devon's part in it.

Chapter Seven

Rylee could tell by the stiffening of Devon's body and the shock on his face, and then his subsequent pull to mask it, that he knew that name and it didn't sit well with him. She opened her mouth to ask, but instead, she bounced from her seat. "Coffee is ready. Do you want some?" She'd turned from him and had already reached for a mug before she finished her question.

"Sure."

She poured two cups of coffee, doctored hers, and brought them to the table, setting one in front of Devon before reclaiming her seat. She didn't want to anger him before she received his help. Biding her time was always tough for her, but she'd do it…for Misty and Mandy.

His long fingers wrapping around his coffee mug drew her attention. The forefinger lightly tapping against the rim caused a small ripple in the dark liquid.

"I'll ask again."

She snapped her head up at his words, embarrassed that her thoughts had turned to his large hand moving over her body and the ripple it could create all the way to her core. Crap. She didn't need her mind concocting stuff like that.

"How sure are you that these girls are there? Just because Westbrook flew to Colorado doesn't mean he stopped at that house." He lifted the mug to his lips and took a cautious sip.

Forcing her mind on the conversation, she cleared her throat, ready to be all business again. She'd done all the research she could to determine the best options for where the girls could be held. Hell, she could be wrong, but she wouldn't give up without trying. "There were several phone calls to the house that coincided with the travel dates."

"Even then, Westbrook could've flown here for parties. Or maybe he has a lover living there. It could be a getaway retreat for him." He picked up his mug and stopped halfway to his mouth, then set it down as if a thought suddenly occurred to him. "You even checked other places before this, so it wasn't your first choice."

Indignation stabbed through Rylee at his doubt, and she wanted to rant at him. Yet, he was right, and she was adult enough to allow her flash of attitude to wash away, albeit with a bit of effort. There was no sense in arguing about her research, or lack thereof. She figured they'd have plenty of time for arguing when it came to their so-called marriage. "I checked the other places he'd been traveling to first because they were easy to search. Their homes having no real security should've tipped me off." Rylee shrugged, hating to admit her failures to him but having to do it so he could see she'd tried. "I didn't want to chance it though, so I cleared them from the list anyway."

Devon nodded as if he understood her need to check everywhere. Maybe that was just how she perceived the agreement because she wanted that to be his response.

"It took me some time to find somewhere to stay

near Carver's place. There are other rentals closer, but this was all that was available at the last minute." She had enough time in a day to hike to the ranch, keep an eye out on the happenings, and hike back before it became too dark to see her way through the forest and trails. Plus, in case anyone was looking, her real name wasn't on a rental contract for anyone to find.

There hadn't been much time to scout before Devon and Kate had arrived. Being in the mountains for a week, she'd lost her way the first few days. She'd never been a Girl Scout. On day four, she'd found the ranch and lost her way when returning to the cabin. Needless to say, she knew she needed help and since she didn't have a compass—a major oversight on her part—she'd made special markers along the route to help her find her way there and back. She'd also cut out as much as she could where the path led off the trail with an ax she'd found by the firewood pile behind the cabin.

The isolated location of Carver's ranch, along with its wide-open surroundings, held her back from rushing to break in without a plan to check for the girls.

Devon leaned his left elbow on the table and rested his chin in his hand. His eyebrows dipped low. "How many other places do you have to check?"

"This is the last one that I pulled from Dave's information."

Silence followed her admission, and she wrapped both hands around her mug and gripped it tightly to keep from fidgeting. Rylee was thankful the cup had cooled enough that she felt no discomfort. "I feel in my gut that this is the right place."

She experienced a shot of disappointment to the

stomach at the doubt clouding his eyes. A doubt she'd felt a time or two wondering if her gut told her it was the place because she had no other leads to follow. She straightened. He didn't need to believe her. Their agreement was for him to help her in exchange for.... She gulped at the thought of what she'd agreed to.

Devon eased back in the chair, his broad shoulders wider than the wooden back of the seat, and nodded. "Okay. But we're not running down there and breaking into the place. We do this my way."

Rylee took the demand as her being unable to handle it and bristled. In truth, she wanted to laugh out loud at the absurdity of the situation. She could only imagine what he'd do if he knew she'd almost been caught searching the second house. He'd probably send her to the FBI and walk away or take over. Although, it sounded like he planned to take over anyway. Well, she'd see about that. She might have almost been caught, but she hadn't. She knew what the hell she was doing. "Your way?"

He drained his cup and stood. "Yes." He didn't expound as he walked to the sink, rinsed his mug, and stepped to the side, drying his hands on a kitchen towel.

Not wanting to allow him to stop their conversation, or have the last word, she approached the sink and dumped her lukewarm beverage before washing her own cup out. Now what? Her stomach grumbled. The day was half gone, and she hadn't had anything to eat yet.

"Are you hungry? I have stuff to make sandwiches."

He rubbed his belly and nodded. "I could eat."

Rylee retrieved the fixings from the refrigerator,

and they made turkey sandwiches—dressed exactly the same with lettuce, tomato and mayonnaise—then ate in silence. She could tell Devon was deep in thought and she didn't want to risk interrupting him and have him decide this was a waste of his time.

After they cleaned up their mess, he turned to her. "Let's sit out front for a bit."

She stared at his jean-clad butt as he made his way to the front door and then called out to Angel. He opened the door and the dog zoomed past him. Devon turned to her with an easygoing smile that could melt butter. "Coming?"

Clearing her head, Rylee joined him outside in the sunny fall afternoon. A small shiver escaped her when he touched her arm.

"Cold?" His worried face touched her.

Shaking her head, she couldn't tell him that his touch affected her so. "No. Just the abrupt change from inside." Somehow she doubted he believed that since, while it was warmer inside, it wasn't that cold outside, plus she wore a flannel shirt.

"Come on." He led her to the hanging porch swing.

The close confines of the piece of furniture bothered her. She had to remind herself that they were just two people and people sat beside each other all the time without any issue.

When he settled himself to the far left, she released the breath she'd been holding and slid to the far right. That left ample space between them.

Then, he turned and slid one arm along the back of the bench and pulled up a bent leg on the seat. His hand rested on the back of the swing near her shoulder, and his knee touched her thigh. She faced forward, watching Angel sniff around the bushes and trees. She would not let Devon see his proximity made her nervous.

It was impossible to deny, though, that no matter how things had transpired between the two of them, she had a deep longing for the man. Then again, what woman wouldn't? Not only did he have a well-defined body, when he smiled with his eyes and sensual lips, she got that tingling feeling inside and the belief he wanted only her.

A chilly breeze ruffled a few strands of her hair and left a refreshing scent following in its wake. She inhaled and distinguished the strong scents of pine and spruce trees, and almost sighed at the essence of sagebrush. It brought out images of earlier pioneers and mountain men making this their home. She'd have loved to be there, forging the way, but she'd have been trouble because she wouldn't have worn a dress all the time or lived by all the stupid rules that held women back.

"It's beautiful here." Devon's voice jerked her back from imagining herself in buckskins, driving a father, or husband, crazy.

Husband. It felt odd saying she had one, even though she'd known for so long. Without remembering the ceremony, it didn't feel real to Rylee. But, it was.

"Did you travel growing up?"

"Yes…with Madison's dad. He married my mom when I was thirteen. Madison is a year younger than me, so we had a good time together."

"What place did you enjoy visiting the most?"

A frown formed on her lips. "You'll think it corny, but it was Epcot Center at Disney."

Devon's eyebrows rose in surprise. "Epcot? That's not a typical young girl's dream."

Wistfully, she sighed. Telling this man her private dreams seemed second nature. It was an oddity she didn't wish to figure out if she didn't have to do so. "I fell in love with Paris and wanted to live in France and pretended it was where I lived." She shook her head. "I know it was silly."

"Did you learn French?"

"*Parlez-vous français?*"

A chuckle emerged from him. "You were devoted. Maybe we can visit sometime. France," he clarified, "not Epcot."

"We'll see." She brought herself back from her grand memories to the man beside her.

"What about you?" she couldn't stop herself from asking…from wanting to learn something about the man who put her body and mind into a free spin.

"Did we travel?" He nodded. "Oh yeah. Dad made sure we saw a lot of the world."

"Did you have a favorite place?"

Taking a moment, she thought maybe he couldn't decide. Devon must've seen a lot to have such a tough time choosing his favorite.

"Vegas," he said softly, shocking her senses. Before she could formulate a response, he changed the subject. "Do you fish?"

Fish? That was out of left field. She turned to him. "Fish?" Maybe he meant it as a euphemism, like fishing for information to help them find the girls.

He looked at her with a boyish grin that made her insides do a little flip-flop. "Yeah. Rod and reel, hook 'em, and fry those bad boys up. Fishing."

She couldn't help but laugh at his description. "Not since I was a little girl."

"We can grab some rods when we're in town."

A slight edge of panic reared itself, and she squashed it as much as possible. No one would be looking for her. No way did Chuck and snub-nose tell anyone about her. That'd be suicide for them admitting they'd held a gun to their heads to get them there. "Why do we need to go into town?"

He shrugged and turned his gaze to where she'd last seen Angel. "I need some things. Do you have the stuff to make S'Mores?"

What the…. Did he think this was a vacation? "Devon," she huffed. "We're here to see if the girls are at that ranch. I don't see how fishing and S'Mores will help with that."

He turned his focus on her with twinkling eyes that promised enjoyable mischief. "Are you saying you're not going to live up to your part of our bargain?"

Damn him. "Of course I am, but…." Her voice trailed off when she couldn't think of an appropriate rebuke.

"Good." His gaze traveled to the hair brushing her shoulder, and his hand reached out to touch it. "What'd you do with the ring?" His soft voice almost mesmerized her.

"It's, um"—she looked down and gazed at her naked left ring finger—"in Baltimore." When he didn't respond, she rushed to add, "I can get it back to you if you want it."

His hand froze and the tantalizing goose bumps that had been sprouting over her, as his hand lightly grazed her shoulder, disappeared. His voice commanded her attention. "Look at me, Rylee."

Slowly, she raised her eyes and fell headfirst into his warm expression.

"I'd rather you were wearing it."

"I—"

"It's okay. We'll figure it out later."

"I—" What the hell was wrong with her? She couldn't get a word out of her mouth. Worse, Rylee had a guilty twinge stealing through her for not wearing the ring. But why would she? She'd asked for the annulment.

He settled back to toying with her hair again. "I have some tapes to show you of us."

Rylee jumped up. Panic flooded her. "We made—" She wrung her hands. "We made sex tapes?" she asked, full of fright at the idea. Good God, she'd been even drunker than she'd thought.

Surging to his feet to meet her, he shook his head. "No, no, no," he all but shouted. A flush of red crept up his neck. He was embarrassed, and she had to admit, his reaction endeared him to her.

Devon's response set Rylee at ease, yet apprehension settled in while they sat back down. The plan was to get his help, show him they wouldn't work, and get him on his way.

Make the plan. Stick to the plan.

Frustration welled inside her as his hand returned to her hair. If only she could snatch it out of his hand without seeming too much like a bitch. Then again, maybe that would get him to forget about the two of them. Although a small part of her started wanting there to be a two of them.

She cleared her throat and her wayward thought.

"What about the girls? I want to see if they're in that house."

"When are you going to tell me the rest?"

Her insides froze with ice cascading through her veins. How could he know there was more? She couldn't be that transparent. If she told him they wanted her, he wouldn't let her help. Besides, there was no guarantee anyone would continue to look for her. They also didn't know where she was. Nothing would come of that. She relaxed her muscles, certain she was out of danger. He didn't need to know. "There's nothing else to tell."

"Um hm." Disbelief saturated Devon's response.

She didn't care what he thought. As long as he helped her.

"I'd like to bring in my brothers for this."

Again with the bringing in someone to help. Didn't he believe he was enough to gather evidence? "No." She may have said it more forcefully than she'd planned, but he needed to understand her stance. "Not until we're sure they *are* there. I won't pass off finding their location only to have the girls continue to slip through the cracks. Besides, I've had FBI training, and you've had—" She broke off with a questioning look on her face, knowing all of HIS had some law enforcement or government background.

"CIA training." He paused and shrugged. "Computer training," he filled in.

"Oh." Disappointment sliced its way through her brilliant plan. He'd said he did computer stuff, but she'd hoped he'd been trained as an agent somewhere. If the girls were there, and there was time, they could bring in the Hamiltons. But to find them, they needed to get inside, and that meant someone who'd been trained for scenarios such as this.

"Believe me. You need my skills."

"What are they?"

His hand left her hair and clasped around the nape of her neck and then pulled her to meet him. He moved closer slowly and his eyes bounced from her eyes to her lips and set a burning desire for him to kiss her. *No.* She couldn't allow this to happen, yet she wanted it with every fiber of her being. Deep down, she knew it would happen at some point, but she wasn't ready yet. Everything was happening too quickly.

"Oh? What...are they?" Her eyes drifted to his devilish grin and the yearning in his eyes, and a delicious shudder ran through her.

"This."

At first, his lips lightly touched hers, but it sent a hot sensation that rocketed through her body. When he applied more pressure and moved his mouth over hers, her eyelids drooped shut and she eagerly followed his lead, allowing his tongue to slide into her mouth at his gentle probing. A sweet, violent shiver wracked Rylee as he shifted their heads and deepened the kiss.

She should stop this...needed to stop it, but the longer his lips locked on hers, the weaker her resolve to separate them. Her heart pounded in an erratic beat. Swamped with lust and longing, her desire for him was so intense that it burned from deep within her. If this was what flared between them, then she could see how her feelings for him must've been deep that night.

He lightened the kiss and nibbled on her lower lip for a moment before he pulled back.

She opened her eyes to a grin that touted he knew

she sported the lingering effects of a well-kissed woman.

"And...." He sprang from the swing, sending her rocking back in the seat and almost losing her balance, and walked inside the cabin.

Dazed from the kiss, curious, and a bit confused that he walked off without answering, she followed him inside and stumbled over her own feet. So disconcerted was she at wanting more, she couldn't speak. What was happening?

Devon emerged from the spare room. Had he been leading her there? Disappointment lashed through her when he proudly produced a laptop and a SAT phone. What the hell was wrong with her?

He set them on the table and opened the laptop before looking at her. "This," he said matter-of-factly, pointing at the computer, "is the other."

She had to figure out which he was better at—handling the computer...or her body.

Chapter Eight

Rylee kept herself occupied in the kitchen while Devon typed away at his keyboard—cursing under his breath from time to time. Watching him sitting strong, his long fingers teasing the keys, had left her hot and bothered. Granted, it was probably heat left over from the kiss. Wow! What a kiss it had been.

It hadn't brought back any memories, but her body had hummed like it was welcoming home an old friend. If her body reacted that way in all aspects of being near him, she could understand their coming together so quickly. The energy that zipped between them would've driven her to his bed. So, when had love come into play?

She'd be patient. If it came, it came. If it didn't— well, she'd deal with it then. Right now, she needed to be focused on rescuing the girls and not her all-fired desire for Devon Hamilton.

Opening up to him had surprised her. It wasn't some secret Rylee had to keep that she'd shared with him, but the fact she had shared with him was significant. Worse, she'd wanted to tell him more. Even though it shouldn't, being so comfortable with him frightened her to her core. She could only imagine how it must've been when they'd first met if she was willing to open up so easily.

Not wishing to deal with her personal life any

longer, curiosity sprang forth, and she had to know what he'd discovered. She brought two small plates of grapes and sliced apple and set one on the table near his computer and then she sat down beside him with her own plate.

He didn't look up. Just kept stroking the keys like a magician casting a spell. Images of those hands on her body had her shifting in her seat. She knew they weren't memories; they were fantasy because they occurred in the cabin. In her daydream, he stood from his seat and kissed her deep and fast while his hands roamed her body. Then he carried her off to bed. Hard as she tried, she couldn't wash the vision away, and her body craved the satisfaction his earlier kiss had promised.

That happened to be when Devon looked up at her with raised eyebrows. Her face heated at where her thoughts had been. If only he knew…. When she fanned herself, a smirk grew on his face. He grasped a grape and sucked it into his mouth—slowly—watching her the entire time.

Holy cow. Now why did that appear seductive? She thought only women doing that for men made it erotic. Damned if it didn't build on the fire inside her calling out for him.

Fighting not to react, she smiled as best as she could. "How's it coming?" She thought her voice sounded calm, cool, and collected. Based on his chuckle, she could've been wrong. The man knew she wanted him and was toying with her. Damn him.

She froze when he reached out and lightly stroked her cheek with a finger. "Thank you for the snack."

Squirming again, but keeping her cheek resting

near his hand, she cleared her throat. "I—" She paused and cleared her throat again. "I wondered if you'd found out anything."

His hand halted its movement and a frown formed. Now she'd done it. She'd ruined whatever heat he felt for her. That shouldn't bother her. She knew that even though she wanted him, they needed to wait until they got to know each other better. He would understand that.

"Nothing much yet. I'm mostly double-checking what you've found out so far." He scooted his chair back. "Come here," he demanded.

Affronted, she refused to move and give in to him. Nothing good could come of her being that close.

Devon cocked his head and gave her a boyish grin. "Please."

Unsure what drove her, she rose from her chair and stood by him. She gasped when his hands clasped her waist and he deposited her on his lap. Instinctively, she slung an arm around his shoulders.

"Better." He nibbled on her neck, and she almost flew out of his lap. His touch…his lips on her ignited a brushfire within her that she wanted him to tend. Wanted him to put it out.

Before she realized it, she'd arched her neck to provide him better access to her throat and was running her hands through his hair. A sigh slipped between her lips, and her body cried out for more.

When his hand covered her breast, she bounced out of his lap and stood out of arm's reach. Her body may be ready, but she wasn't. "I—" She reached forward and hurriedly grabbed her nearly full plate. "I'll just clean up." Escape was her only option, at least in her mind it was. When she reached the kitchen, she was so hot for him that her skin felt as if it were on fire. She reached inside the freezer and removed an ice cube. As she ran it up and down her neck where he'd been nibbling, she heard his laughter from the table.

****

"Son of a bitch!" Devon ground out and then surged from his chair and began to pace. He absently wove his unsteady hand through his hair and considered what he'd found. The Robert Carver he knew *was* the owner of the house and had named it Canyon Creek Ranch. The property had been in the family for two generations. There was nothing nefarious about that. Even former CIA bosses deserved to own a home. But still.

Rylee had to be wrong about the girls being there. Carver might've left the agency not long after Devon had, but it'd been to retire, not to sell young girls. Even the thought that his old boss might have the girls held captive was beyond his scope of belief. Yet, Carver had some tie to Westbrook since he had visited. Lovers? He'd never considered Carver's preference, but he had never married. Friends? Possible, but the more he considered it, the odder that idea sounded with Dave's father being a criminal. Business partners? Not in the way Rylee thought. Devon wouldn't allow the anger he felt for Carver to cloud his judgment in this case. Human trafficking was a big jump from covering up a covert agent's murder.

Instinct told him not to share that he knew Carver, and who he was, with Rylee yet. If they found out the girls were there, he'd explain his relationship with the man. Otherwise, she might not trust him to be sincere in his search.

Carver though. *Fuck!* He wanted to scream at all the memories he'd pushed aside because of that man.

"Devon?"

Rylee's sweet voice stopped him in his tracks. He dropped the hand from his head and smiled at her. Each moment with her told him that while they weren't in love, they could be one day. She'd start to let him in completely.

"Are you okay?"

"Huh? Oh, yes." He walked to her, SAT phone in hand, and she backed up to keep him at arm's length. *Dammit.* He'd pushed his luck earlier, but he couldn't help himself. Being close to her was difficult because he wanted to touch her constantly. She'd enjoyed the hell out of the kiss, as much as he had, so her pushing him away cut deep. "Call the cabin's owner and have the phone line and internet connected tomorrow. Internet is shit on the SAT phone." Let her think that was his frustration.

Rylee nodded and reached for the phone, carefully avoiding touching his hand.

Hellfire. "I need to make a call." Devon heard the gruffness in his voice and didn't care. He entered the guest room and snatched up the second SAT phone. He would not let her get to him. He'd show her the girls weren't there and then they could work on their marriage. *Hell.* Just as he knew she wouldn't, he couldn't just drop it either. They'd look for leads to the girls. He'd tear apart everything he could of Dave's and even Brent's lives. He'd agreed to help her rescue them, and he would do whatever he could to make that happen. That came with its minefields, but he'd worry when he had to.

Stalking past her, he thought of how to handle the request he had to make. If his asking for anything got back to the wrong person, the entire HIS team would be swarming and he'd never get a chance to get Rylee to trust him. He wanted them in on this…needed them, but now, there was nothing they could do except completely fuck up his chances for a happy—and lengthy—marriage.

He took a deep breath, dialed, and hoped this gamble worked. He silently apologized in advance to his brother and sister-in-law for corrupting their employee.

"Hello." Mrs. Kessler, the older woman Jesse had hired when Reagan was a baby to help care for the little girl after his brother's wife's death, had a smile in her voice. When he married Kate, Mrs. K., as they'd come to call her, had already become part of the family and spent her time keeping the men in line. Devon recalled many times she'd chastised him for one thing or another. Mostly getting his hair cut when it'd been longer. Maybe growing up without their mother had them adopting her as a pseudo-one. No matter the reason, Kate may rule the roost of her home, but Mrs. K. held the wooden mallet when it came to the Hamilton men.

"Hi, Mrs. K., this is Devon."

"Devon Michael Hamilton!"

He cringed at the use of his middle name.

"What's with you running off? Are you going to be home in time for Jason's game on Friday?"

He stared out at the red, gold, and brown leaves on the trees but failed to witness their splendor. One leaf caught his gaze as it drifted, floating here and there before it landed on the ground. He silently sighed. Leave it to Mrs. K. to make him feel properly chastised, like a six-year-old boy who'd been caught trying to kiss a girl, with only a few words.

As for getting home for the game, that wouldn't happen. He hated not being there to support his nephew. Kate and Jesse adopted the kid after he'd lost his parents while he'd been in the hospital. With his leukemia in remission, and the sports training provided, his nephew had his big wish—to play football as quarterback. He wasn't strong enough to last an entire game yet, but he started every one of them at his school. Jubilance surged through Devon at what the boy had accomplished. He'd find a way to make it up with him. "Sorry, I won't make it back, but I'm sure Kate will tape it for me."

The woman snorted. Devon shook his head and bit back a chuckle. She'd actually snorted. "She tapes them all even though you're all there. Did you want to talk with Kate? Jesse's gone, but I'm sure you knew that."

"No. Actually, I wanted to talk with you. I need a favor, and I'm counting on your love for me to see it done." He hoped the boyish charm he'd tossed in there would do the trick.

"Me? Are you in trouble?"

He chuckled, guessing it depended on what trouble constituted—wanting a woman who didn't want you or chasing kidnapped girls. Yes, he was in trouble. "No, of course not. I just want to do some stuff in the mountains and don't want the family interfering."

"I won't lie to them, Devon Michael."

Damn. She'd perfected the first and middle name

thing with them. "I'm not asking you to lie. If they ask you directly, then you answer honestly. I'm asking you not to volunteer the information. Can you do that? For me, pretty please," he cooed with a laugh.

She chuckled. "You think you're funny, don't you? Well, you're lucky I'm in a giving mood. Now, what do you need from me?"

"I need you to pack up some equipment and send it overnight to me."

"Some secret spy stuff? Humph. Sounds like trouble to me."

Devon could visualize her standing with her hand on her hip giving him the look that made him want to confess to pulling a girl's braids in his second-grade class. Ah, he missed tormenting little Charlotte.

"How do you expect me to get it to the post office without them knowing I'm leaving?"

"I'll send the mailing labels for you to print and stick on the boxes. I'll schedule a pickup so you only have to ensure the boxes are ready."

"Ooh, does this mean I get to play on that fancy computer of yours?"

His gut clenched at the thought. Yet, the little things were all it took sometimes to keep the woman happy. "You do get to be on my computer, but please take care of my baby." Rylee had no idea what kind of sacrifice he was making for her. Like the laptop with him, no one was allowed on his computer. A cold shiver snaked up his spine at the idea of someone intruding in on his space. But this was important to Rylee so he would endure. "Grab something to write down everything."

"Hang on." The sound of rustling and then paper

crinkling told him she was probably shuffling through the desk drawer off the kitchen.

Devon rattled off items, instructions, and a stern warning—as stern as he dared—about care. He hesitated at weapons, not wanting to ask for them and have Mrs. K. say anything. The weapon Kate left and Rylee's would have to be enough if they ran into trouble.

After ending the call with his co-conspirator, he decided he'd best call Kate like he'd promised and get it over with. Besides, it would keep her away from Mrs. K.'s plundering in the war and storage room.

"It's about damn time you called me." He couldn't decipher if Kate's voice carried more anger or concern. Oh well, he deserved it all, especially with his last act.

"Hello to you, my wonderful sister-in-law."

She huffed at him, clearly not appreciating the charm he'd infused in his words. "What's going on?"

Not ready to skirt the truth, he pressed on as though she hadn't asked. "How's Megan? Has she dropped that kid yet?"

"Don't even try. She's not due for another month. What's going on?"

He sighed and dropped in the porch swing. "There's nothing else."

"Bullshit."

"Kate," he said as firmly as he could muster, "leave it." After it left his mouth, he knew that he shouldn't have wasted his breath with that remark.

"Humph. Are you at least staying? What about the annulment?"

"Of course I'm staying. I'm not letting her get away that easy. She married a Hamilton. She'll learn what that means soon enough."

He got the laugh he'd hoped from her. Kate and Jesse's relationship hadn't been all roses at the start. In fact, he'd moved in on her when she'd have preferred he hadn't.

Maybe Kate would relax about Devon and Rylee's predicament and leave it to him to resolve.

"Good," Kate said briskly.

"What about Arthur and the FBI? I'll move her if they're coming." They'd dealt with fallout from FBI leaks before. AJ's cover had been blown, putting his and Megan's lives in danger. Devon wouldn't subject Rylee to such a chance.

"You wound me, Devon. I told you I wouldn't rat her out. Besides, they don't suspect her, or as far as I can tell, know she was there. They just want to talk with her. Arthur didn't push me."

"I doubt he would right now, but keep an ear out. I agree that she can't help them. It'll only put her life in danger if the wrong person found out. You need to know if one of those goons blabs to the FBI though." He'd pushed that issue to the back of his mind with research today. His mind had remained focused on the girls—and his marriage. He had to get back to why the goons picked up Rylee in the first place. Gut instinct told him that someone knew she'd been there and she was in trouble whether she realized it or not.

"Ye of little faith, I asked about them today—in a roundabout way. The two who worked for Dave stated that they weren't working for him that night and had no clue of his whereabouts."

Good. That eased his mind a smidge.

Rylee walked out of the cabin and the need to

protect her almost consumed him.

Angel dashed past Rylee, barking at a squirrel darting across the yard. He liked that mutt. No matter how jealous he was of Brent's relationship with Rylee, he respected the man for rescuing the dog from the shelter. Most people would've probably bypassed the older dog for a cute puppy.

"Rylee sends her love."

Her head snapped around to him and a surprised expression blossomed on her face.

He smiled, knowing she was curious about who he spoke with and almost left her guessing. "I'll talk with you later, Kate."

Rylee's shoulders dropped and relief visibly passed over her.

Devon ended the call, lifted himself from the swing and ambled toward her. She cut a fine figure and from the side, her jeans and flannel shirt contoured to her curves. His mouth watered at the thought of her without them. The visual overtook him and his body reacted.

"Did she buy it?"

Silently counting to ten to relieve his disappointment that he couldn't touch her, he raised his eyebrows in question. "You mean that nothing is happening? She said she did, but I don't think she actually believed it. You should know her better than that."

She nodded. "True. Do you think she'll come back or send anyone?"

Shaking his head, he frowned. "No. Not as long as we keep in touch with her."

"Good."

He wanted to pull her into his arms, but he had to

get the e-mail to Mrs. K. so he could receive his equipment tomorrow. If they wanted to get busy finding the girls before they could be sold, he had to have those items. He had a trick or two he wanted to try before they attempted to break in and search. "How long before dinner is ready?"

"About half an hour. Is that okay?"

"Perfect. Thanks for cooking." He cleared his throat. "I have a few things to take care of real quick and afterward, I'll help you cook. Then, we'll enjoy our evening together."

She fidgeted, her body swaying slightly. "Will you tell me what you've found out today? I don't like being kept in the dark."

"Not tonight." He kissed her cheek and swept past her into the cabin before she could respond. There was nothing more they could do for the girls tonight. As for them, though, he had other plans for their evening that involved him and Rylee getting cozy.

Chapter Nine

Kate stood in the doorway with her arms crossed, watching a UPS truck depart until the rain blotted it from view, and then turned to observe the older woman. The one she'd seen packing in the war room.

Mrs. K., walking with her shoulders hunched down and head bowed looking at the ground against the weather, was almost at the front door before she noticed Kate. The woman nearly tripped over her feet when she stopped in a rush. With the older woman's gray hair nearly plastered to her face, it almost covered her eyes, but Kate could make out the shocked expression of getting caught splashed on the housekeeper's face, and it almost made her laugh. She'd learned a great deal from Mrs. K. the last year on keeping an eye on the household.

In fact, she raised one eyebrow and used the stern voice she'd heard Mrs. K. use. "Come inside where it's dry and tell me what you're doing."

"Nothing important," the woman rushed to say as she followed.

"What did you ship?" If she hadn't known that it had to be for one of the men, she'd never have been so bold with Mrs. K.

"Nothing important."

Somehow, she doubted that. "Did Devon have you send him something?" It had best not be her dear husband sneaking something under the radar.

"I—" She broke off and her shoulders slumped, but this time it was in apparent defeat. "He did and I worry."

"What kind of stuff?"

The housekeeper reached into her pocket and extracted a list of items.

Kate scanned the damp sheet. *Son of a bitch. I knew Devon was hiding something.*

"Did he ask you to hide this from me?"

"No." She shook her head. "He told me I had to tell you if you asked, but not to offer."

Taking a deep breath to control her rage, she held it and counted to five, then released it. "Thank you, Mrs. K. I'll take care of it."

"You just make sure he gets home safe," she said, hurrying away. Escaping was more like it.

Kate smiled. The older woman was a bit spry when the situation warranted. After locking the front door, she retrieved her cell phone from her pocket and dialed while she walked to her and Jesse's bedroom.

Devon was in a buttload of trouble as far as she was concerned.

"Hello."

"Your brother had Mrs. K. go behind my back and do something," she said to her husband.

Jesse heaved a sigh. "What did AJ do now?"

She shook her head, even though she knew he couldn't see. "Not AJ."

"Well, Brad's with me."

"No," she huffed. "Devon."

Laughter streamed through the phone.

"It's not funny. I think Devon and Rylee are up to

their ears in something."

"I thought everything was okay and that's why you came back."

She hesitated. How much should she tell him? "Well, since then, he had Mrs. K. ship him some things."

"Hmm. I've been wondering. Why did *he* stay with her and not you?"

"He wanted to give their marriage a chance." She slapped a hand over her mouth—too fucking late. It was the one thing Jesse didn't know in the Hamilton world, and she'd just spilled that secret. One she'd promised to keep until Devon was ready to announce it.

"Their what?" he roared.

She pulled the phone away from her ear and winced. Putting it back, she left it far enough away to hear but not have her eardrum busted if he yelled again. "I wasn't supposed to say anything, but I am worried about them."

"When did they get married?"

"It was while he was in Vegas. Right after we'd met," she hurriedly added, remembering working with Jesse before their trouble had begun.

"Hell. I shouldn't have let go of what happened when he asked. That must be why he fucking didn't want me to look into it."

A shattering sound reached her ears, which she hazarded a guess was a glass from Jesse's hotel room hitting the wall.

"I don't know about that, but he wanted to handle this himself. Only," she paused and winced, prepared for more outrage, "she asked for an annulment."

"Rylee fucking did what?" Heavy breathing, not

the kind meant to scare someone on the phone, but the kind where someone was in an emotional uproar, bled over the receiver. "He'll have to handle that himself," Jesse finally said in a calmer voice than she'd expected. She wouldn't want to be Devon Hamilton when his big brother called next. "Why do you think they're in trouble—except from the ass kicking he'll receive from me?"

She told him everything Rylee had shared.

"If no one knows she's there, then she's safe. Besides, Devon would send for us to protect her if he felt she were in real danger. He wouldn't do it by himself."

Unfortunately, she had to concede that point. She'd never been told why he didn't go out in the field, but she remembered the fearful expression on his face when she'd handed him the Beretta. "Something's not right though."

"I don't see what makes you say that."

Wasn't he listening to her? Everything made her say it. But what hit home was the list of items Devon requested. "He asked for the drone."

"Fuck."

"My thought exactly." That was Devon's new spy toy, and she couldn't believe he'd take it out just to play.

"Let's think logically. Maybe they're using it to view parts of the mountains they can't reach? He could be trying to impress her. Really, what kind of trouble can they get into up there?"

Kate snorted. "Famous last words."

His voice softened. "You're right, sweetheart. Okay, there's nothing to bring us all back, and he'd kill us if we just showed up. I'll talk with him later and see what I can find out."

"Don't tell him that you know about them being married. He'll kill me if he finds out I told you."

"I can't guarantee that, sweetheart. In the meantime, you've got AJ and Jake there if—and I mean *if*—Devon calls for help."

"But—"

"No. You do not crash. They could truly be working on this marriage thing. Don't worry, though. I'll put everyone on standby. We're all due to finish up in the next couple of days, anyway."

"I'll call Rylee and see if I can get anything else from her." She'd at least let her friend know that she and the men would be there for them. Plus, she'd offer to return. Rylee hadn't wanted to be alone with Devon, anyway. Maybe—

"Devon's smart. He won't do anything to put them at risk, so there's no need to worry."

"Then why are you worried?"

Jesse eased out a slow, heavy breath. "Probably the same reason you are. I love him." He paused. "He's a Hamilton. We take care of ourselves and our own, and it sounds like Rylee is Devon's. They'll be fine."

An inkling of suspicion that her husband said it just to make her relax struck her. She'd learned to figure him out. He was just as worried about his brother as she was.

They spoke for a few more minutes before she called AJ and Jake and got them up to speed on her hunch. Unfortunately, they agreed with her husband that she shouldn't worry. Yet, they didn't know about the marriage.

Chapter Ten

The campfire crackled, the sound mixing with the chirping of crickets and the hushed whispers of other wildlife. The firelight stood bold in the darkness, its illumination dancing off the cabin and surrounding woods and giving them a fiery gold glow for the briefest of moments before it flickered, shadowing an area and then relighting it.

Calm and peace surrounded Devon, and he wanted to grab it and hold on to it, allow it to absorb within and retain itself there, but the spirited woman sharing this retreat kept the blood pumping hot through his veins with nothing more than her being in the vicinity.

What to do in a relationship with a woman had never been this difficult to decide. He'd never wanted anything serious, despite the fact he'd dated a few women for brief periods. But with Rylee Hawkins—no, Rylee Hamilton—something was different, and it wasn't just his not wanting to have an annulment behind him.

Devon stared into the small fire they'd created in the outdoor patio steel fire pit, wondering if he was doing the right thing trying to salvage something of their marriage. As far as he knew, it could be just lust and burn itself out within months… weeks… or even, heaven forbid, days. Then they'd be stuck together and probably come to despise each other. He expected she'd then ask for a divorce. He definitely didn't wish that for himself.

He wanted…craved with everything he was, to have what his brothers had found with their wives. That level of head-over-heels in love that lasts a lifetime. Like many, he hadn't believed in such a love that encompassed his whole heart and beat with a soul mate. Yet, he'd witnessed it come to life with Jesse and Kate, AJ and Megan, and Jake and Em.

He had to believe that he'd married Rylee for more than lust. The question that still rattled around his mind was had he been in love with her when they'd wed, and if so, why didn't he have that same feeling now? He didn't have that answer just yet, but without hesitation, he wanted to be with her, and deep down he knew it wasn't just lust. There was something else there. Yet, it wasn't full-blown love either.

Convincing her they should try wasn't going to be easy. Sure, she'd agreed that she would but he hadn't believed she really wanted to give it any effort. In fact, he expected she'd pull out another copy of the annulment papers as soon as they found the girls. Something just drove her to not want to be married. He had to find out why…and soon.

He wouldn't allow her to shut them down too early though. He'd show her they had something, and together, they'd figure it out.

"You've burned that almost beyond recognition."

So lost in his thoughts, Devon started at the sound of Rylee's voice. Sitting on a blanket on the ground with his knees pulled up and his back leaning against a yellow Adirondack chair, he held the wire hangar toward the fire. A black object that was once a white marshmallow rested in the flames on the hangar's tip. He jerked the inedible item back and blew on it to extinguish the flames that ate through the mushy treat.

Rylee's melodic laughter drew his attention. Her face shone in the light, and the reds in her hair almost looked aflame. She had donned a navy blue jacket to ward against the evening chill, but his mind still pictured how enticing her chest had been in her snug flannel shirt. All day he'd wanted to reach out and rip the buttons off the shirt, spread it open wide and bury his head between her glorious breasts.

His groin tightened, and he shifted to disguise his thickening need for her. Christ, he was nearly thirty-two years old. He should be able to control his libido better than this. Not that he didn't desire her all the time since he'd been here, but his body chose certain times—like now—to put it on full display.

Always rationalizing things, his mind reminded him that she was his wife and there was nothing wrong with seducing her. She'd been putty after their kiss earlier.

Rylee cocked her head in question and a stroke of concern wove into her voice. "Devon?"

He opened his mouth to speak, but those damn eyes of hers held him captive. They stared deep into each other's gaze, and their breaths rasped loudly in the night air. He searched the depths of her eyes, looking for something he couldn't name, and his heart pulsed with the flickering golds and browns that made up the whiskey shade of them. As he pulled himself out of the depth of their fiery beauty, her eyes began to change… to darken… to dilate… and he knew why. *She wants me.*

A tiny smile curved the corners of his lips and satisfaction settled in his being. Although he wanted to snake his arms out around her, he told himself to be patient. To lighten the mood, he laughed at himself. "Wow, I guess I cooked this one a bit too much." Not wanting Angel to burn herself on the hot inside, he chucked the ruined food into the fire, grabbed a fresh marshmallow from the bag on the blanket between him and Rylee, and tossed it to the mutt who'd been lying patiently to the side.

"Uh, okay. I was worried for a second."

If she'd known what he'd been thinking, she probably would've bolted. "I was just thinking how great these will be when we pick up the stuff to make S'Mores. Just think of the gooey, chocolaty goodness." That only incited visions of licking her fingers with the tip of his tongue, then sucking it off her lips, tasting her succulent sweetness.

He had to reach down and adjust himself regardless of if she observed it or not. His dick was painfully hard thinking of her tongue doing the same to him. *Dammit!*

Rylee cleared her throat. "Since we're getting to know each other, tell me, what was it like growing up with so many brothers?" Her nervousness should've surprised him, but she'd seen him make himself more comfortable in his jeans, so he gave her that emotion.

"Hmm." His eyebrows dove into an inverted arch. "I'd have to say mostly it was great. I mean, there were times when not getting a moment to yourself became a problem. Usually though, I could slip away without anyone noticing. Since our dad worked so much, Jesse took responsibility for all of us. The twins kept his hands full. They fought like cats and dogs one minute, then were conspiring together the next."

She twirled her marshmallow. "What did you do when you were alone?"

"Read. Mess around with programming. I knew pretty early that while my brothers were very hands-on with things, I was more comfortable behind a keyboard."

"Jesse used to rave about you and the work you did for HIS." She looked at him quickly. "I didn't know then."

He shrugged, ignoring her added statement. "When we were in high school, Jesse tried to get me to try out for a sport. I did eventually—track, but he didn't consider that manly enough for a Hamilton. He didn't understand what I could do with a computer, so I hacked into his e-mail one day—right in front of his eyes—and explained how I planned to make my mark on the world, and he never bothered me about it again."

She raised and lowered her eyebrows playfully. "Anything juicy in the e-mails?"

Devon chuckled. "I didn't read them, although most were from girls. Anyhow, when I wanted to join the CIA and do computer instead of fieldwork, he didn't bat an eye. He even told me he was proud of me."

"That sounds like Jesse."

He wanted her to have that much satisfaction… no, pride…no, confidence in him that she had in his brother.

After removing his marshmallow from the fire, he blew on it to cool it off. He split it open and continued to let it chill. Just when he got it to a manageable temperature, Angel bounded over, pushing on his chest to get to the treat. Instead, she knocked him askew and the marshmallow smeared on the side of his face.

Settling the dog off him, he sat back up and began to wipe at his cheek, noting Rylee bouncing with laughter. "It's not that funny," he growled.

Surprising him, she moved closer and softly pushed his hand away. "Here, let me." She proceeded to gently pick marshmallow from his cheek and hair. Her touch didn't ignite the fire he'd been feeling. Instead, it touched his heart, made him have that warm and fuzzy feeling he'd heard people talk about. She had a loving touch.

"Did Angel hurt you?" she asked softly.

Devon shook his head. "No."

She pulled back. "Stay still so I can get this all out. You're lucky it wasn't still hot. All the gooeyness—as you called it—would've burned you. As it is, you're a bit red, but not anything that's permanent."

The fire lit up Rylee's face. Damn, she was beautiful. And this caring and affectionate side of her, that she'd been trying so hard to hide, only made him realize even more that she was meant for him.

Continuing the cleaning, she sighed. "She's really a good dog. I think you're giving her that marshmallow may have spoiled her."

He didn't care if that was the case since it resulted in Rylee taking care of him. He'd suffer through anything for that to happen.

After she finished, she graced him with a brilliant smile. "All done." Before he could reach for her, she moved back to her position and placed her marshmallow back in the fire.

"Thank you," he managed to say around a dry

throat.

"You're welcome."

Heaving a heavy sigh, Rylee pulled her marshmallow out of the fire and blew on it. "I thought we'd go check on the girls tomorrow."

His heart sank with the switch in topic. "We will, but first I need to go to town and pick up my equipment. While we're there, more food would be good since I don't know how long we'll be here, and we're going camping."

"The stuff you had sent?"

Proving the girls were here, or not, was important to him, but he couldn't do anything tonight. He wanted to put this time to good use getting her to open up to him. "I'll show you tomorrow. Now," he stated and reached for another marshmallow, "let's see if I can make one of these for my woman."

The change in the body beside him couldn't be missed. She tensed, her body visibly snapping straight, her jaw tightening.

He fought not to laugh. "Don't go getting all crazy on me. I was just joking with you."

Rylee narrowed her eyes at him and relaxed, somewhat, but didn't smile. "It's not funny. I don't think…." She swallowed, the lump visibly sliding down her long, creamy throat. "I don't think…."

Devon wanted to grab her and kiss her senseless, but knew he couldn't yet. He had one trick up his sleeve that he prayed helped, and that—the tape of them—could wait until tomorrow. "Then don't think." He laid down the marshmallow and holder and leaned into her. His prior notion of not kissing gone. "Rylee," he rasped and reached up with one hand and touched her cheek.

Chapter Eleven

The tense silence filling the car was heavy enough to all but smother Rylee's air passages as she sat in the passenger seat on their drive into town. Devon hadn't spoken to her since she'd walked away from him the night before. Okay, she'd fled after she said she wouldn't do it again.

Initially, when he'd put his hand on her cheek, she'd turned into it, attempting to regulate her heavy breathing. It had been surprising he couldn't hear the thumping of her heart over the crackle of the fire. Damn, but it taxed her to fight her growing attraction to the man.

Then, his eyes had darkened and darted to her lips.

For one breathless moment, she'd thought he'd been about to kiss her, and she hadn't planned to stop him. She'd wanted his lips touching hers again, his mouth covering hers, and his tongue stroking inside her mouth. A delicious shiver had made its way through her at the thought, and she'd wet her lips in anticipation.

Then he'd gone and broken the spell. Ruining it all.

"Rylee, I know you said you'd give us a try, but what's holding you back?"

At the question, her heart had plummeted to her toes. There was only one thing to do and that was to tell him the truth. Maybe after hearing it, he'd understand and give her the annulment. Maneuvering her face free of his magical hold, she responded in as firm a voice as she could. Hell, she'd just been ready to kiss him so it didn't sound too strong to her. "When I marry, I want to marry for love. I don't want to be like my mother who married and divorced six times because she thought she was in love when it was just intense lust that burned out in no time. I want the love you see where couples are in their nineties still as enamored with each other as the day they met."

He took a deep breath, held it, and exhaled slowly before speaking. "You do realize you have already married. And, since we don't know for sure, it could've been for love."

"No." She shook her head. "It was a drunken mistake."

Narrowing his eyes, he spoke with a tight jaw and what appeared to be extreme control. "I think you know better than that. You didn't look drunk in the tapes, and the preacher and his wife didn't say you were."

"Then why did I blackout?"

He shook his head. "I don't have that answer. But I do know that by getting this annulment, you're starting off in your mother's footsteps."

"Don't say such a thing! The annulment wipes out my poor lack of judgment. It doesn't count as a divorce." She surged to her feet and raced to the cabin, slamming the bedroom door behind her like a child. He was wrong. She wouldn't be like her mother. An annulment didn't count.

He's right. Maybe you should try, a voice whispered in her mind. *No. I don't love him. I want to marry for love.*

After that, she'd remained awake, listening for

Devon's return to the cabin. He hadn't even slowed his footsteps when he'd walked past her door.

This morning, he'd only said what was necessary, and it'd been clipped words.

It had taken her time to realize that she'd called marrying him "a mistake" and "poor judgment." Of course, Rylee needed to apologize, but the words remained lodged in her throat. She had to try. "Devon—"

"We'll hit the UPS store first. Before we pick up groceries, I need a few electronics. Do you know anywhere to go?"

She hadn't been in town except to grab the food on her way through it. "No." She also didn't want to stay out in public for long. No one may have seen her at the accident, but the two goons knew she'd been there. And who knew if they blamed her for their boss's death. Preferring to remain careful, she'd not returned to the quaint little town.

She wasn't stupid enough to disregard that if Robert Carver had the girls, he might also have the name of whomever Dave and his asshole father had planned to sell her to. She had to be careful, that was for damn sure.

She'd get with Arthur after this was over to see if he could resolve that issue for her so she wouldn't have to look over her shoulder. She wasn't one of his agents any longer, but he'd been kind to her and she knew he'd help. Besides, he wouldn't want her sold. She shuddered at the thought. It wouldn't happen.

"Kate called me last night. She found out Mrs. K. sent you stuff. I can't believe you used her."

"Yeah, well, I didn't have much choice. Had I

known she'd get caught...." He shook his head. "Jesse called me, and I think he knows about you and me. He didn't say it, but he was too pissed off at my just staying up here with you for no real reason."

"Are they coming?" Part of her wanted them to, while the other begged for them to stay away...for now. She was responsible for those girls, at least that was how she saw it. And, her gut told her a bunch of people creeping around the woods would scare this man off. *If they're there*, her mind tried to remind her.

Rylee closed her eyes for a moment and prayed they were. She couldn't take not finding them.

Devon glanced at her and back to the front, but not before she noticed his frown. "No, they aren't coming."

She nodded. Satisfied. "I promise we can tell them if the girls are there."

"Oh, my dear Rylee," he bit out. "We'll tell them then, *or* if I decide things are too dangerous, whether you like it or not. We can locate the girls, but it'll take more than both of us to rescue them. And I think you know that."

That stilted conversation again. She had to think of something to help get them back on civil footing. "What was it like growing up as a senator's son?"

He looked at her, then back to the road. "When we were young, it sucked. Our dad worked so much and we couldn't participate when he entertained. However, in my teens, I rather enjoyed it." A smile crossed his lips. "I met some very interesting people. I actually met the French Ambassador."

"You didn't mention that when I told you my dream of living in France when I was young."

A quick glance at her, and he focused his gaze

forward. "I hadn't thought about it until now. He's not the ambassador any longer. In fact, I'm not even sure he's alive. But he did make France sound like a great place."

"I knew it," she said confidentially.

Laughter bubbled out of him. "I said we'd visit, but we're not living there."

That wasn't the first time he'd said "we" when referring to the future, but it stopped her from speaking more on the subject.

"So, your sister is Madison Maxwell. I have a brother who drools over her. Do you think she can visit sometime? I'd love to see him fall all over himself."

"Most men drool over her. She's gorgeous. Yeah, I can invite her to visit." She didn't add that it would be to her home and not their home.

"Are you two close?"

Rylee nodded. "We are pretty close for living so far away from each other. I consider her my best friend."

They arrived in town, and at their first stop—the UPS store—Devon turned to her. "I have a very important question."

Automatically tensing, her mind raced through all the possible things he might want to know. As long as he didn't get back to the accident.

"What are you wearing that has made the car smell so damn good I've had to fight to keep my hands on the wheel and not you?"

Stunned to silence, it took her a moment to process. "Beau—" She cleared her throat. "Beautiful by Estee Lauder." Since her mouth couldn't hold back, she rushed to add, "But I'm also wearing Pink Cashmere lotion from Bath & Body Works." Lord, he didn't need that last bit of information. He meant the perfume.

Devon raked his gaze over her and her body responded as if he'd just used his hands to rub that lotion over every square inch of her. She shifted to alleviate the growing warmth and dampness between her thighs.

"I like them." He opened his car door, but before he stepped out, he added, "A lot." Then he left her alone to gather her senses and follow. The man's changing moods was not what she'd expected, but he kept her on her toes and she was beginning to enjoy it.

Together they filled the back seat with the packages waiting for them. Curiosity was killing her, not knowing what he had sent. What kind of stuff did he plan? As far as she was concerned, they just had to get in and out without anyone seeing them. She couldn't imagine what he'd need.

On the sidewalk, a prickling sensation skipped along Rylee's spine and continued up to the hairs on the back of her neck. The overwhelming feeling that she was being watched almost knocked her breathless. She slowly turned her head, taking in the area and scanning every face. Her FBI training had taught her how to assess her surroundings, and she didn't miss a thing. She also didn't notice anyone suspicious.

Maybe paranoia had taken hold and was trying to shake up her resolve to search for the girls. Yet, part of her wondered about Dave's plan. He said he'd be bringing her to the twins. If she allowed herself to be captured, could she save them? All three of them?

That was by far her stupidest idea. First, she didn't know for certain the girls were here. She crossed her fingers in juvenile hope. Second, getting herself captured was ludicrous. The risk was too high that she'd fail and lose herself in the process. No, finding them and then bringing in help was the trick.

Devon followed her scanning of the area. "Is something wrong?"

"No."

Did she imagine it or had he stepped closer to her and stood more rigid? She told herself not to dream up something that wasn't there. He probably did it because they had entered an area with an increase in foot traffic. "Here's the grocery store." She split off to the right, and her mind eased when he remained close to her.

She wasn't sure which of them was on alert more—her or him.

Down the soup aisle, a woman searched the shelves while her toddler kicked his—she guessed a he because the child was dressed in a blue jumpsuit—feet in the buggy. The little one kept opening and closing his hands and babbling, "Hi. Hi."

Rylee couldn't help but smile and wave to the child. "Hi there." Her voice was soft and held laughter. It held a childlike quality—one that adults used when speaking with a baby or toddler.

Devon cocked his head at her, gave her a surprised look as if watching an alien, and then he smiled, his face lighting up.

She shrugged and winked at the child as they passed. That interaction eased some of the tension from her shoulders. Her smile faltered when they came to the head of the aisle, her gaze landing on a man standing at the door of the small grocery store. The tall, menacing goon of Dave's wasn't looking at her, but he was looking for something…or someone. Her heart pounded and rushed the beating of her pulse. What was his name again? Clark? She almost snapped her fingers. Chuck. That was it.

She slipped behind Devon, hoping the man hadn't seen her. She had to find an escape for them. Her palms turned clammy and she wished she'd brought her weapon because she had no doubt Chuck had one under his jacket since it was too warm to wear one. "We, uh, have to get back to the cabin, Erik—the owner—said he'd schedule the internet connection for this afternoon." Peeking around Devon before he moved, she relaxed a bit to see that the man wasn't in sight. Was the other one here too? *Fuck!*

Rylee twitched and kept her eyes moving during their checkout. It seemed to take forever, and Devon kept up a running commentary with the cashier.

"What's the oddest combination of things you've seen people buy?" he asked.

The young girl checking them out tilted her head to the side in thought. "Hmm. I'd say someone came in and bought a can of corn, a magazine and duct tape. Darned weird, actually." The cashier shrugged.

"Wow, as a journalism student"—he'd established that with her at the onset—"you could make a great story from that." He spread his hands apart as if displaying a news headline. "Captive is taped and forced to eat canned corn and read— What was the magazine?"

A crooked tooth smile split her face in excitement. "And read the *National Enquirer*." She laughed and quoted their total.

Devon paid and they left. Luckily, they'd been

blessed without one of the Westbrook muscles entering the store.

She didn't relax as they loaded the car with their purchases and began their trip up the mountain. Watching the side mirror to make sure no one was following them, she jumped when Devon spoke.

"Are you going to tell me what that was all about?"

"What?" *Dammit.* What should she tell him? Nothing yet. It didn't seem the right time to tell him. With his level of protectiveness, if she told him about the guy from her kidnapping, then she knew full well he would call in his brothers and she'd be put into protection. He might even call in the FBI. While she wasn't going to put herself into any more risk than necessary, she needed to see it through. It was a burden he wouldn't understand.

"Rylee, what the hell is going on? Something, or someone, spooked you back there."

She feigned innocence. Chuck may not have even been there for her. They had no idea she was in town. As long as she kept hidden and took no more trips out, she was safe. "Nothing spooked me."

"Then what—?"

"Don't hit that squirrel on the side of the road!" Rylee shouted and pointed ahead of them.

"Shit." Devon swerved to miss the animal scurrying across the asphalt.

To head off more on the topic, she asked him, "Have you ever eaten squirrel?"

He shook his head as if to clear it. "Did you say squirrel?"

"Yeah. I've heard people say they've actually eaten it. Me, I can't see doing that."

"Must be a country thing." He glanced at her. "No, I haven't eaten it. It could be interesting."

"How about rabbit?" She kept on with different food choices to keep the conversation active with no room for him to ask her about her experience at the grocery store.

When they arrived at the cabin, Rylee hurried to let Angel out. They brought in the shopping bags, and she went back outside to find the dog while Devon put away the groceries. With Angel not in sight, no doubt foraging in the trees, she occupied herself with collecting firewood and taking it inside. Devon would probably balk, but she was quite capable, but more than that, she liked to feel productive. She'd done it before he'd arrived.

Around the side of the house, she filled a wheelbarrow with cut logs, all the time expecting him to show up behind her. Her muscles worked and sweat dripped down her back, but she lifted the cart handles and shifted the heavy load to make it easier to transport. Sure enough, when she'd made it to the front of the cabin, Devon stepped outside and immediately rushed to take over.

"I've got it." He reached for the handles.

Rylee shrugged and allowed him to do it. If it made him feel better, she could suffer his macho man attitude. Walking around the yard, she called for Angel. Coming upon a mostly dead tree about four feet high, she kicked at the base of it until it toppled over. Before she could bend over to pick it up and drag it to the woodpile, Angel emerged from the woods with something in her mouth.

The dog approached Devon—traitor—and sat with

her tail wagging and a gray ball of fur between her jaws. She wondered with amusement if the dog had a squirrel for them.

Devon reached his hand out. "Drop it, girl," he told the dog.

Angel, clearly not understanding, did no such thing.

Squatting, Devon talked soothingly and once again extended a hand toward the dog. She wanted to reach out and grab it to keep him from being bitten. Couldn't squirrels carry rabies? She didn't want to tell Kate that she'd had to rush him to the hospital.

This time Angel obeyed, except she dropped the creature on the ground instead of in Devon's waiting hand. Devon praised the girl and leaned his head down to inspect the wild animal. If it were a dead squirrel, she didn't care how interesting Devon thought it might be, she was not cooking it for dinner.

With the little gray ball of fur in his hands, he turned to her, stroking the small animal's head. "I guess Angel likes cats."

She released a quick breath that he hadn't been bitten. The unmistakable sound of purring vibrated through the air, and she fell in love with the fluff ball and its big eyes looking at them with hope. "It's so tiny." She reached out and stroked the kitten's head.

"Help me look around for its momma or more little ones."

They searched the area where Angel had emerged from the woods, but found nothing. Thank God that Angel brought it to them or it would certainly have died on its own.

Devon cooed to the kitten as he stood and

inspected it before handing it over to her. It couldn't be more than a couple of weeks old. She hoped they could keep it alive without its mother. "Meet Max. Maximus actually, but Max for short."

Flabbergasted that Devon had named the kitten, she asked, "You're keeping it?"

"Him." He nodded. "And yeah, *we're* keeping him." He reached down and petted Angel. "Is there anything wrong with that?"

"Of course not. I think it's…great." Great that Devon happened to be a sexy man with a protective streak and a heart of gold who rescued abandoned animals. She'd wanted to fall in love with her husband, and how could she not fall in love with this man? The thought startled her and she stiffened her spine. She had to give their marriage a try. If she ended up like her mother, then so be it. Devon came across to her as someone she might succeed with.

Chapter Twelve

Leaving Max to his bowl of milk and the bath Angel seemed to think necessary, Devon began the chore of unpacking the boxes from home. Yet, his mind couldn't let go of the fact that Rylee had been fearful in town. Something had spooked her, and he couldn't get her to spill.

Had she seen someone who would recognize her from the accident? He mentally shook his head. She said no one saw her. He had to agree or they'd have killed her right then and there. But the two who'd put her in the car were still out there.

Gaining the information from Rylee about what put her on edge was impossible. Devon would have to keep an eye on her, closer than he already was. He'd love to lock her in a room and call his brothers to check this out, but he also wanted a chance with her, and bringing them in would ruin that. He would give up the opportunity for them if his gut churned that she was in danger, not just the imagined danger that he had.

"What's that?" Rylee asked as he pulled his baby from a box.

"That is what we are using to see what we can at Canyon Creek Ranch." He unfolded the wings of the black piece of equipment and showed her the drone they'd fly over Carver's place. The one he hoped captured what they needed so she never had to go near the place. He reached into the box and pulled out a camera. Waving it with care and smiling, he added, "Infrared camera."

Her face brightened with pleasure. "Sweet." Then she looked crestfallen. "But there's only a spotty cellular signal in that area. Believe me, I tried."

His smile grew. He always acquired the best equipment. "My Viper Air Elite UAV has its unique software. No 3/4G or WI-FI needed," he said with a pride-filled voice.

She slapped her hands together quickly and then fisted each in front of her chest in excitement. "Yes!"

Hell, if this toy made her happy, he had plenty more to share, and he'd take her to a dark closet and start with the one in his pants. *Shit! Why can't I keep my mind out of the gutter with her? Because she draws me in like no other.* He just had no idea how to handle that concept. He cleared his throat. "We still should be where I can see it, though."

The look of confusion on her face told him the raspiness in his voice hadn't been imagined. "Do you want me to open one of the other boxes?"

Anything to keep her from figuring out where his mind had launched itself. "Sure. Be careful though."

"What's in these?"

They both straightened at the sound of an approaching vehicle. Panic passed over her face before she shuttered it and tried to look calm and unnerved.

Rylee's gaze pierced his with strength. Damn, the woman was amazing in how quickly she could bolster her courage. "The phone guy."

Nodding and grabbing the equipment on the table, Devon dropped it into a box and then carried it to the bedroom he'd commandeered since the loft was awful for someone with his height. "Bring those boxes in here," he tossed over his shoulder. After setting his load on the bed, he turned and was hit square in the chest. He reached out to steady the box, and Rylee, who held it.

"Sorry," she whispered.

Smiling, he accepted her load and placed it beside his. "I'll get the door."

"I can get it." She attempted to precede him out of the room, her path intent on the front door, but he stepped in front of her.

"I'm sure you can, but I'll get it. You can stay in your room."

Beside the front door, he peeked around the curtains on the window to witness a stout, bald, African American man exit the phone company truck.

"I what?"

Turning to her, he caught a vision of her in a temper with her hands shoved on her hips and her face reddening. He didn't relish being on the receiving end when she erupted, but she was damn cute and it turned him on all the more. "We don't want anyone to know you're here, right?"

"Well, not anyone that matters. As for this situation, I hate to break it to you, but the man will be looking for me since the owner gave him my name."

He heaved a heavy sigh and pinched the bridge of his nose between his thumb and forefinger. "Rylee—"

Three loud knocks bounced off the door, interrupting him.

"It'll be okay," she said. "But"—she smiled in a sweet manner telling him she was just placating him—

"I'll let you open the door if it makes you feel better."

He groaned. She needed to be flipped over a knee and given a good spanking. His jeans were embarrassingly tight. *Dammit. Get your mind out of the gutter.*

The telephone technician—Daniel—was in and out in less than an hour, leaving Devon connected to the internet and smiling when he found out Rylee had registered under a false name.

Ready for their mission, they left the cabin and trudged through the forest. He wished he'd brought the ax and cut away more of the trail they'd created for their trek to Canyon Creek Ranch because he wasn't excited about scratching up his UAV with branches and bushes that leaned in their path.

Rylee turned her head back to him with concern creasing her brow. "Do you think Max is okay with Angel? Should we have separated them before we left?"

Devon chuckled. "I wouldn't worry. I believe that dog has adopted the little tyke."

They continued, with, his discomfort, Rylee leading since she knew the way. There were few places wide enough for them to walk side-by-side. "I found a cave of sorts. Mostly just an inset, but deep enough."

That piqued his interest. They should have some place to go if someone came to the cabin looking for them or— "Show it to me on the way back. Maybe we can camp near it."

She looked up at the afternoon sky. "I'm not sure we'll have time."

Following her gaze, he viewed the brilliant blue sky nearly desolate of clouds. He couldn't have asked for a more perfect day to fly his UAV. "Tomorrow works," he conceded.

They reached the ledge and Devon's nerves tightened into a kink that settled in his shoulders and neck. "I know we are a distance away, but we'll stay to the tree line so we won't be seen."

"What do you want me to do besides stand here?"

Raising one eyebrow and a corner of his mouth, he watched her expression change and her face redden when she realized his thoughts had nosedived. Enjoying watching her embarrassment, he winked to irritate her. "Plenty, but right now, just have a seat."

He wasn't sure, but he thought she muttered something like, "Pig," under her breath. It pulled out a chuckle from deep within his chest. He sat beside her, removed his laptop from the bag, then opened and powered it on. After confirming his connection between it and the UAV, he relaxed a smidgeon, kicking himself for not confirming before they departed the cabin. "Okay. We're ready."

The excitement on her face sent a pulse of pleasure radiating through him. He wanted to find the girls for her. But, if they were there, that meant Carver was involved. He didn't want to believe it. Neither scenario gave him a full happy ending. He'd either still be searching for the girls or he'd be chasing his old boss.

Pushing it all aside, he controlled the UAV and lifted it off the ground. Although his plan would give minimal opportunity for Carver to notice it unless he was searching specifically for a drone, Devon sent a prayer up that no one would see it, except he and Rylee, of course. It was a chance he was willing to take that it'd be sighted because it didn't put Rylee in harm's way.

"Clarise, huh?"

"What? Oh." She laughed at the name she'd registered with. "It's one of my sister's friend's clothing lines. The designer once told me the clothes are perfect for me, but I'm partial to my jeans."

"I'm partial to them also."

Surprise filtered through him. Turning to her, he raised his eyebrows up and down suggestively.

"Do you think they'll see it?" she asked, skillfully changing the subject.

He shrugged. "I hope not. We can fly high enough with this one it shouldn't attract attention unless someone looks up. But to be safe, I'm only doing one flyover in each direction."

"Is that enough?"

"It'll have to be. Otherwise we risk alerting them that someone is watching." He looked down at his screen. "Here we go. We're approaching the barn."

Outside the barn, which was empty as the two horses were in the corral, stood one body. By the size of the heat signature, it had to be a man or a rather large woman. They decided it was a man.

"What about inside the barn? There could be someone there." Rylee's breath fanned his cheek when he turned to her voice, which sent heat sliding down his body. He caught a whiff of her scent wrapped around her and almost dropped his laptop. He planned to buy her a warehouse full of that perfume and damn lotion. He mentally slapped himself for allowing his mind to wander. *Pay attention.* "No," he said, working hard not to sound breathless, "the IR would've caught it."

"Okay."

Not realizing what she was doing to him, she didn't

move and when he looked closer, he could see down the front of her shirt. This one, he noticed, had snaps in place of buttons. The creamy expanse of her flesh beneath and the tops of her breasts almost pulled him away. Oh, what he wouldn't give to pull her close and to the ground. He jerked his head back and cleared his throat at his horny thoughts. Thankfully, he hadn't crashed his drone by not paying attention to it. He was acting like a sex-starved teenager and he had to get that under control. "Here's the house coming up."

Watching the screen with avid interest, disappointment snagged him at the emptiness of the ranch house.

"It didn't show anything. Does that mean no one is there?"

"It does." At least no one with a heat signature. He wouldn't allow himself to think of any other option.

"Damn! I just know they are there. Check it again," Rylee directed. "Please." Her tone was earnest.

A heavy sigh escaped his lungs in a loud, slow exhale. "Rylee, the only person there is whoever is at the barn."

"Then I guess all that's left is going in to see if there are any clues leading to them."

Without conscious movement, his jaw tightened and he hissed a response, "Bullshit." He inhaled deeply and released the breath in a soft whoosh. "Let me get the drone back and we'll talk about this when we get back to the cabin."

"I know they were there."

Silence bled between them when he recovered his UAV. Carrying it and his laptop, the long hike back to their little getaway gave him time to sort his thoughts on the issue and he didn't hold back that thought when they walked into the cabin. "It's time to bring in my brothers."

"No. They weren't even there. Remember?"

He narrowed his eyes at her. "You think they've been there though. You've said that already." He didn't have anything that gave him that impression, but he wouldn't discount any possibility. Those girls needed the Hamiltons.

"We have to go in and see what we can find out about where they might have gone. Then"—she stretched out the word—"we call in your brothers and Kate."

"Dammit, Rylee! This isn't a game. If Carver did have them, then that man by the barn could be a guard on a shoot first and ask questions later order."

She shrugged as if tossing aside what he'd said. "I know how to get us in. It's easy."

Screaming a big, "Hell no!" was the first thing that came to mind, but Devon decided he needed to remain calm with her. He needed her trust. "You've given this some thought, haven't you?"

"Yes. It'll work. We go in as lost hikers."

He wanted to grab her shoulders and shake some sense into her. He had to wonder if this was what AJ went through with Megan when she wanted her story no matter what. "No."

"Would you do it if it were Kate?"

He shrugged one shoulder. "That depends. Kate tends not to listen."

"Well, first, I've been trained as an FBI agent like she was, so I can handle what comes my way."

Nodding, he conceded the point, but it didn't mean

he wanted her to go into possible danger. Hell, he didn't want to go into it himself.

"Second, there's only one person there, and we're just asking for water and directions."

Devon could be overreacting as it was, like Rylee said, only one guy. He was used to his brothers doing this stuff and it unnerved him to think of doing it with or without her.

"Nothing that would pique anyone's interest," she added.

Nothing except the homeowner knowing who Devon was.

Chapter Thirteen

Over a dinner of chicken fajitas, Devon continued his attempt to get to know Rylee. The more he talked, the more she felt they were a part of each other. Stupid though it seemed considering their situation.

"How many stepdads did you have?"

"Four. Mom was married before she wed my dad." She smiled and once again felt that strange level of comfort telling him something she liked to keep hidden from others. "I don't remember my first stepdad. I was too young and he wasn't around long. Mom says he liked to drink too much." She shrugged. "I think at the time she liked to drink too, so he must've had a real problem."

Devon grunted.

"Stepdad number two I remember a little. I was still small and he wasn't around long either. I can't remember what Mom said the problem with him was. I do remember he used to bring me presents and liked to hold me on his lap."

"Like Santa Claus or some pervert?"

Rylee shrugged. "I couldn't remember, but I'd lean toward Santa Claus. Now, stepdad number three was a piece of work. I don't know what Mom saw in him." She shuddered. "I'll tell you about him another time."

"Did he hurt you?" Devon's hoarse voice, filled with emotion, caught her by surprise.

"No. He never laid a hand on me." Taking a deep breath, her thoughts of her next stepdad brought a smile to her face. "Madison's dad was the best. He loved his daughter, but he treated me just as well as he did her. He and my mom are still married." She sighed wistfully. "She finally found her dream of true love."

"We'll get there," he assured her.

Unsure how to respond to his statement, she ignored it and bit into her dinner.

They finished in silence, and after the dishes had been cleaned, Devon collected the dog from outside. Rylee picked up Max, reveling in the comfort of his purring, and then sat on the couch.

The door opened and Angel rushed to her and sniffed the kitten. It appeared Max had a new momma.

"It gets dark as hell out here." Devon walked over and rubbed the top of Max's head.

"No city glow." She looked up at him. "Would you light a fire in the fireplace?"

"I can do that. Are you sure though?" Devon asked. "It's not that cold inside."

"It will be later, but it's more for ambiance." Rylee shrugged. "The cast iron fireplace is something I love about this cabin and the mountains."

Devon bent over, his jeans tightening across his butt, and Rylee's mouth watered. Being attracted to him had never been the problem.

Fire blazing, Devon dropped down in a chair facing the sofa. He swiped a hand over his face, and his other petted the dog sitting beside him. Rylee had a feeling the second hand moved without thought. Angel just might have a new papa.

"It's been one long day," he said.

Rylee stood. "It has. And it's time for the little one to sleep." Angel bounded beside her and followed her every movement with Max. When she laid him down on the dog's bed, Angel curled up next to the kitten and cleaned it.

Devon laughed. "They get along great."

"I'm so glad Angel found him."

"I am, too. What do you want to do? Watch a movie? Read a book?"

She wet her lips, nervously. "You said you had a tape of us. Can I watch it?"

He appeared stunned by her request, but quickly recovered. "Hell yeah." Devon surged from his seat and brought his laptop from the table and settled to the left of her on the sofa. He placed the computer on his lap and after a couple of mouse clicks, she and Devon were pictured on screen. "These are security tape remnants that I was able to pull. I just pieced them together so you'll see jumps here and there." He rubbed the back of his neck with his left palm. "Are you sure you're ready?"

She hated that he was wary of how she'd react. Not being willing to learn more about them had given him the wrong impression. Well, right at the time, but wrong overall. Things had changed. No more running and hiding from her life. "Yes. I'm more than ready." She smiled what she hoped was her sweetest smile.

After searching her eyes and finding whatever he sought, Devon scooted close enough their legs touched and pressed Play on the video, then he tossed his right arm behind her on the back of the sofa. Ignoring the goose bumps from his closeness, she focused on the computer screen.

They strolled down the strip, hand in hand, and sometimes arm in arm. No matter where they were—in front of a casino, a store, or a restaurant—they constantly sought out the gaze of the other.

She looked to Devon, who watched the screen with a glassy-eyed stare, before returning her gaze to the video he'd compiled. She didn't look drunk. Neither did he. Yet they'd married. If they'd been in as much lust as she'd witnessed, they could've just gone to one of their rooms—no wedding ring necessary.

Although confused about their decision, seeing the two of them so euphoric flipped something in her heart. The couple on the screen appeared to love each other, and they belonged together. That was what she wanted. She sighed. It appeared that she'd had that closeness and couldn't remember the joy of it or feel the love she witnessed. With a surge of feeling, Rylee knew she *would* be his wife, and they'd get that love back.

The Rylee and Devon in the video stopped, embraced, and kissed. Not just kissed—nearly made out right in the middle of the sidewalk. Watching it heated her blood, and she became more aware of the man beside her...the man she'd been intimate with.

"Rylee," Devon said softly and leaned closer, obvious that a kiss was what he desired.

And why wouldn't he after watching the video? Although nervous, she wanted one as well and wouldn't allow something trivial like how his presence loomed so close that he consumed all the available air to stop her from receiving his kiss. Heck, she'd be surprised if he couldn't hear the thumping of her heart over the crackle of the fire, it beat so strongly for them.

Craving his touch, Rylee tilted her head in his

direction for the kiss he looked ready to deliver. She wanted to tell him without words that she was giving their marriage a chance, too afraid her voice may crack should she vocalize her wish.

Their lips met, and that crazy story built for die-hard romantics about seeing fireworks was real. Lights flashed behind her eyelids as he kissed her lips, feathery light at first, just enough to tease…to torment. She allowed him the lead, but she would by no means be a passive participant. When his hand snaked behind her head, she seized the opportunity and inclined her body into him.

Pulling back, Devon peered into her eyes with a big question in his. *Was she sure?* she read. She hoped her answer—*Yes, without hesitation*—showed brightly for him to read. In case only she understood, she smiled and wrapped a hand into a tight fist, grasping his shirt in its clutches, and pulled it—and him—back to her. "Kiss me…*husband.*" Tagging on the endearment hadn't been planned, but by the look of first shock and then pleasure on his face, she was glad it happened.

"By all means, *wife*," he whispered against her mouth. His tongue played at the corners of her lips, taunting, until she sighed and parted them. He took advantage and delved inside, his tongue stroking deep, inciting a small wave of pleasure to ride through her lower abdomen.

A raw, intense urge from deep inside unleashed itself and the need to mold their bodies together, his warmth against her increasingly heated body, took hold, and she shifted closer again, trying to obtain that needed contact. Appearing to have had a similar thought, he lifted Rylee and slipped her onto his lap. In that position, she became keenly aware of his growing erection and she sucked in a breath of surprise that she'd affected him so deeply...and so quickly.

"Better," he murmured before retaking her mouth. His tongue swept deep inside until she tasted the essence of Devon. It was masculinity, strength, and a sweetness only the best of men possessed and allowed a woman to see. Good God, and this was her husband.

Something about him called to her inner being...to her soul. She let out a moan and took control of the kiss, their tongues dancing like they'd been partners in intimacy for years. When he turned her head and tried to resume control, she allowed it, surrendering herself to him, waiting to see where he led them.

A grunt of protest slipped between her lips when he broke the kiss. That wasn't where she wanted him to go. She shifted on his lap to find some relief from the carnal ache that had seeped into her core.

"Easy," he rasped against her skin. Leaving behind butterfly kisses, he nibbled and trailed his lips to the corner of her mouth, her cheek, down her jawbone and throat. When he reached the thrumming pulse on her neck, he left goose bumps skittering across her skin.

"You're mine," was heard on a growl before Devon nipped at her throat and then earlobe.

Eager, and much too excited, Rylee pulled his shirt from his pants and slipped her hands underneath to his lean, muscled chest. Her palm slid over the heated flesh, fingertips passing through short hairs, and she felt the shudder go through him.

The slide of his hand under her shirt halted her exploration and when his hand grazed the underside of her breast, she thought she'd skyrocket off his lap. Heat infused itself between them and latched onto the fire building inside her. She shifted again and was rewarded with a tortured groan.

Pushing aside her bra, Devon palmed her breast and flicked at the tip of her nipple, which shot a wave of pleasure to her core, amping her need for him. A need she planned to fill in a few short moments.

Slipping her hand into the waistband of his pants, her fingers brushed his hard length that throbbed for her waiting hand. She fumbled with the buttons and when she reached the zipper, Devon grabbed her hand and eased it away.

"We need to stop now, or it'll be too late," he said as their breaths mingled, their lips so close.

Her rapidly beating heart and libido didn't want to agree. Rylee rested her forehead against his shoulder, her ear pressed to him, listening to the erratic beating of his heart. Attempting to regulate her heavy breathing was more of a challenge because of his closeness, yet she refused to climb off his lap.

"I don't know what changed your mind about giving us a try, but I'm glad you did." He turned and with his lips pressed to her hair, whispered, "Let's wait to move to the next level until we're more comfortable with each other. I don't want it to be just…sex with us."

Christ, this man couldn't be more perfect. She was glad she'd decided to give them a chance. Waving a hand in front of her face as if fanning herself, she joked, "I'm warm…hot, actually. Maybe we should bank the fire."

His chest rumbled with his laughter.

She could get used to Devon Hamilton.

Chapter Fourteen

The cacophony of heavy raindrops on the roof and subsequent bouts of clashing thunder woke Devon at an early hour. Lying in bed, naked as always, but with the sheet covering his midsection, he pulled his hands behind his head and stared at the ceiling.

They'd almost had sex the night before. If he hadn't stopped her, she'd be lying beside him now, watching the sunrise. That was what he wanted. Why the hell had he stopped her?

Sighing, he knew why—he wanted her to have a better connection with him. Otherwise, he feared she'd regret her actions or worse, blame him for trying to wiggle out of the annulment, because once they had sex, that possibility was off the table. And, he wouldn't discuss divorce.

It had been a good sign she'd taken to the tape so well. It meant she accepted they'd married under normal pretenses. Her opening up to him was also a positive. What mattered was they were together with a chance to build new memories.

Another roll of thunder boomed closer than the last. Rylee would be upset, but they weren't exploring today. No way in hell would he hike in that weather unless he knew for certain the girls were there. And, in that case, he'd have HIS in tow. It was a waste to have them scout out a house with only one person in

residence. Devon just prayed that one person wasn't
Robert Carver.

Although he couldn't completely let it go,
something inside him told him the man at the ranch
couldn't be Carver, because the Carver he knew
would've required help around him. The man had
always had lackeys, even to get his coffee. In fact, the
man used to brag about how he'd never cooked a meal.

A weak meow sounded beside his bed and he
almost jumped out of his skin. Peering down, he saw
Max looking up with big eyes. He picked up the kitten
and put him on the bed. "Sneaky little bastard," he
muttered. It also meant Rylee was up because the little
tyke had slept with her.

Looking forward to a day with his wife, cooped up
so she couldn't run away, he swept the covers off and
tossed his legs over the side of the bed. Max moved
toward him and he reached out and snagged the kitten
before he made Devon's lap his bed. "Oh no. There will
be no moving around in that region. You could scratch
something and then I'd have to drop you back in the
woods." The last part was a total lie. His wife was
already attached to the kitten. He was too, but the pet
didn't need to know that if his lie kept him off Devon's
balls.

Max answered with a yawn and stretch, his little
butt pushed up in the air, and then he pranced to the
pillow where he circled and curled himself into a ball,
laid down, and closed his eyes.

Devon shook his head, stood, and reached his arms
above his head, stretching. That was the moment his
wife chose to push his door open.

"Oh." A look of shock slapped her face. "I, um—"

Her eyes raked his body from head to toe and stopped where he still sported his morning wood. "I just planned to sneak Max out. I'm sorry he got in." Heat crept down her neck.

He dropped his arms and instead of covering himself in modesty, he strode to the dresser and opened a drawer to pull out new clothing—like walking around naked in front of her was an everyday occurrence. "Yeah, well, he's comfy now. You may as well leave him." Christ, it was difficult to act normal when he had a hard-on and she was right there. If things went well today, he wasn't stopping tonight.

Realizing she still stood at the door, he turned toward her as he stepped into his underwear, smiling inwardly at the hungry look in her eyes. "Was there anything else?"

Her gulp was visible to his eye. "No." Slowly, she shook her head. "I'll start coffee and breakfast." Without waiting for a response from him, she spun on her heels and raced from the room.

His hearty chuckle followed in her wake.

Dressed and carrying a purring machine, Devon stepped from his room and into the kitchen area. He took the spatula from his wife and deposited Max into her arms. "I'll finish."

While not a gourmet chef, he held his own in the kitchen. Her eggs just needed more seasoning, but tonight, he'd make her a nice dinner. Candlelight and soft music—only the best for Rylee. He was pretty sure he'd picked up everything he'd need when they'd been in town.

Devon whistled a lively tune while serving up the eggs, bacon, and toast she'd cooked. He didn't think he'd ever felt this happy, this contented and relaxed with a woman. It was a sensation he'd never experienced. A bit of ecstasy built inside him at the possibility of having what his brothers had.

"Breakfast is ready."

Releasing the curtain on a front window, a loud sigh escaped Rylee. "I can't believe it's supposed to rain all day," she said glumly.

Sitting at the table, he placed a napkin in his lap and picked up a fork. Maybe he should've thought to check the weather, but his wife's nearness had fogged his mind. "Gives us more time to research. And"— Devon raised his brows—"get to know each other." No longer could he make her think the worst of him. "Look, Rylee," he said, "I won't hold you to that part of the bargain. Truth is, I'll help you look for the girls anyway. I just want you to give us a try."

Hoping his words settled her, he tensed when she placed her fork down and stood without a word. She ambled around the table to him, leaned down, and kissed his cheek. The warmth nearly burned him through. "Thank you," she said.

Hands itching to reach out and grab her, he forced himself to be patient. He placed his fork on the table and turned to her. Shock immediately filled him.

Holding out her hand, she said in a low, husky voice, "I'm ready."

It was his turn to gulp. Did she mean? Beads of sweat formed on his brow. "Ready for what, exactly?" He had to clarify, not only for himself, but to ensure she understood also.

A seductive smile spread across her face. "For us to try. I thought we might start in your room."

He launched himself from the chair fast enough that it fell over, and his napkin floated to the floor. He didn't give a damn. He took her hand and all but dragged her to his room. The hell with waiting.

Chapter Fifteen

The stirrings of desire had coursed through her since she'd woken. Heck, had the man not left her the day before with an aching need for him, she'd never had to be so bold. She'd been up half the night wondering if she should make the first move.

When she followed him into his room, he kicked the door closed. The usually trailing Angel had remained on the couch, her tail wagging. Even she'd sensed the change of the vibe in the air.

Rylee's focus was on Devon and what was to come. Her insides tingled at the thought of his hands on her again. Now that she had him, a nervous pulse skittered through her, making her wonder if he could feel her slight tremble.

Pulling her other hand into his, so that he held them both, he surprised her by not moving closer. Her heart lurched in a panic. *Don't let him have changed his mind or stop halfway again.* A bob bounced down his throat in a hard swallow. "Are you sure? Because once you do this, there is no annulment."

Relief flowed freely and a smile grew on her face, while she nodded slowly. She'd never been surer of anything. "I'm sure. No annulment." Her hope was still that they fell in love and she believed it possible. Devon had made her believe it *was* possible. It wasn't just lust between them. Oh, how she could see herself madly in love with him.

He hauled her close until their hands were locked securely between their bodies. Then he lowered his mouth near her ear with his warm breath teasing her neck. He nuzzled on it, eliciting a wave of goose bumps that ran rampant over her skin. "Who the hell am I kidding? I wasn't letting you have an annulment anyway."

Laughter burst forth from her. Rylee should be upset he'd never planned to honor their bargain, but it no longer mattered. It lit her heart that he wouldn't have given up on them.

Dropping her head to the side, she opened herself to his exploration of her throat. His lips were warm, wet, and the kiss a little rough since he hadn't shaved, but the combination was already driving her crazy. Releasing their clasped grip, she slid her hand up his chest to his broad shoulders, then to the back of his neck, where her fingers ran through his soft hair.

Kisses trailed along her neck to her cheek, first the left side and then the right side of her mouth before halting, his lips hovering a mere inch over hers. His breaths, much like hers, came in short jerky puffs, fanning her face. "I plan to make sweet love to you. I promise that no part of your body will be left untouched when I'm done with you."

Her insides quivered with delicious pleasure that flowed outward in waves.

With a groan, he wrapped his arms around her, pulling them closer until she felt his racing heartbeat, a rhythm that almost matched hers.

Elevating herself on her toes, she wound her arms around him. "Kiss me."

The warm shock of him answering her with his mouth crashing over hers stifled her thought. They angled their heads and deepened the kiss, tongues dueling.

Devon's hands slid down her back until they landed on her ass. He squeezed lightly and then palmed them and pulled her until his erection pressed against her belly. She gasped into his mouth. He was already hard and they'd just started playing around. Then again, she was already wet, so it wasn't out of the realm of possibilities.

Breaking the kiss, he gazed down at her with eyes darkening more every second until she suspected the gold in them would be nothing but flecks. "You have too many clothes on," he growled.

"So do you."

"Well, we can undress each other, or we can each undress ourselves at the same time. I guess we could also go with strip tease while the other watches, but I think we save that one for later. Don't get me wrong, I want to undress you, but option two gets us there faster." He tilted his head toward the bed's direction.

She laughed. "Then, by all means, let's go with option two." Immediately, she ripped her shirt over her head. Taking a peek, she caught him already in his underwear before she'd pulled her jeans down. When she reached back to unhook her bra, the sight of him transfixed her. He stood in all his naked glory, with narrow hips, broad shoulders, and lean contours. His muscled and well-defined chest and arms almost had her drooling. Damn, he was fine. What had her almost gasping was his erection jutting toward her. With his hands fisted at his sides and his chest almost heaving with each rapid breath, she guessed he was holding on by a thread.

When he didn't move or offer assistance, she released the clasp and allowed her bra to slide seductively from her shoulders, slowly exposing her breasts with puckered nipples, demanding his attention.

His breath hitched and she smiled a little.

Taking the same approach with her panties, she slid her fingers on each side and toyed with them before she hooked her thumbs into the waistband and leisurely inched them down. Then she stood before him with none of the embarrassment she'd worried would appear. Instead, she absorbed the prevailing current of desire that flowed between them. It was strong and powerful and made butterflies tumble in her stomach.

Devon stepped closer, and Rylee leaned into him, but wrapped her fingers around his girth and completed a couple of exploratory strokes.

He groaned. "Your hand feels too damn good. You need to quit that if you want me to last."

A giggle crested and she allowed it to escape. She removed her hand, but only for the time being.

In a surprisingly swift move, probably to pay her back for the giggle, he reached out and lifted her in his arms, holding her with an arm underneath her back and one underneath her knees. He approached the bed and gently lowered her across the middle.

The way he stood and stared at her made her feel like she was about to be a feast.

A muscle twitched in his jaw. "No place left untouched," he said in a voice that sounded as if it pained him to speak.

She almost cried out, calling him to her fast, but

she could see what it was costing him to go slowly and she wouldn't interfere. Hell, she planned to enjoy the hell out of it. Smiling, she said, "Get on with it."

Devon ran a finger lightly up her foot's instep and she jerked reflexively. He chuckled. He'd pay for that at some point.

Then, his lips touched her toes, languidly taking one in his mouth, and Rylee sucked in a breath as pleasure surged to her core. Who could have imagined such an exquisite stroke of desire could be found in toes?

One hand explored her legs, up and down, each time getting closer and closer to between her thighs while he continued to kiss her foot, then began a hot, wet path up her leg. At the tender ministrations, her legs fell open for him, eager for more.

He lifted her leg and kissed behind her knee, and she moaned as her pussy tightened and her clit throbbed.

Good grief, the man had a long way to go to cover her body. She might not be strong enough to handle it. Then again, she had on their wedding night, even if she couldn't remember it. They'd replace that night with now and many more encounters to come.

When he kissed the inside of her thigh, her clit pulsed with anticipation. He was so close she felt the roughness of his morning beard as it teased her skin. She needed him to continue closer and closer until he took her in his mouth.

Just as Rylee felt the warm air from his breath at her juncture, he pulled away and went to the toes on her other leg. She could just grab him by the hair and pull him up. She swore the man was laughing while he was making love to her leg.

Finally making it back to her core, his hot breath on her nub, she bucked upward, nearly jumping off the bed. "No more teasing," she demanded in a raspy whisper.

"No more." His tongue probed her center and a full-body shiver overtook her. Sliding his tongue up to her clit, he stopped and sucked the bud into his mouth, and she whimpered. If possible, her nipples puckered to tighter beads, yearning for his touch...his mouth.

Nipping, licking, and sucking her nub, he inserted a finger inside her and she grasped his hair and dropped her head back, closing her eyes at the ecstasy cresting like waves through her body. She felt like an ocean with a delectable storm surge building, and only Devon Hamilton could make it happen.

And then it did. Riding a tidal wave of tsunami proportions that swelled from her core to her extremities, Rylee cried out, and her awareness of everything floated with the tide. Weightless. Peaceful. Sated.

"Mm." When she returned to herself, she looked down to see a smiling Devon with his head resting on her belly, watching her. "Come here."

His head shook left to right. "No can do. Still more to cover." With that, he swiftly traced a path from her stomach to her breast. Leveraging himself up on one arm, he used the other to circle her erect nipple.

Her body tingling, she didn't know how much more enjoyable torture she could stand.

Leaning down, he blew on the tip and goose bumps dotted her body. He opened his mouth, acting as if he was about to take the nipple in his mouth but pulled back with a wicked glint sparkling in his eyes. "Nope, arms and back first."

Digging her fingers into his shoulders, she narrowed her eyes. "If you don't get up here and get yourself inside me, we are going to have problems. There'll be other times for you to love my body."

Launching himself off the bed, she must've cried out because he looked at her strangely. "Condom," he explained.

Thank goodness one of them had enough sense to think of protection. The fact he'd brought any wasn't something she could process at the moment.

After ripping open a foil packet and donning the condom, he crawled back on the bed and angled over her, positioning his erection at her core. "Look up at me."

Gazes locked, a swell of heat simmering between the two, he entered her slowly as if testing, then he thrust upward and she cried out at the instant fullness.

A hand lightly stroked her face and his eyes filled with concern. "I'm so sorry. I didn't mean to hurt you. I guess I got a bit impatient."

It took a moment, but she was able to smile and mean it. "I'm okay now. Just the shock." To show she meant it, she moved beneath him.

Dropping his forehead to hers, he groaned. "Christ, you feel so good."

"You do, too."

Slowly, finding a seductive rhythm that created a wake within her, Devon took her mouth again, and their kisses were hotter and deeper than before. They bespoke urgent needs that skittered along every nerve ending within her.

She clutched desperately at his shoulders as their movements quickened, becoming almost frenzied, and the buildup returned.

Separating their lips, they each attempted to capture gulps of air. "I want you to come one more time."

"I'm going to. Real soon." Everything was drawing to her center, drawing tight, ready to explode.

"Then hang on."

Her muscles tensed and her head fell back. Euphoria rushed heatedly through her, sending her on a momentary break from her body while she floated on the crested waves, and then leaving in its wake, a well-loved woman.

Devon slid off her. They both lay on their backs, breathing heavily. She looked forward to starting the day like this every day.

"I need another few minutes before I start on the rest of you."

With nothing else to do for the day, she would happily be his playground. She turned her head to him. "You're on."

Chapter Sixteen

Devon hadn't lied when he'd promised to love every inch of her. Rylee smiled at his exuberance when he'd covered everywhere. By the time the need for food called them out of bed, it'd been a chore to walk on legs of rubber, but otherwise, she'd felt fantastic. Better than she could ever remember.

She could feel the connection between them. It was strong…powerful.

With no hope of the rain letting up, Rylee continued to relax and enjoy getting to know Devon. The word "marriage" began to flow more easily. It had best because there would never be a divorce. Even though they weren't in love, she truly believed she had what her mother and Madison's father began with. Theirs grew to a great love. It could happen to them too.

Sitting at the dining table, she watched Devon work. His long fingers glided across the keyboard and his brow would furl and unfurl as he reviewed new information. He'd successfully pulled everything on Dave's phone. There'd been a great deal more travel itineraries than she'd found which put into question the number of potential locations of the girls. Yet, in her heart, she knew Robert Carver was their man and his ranch was the right place. Or at least it had been.

"There are a lot of places for us to check. I'd like to

get back to my computer at headquarters. I could probably crack Brent's phone there too."

Clearing her throat, she stood and walked toward the kitchen area. "After we search for clues here." She spun around and faced him, pounding one fist into the other palm in frustration. "I just know this is right."

Scrutinizing her, his eyes gave nothing away. Did he think she was crazy? Obsessed? She probably was, but her gut....

"If it's not raining in the morning, we'll go." She brightened and he raised his hand to forestall her. "Then we go back to HIS and find these girls." Devon stood, walked to her, and wrapped his arms around her waist. "I've enjoyed the hell out of my time with you, and we'll get plenty more. I promise. But first, let's find Misty and Mandy."

Rylee's arms wound around his neck and she pulled him close, hugging him tightly. "I could fall in love with you." She hadn't meant to tell him that she'd softened so much to him, that she could see them together. It was true though. He'd flipped something in her heart and she wouldn't fight it.

"That's what I'm counting on," was whispered in her ear.

****

Devon typed a reply to an e-mail of a potential HIS client on his keyboard. While HIS believed gray areas existed, they didn't flat-out break the law—well, mostly not—as a general rule. His dipping into government servers fell into a gray area as far as he was concerned. So, this client's request to shoot anyone who even looked at their boss the wrong way was not something they'd ever consider accepting.

His fingers paused as he thought back to earlier that day. He'd worried when he'd first woken from their nap, wondering how Rylee would react waking next to him, buck-ass naked. He held back the concern and waited for her eyes to open. When she'd woken, she'd curled into him, and then after enjoying exploring each other, she'd climbed onto his waiting erection.

He inhaled and sighed in pleasure. Talk about a morning surprise. She'd turned some type of corner in their relationship, and her giving them a real chance was in the cards.

Wishing he could return the memories of their time in Vegas, he thought maybe he should check out her friends and see if someone might have slipped her something. Yet, the preacher had said the two appeared sober. It had stood out to the preacher because many of his customers weren't.

Maybe she could've just blacked out and enjoyed herself without the restraints she held so tightly. The same type of restraint that kept her worrying about being divorced from him. He wasn't letting her go. She'd learn real fast, if she hadn't already. She was now a Hamilton, and they didn't let family go.

And, as for love. Well, he wanted that too so if it was in the cards—*damn Vegas puns*—then they'd fall in love. Possibly for a second time.

The front door opened and Rylee entered with Angel bounding behind her. "It finally stopped raining."

He looked back down at his work. Inwardly he wanted to hoist her over his shoulder and carry her to the bedroom to fuck her brains out. He shook his head and closed his eyes for a moment to regroup his thoughts.

By banging the kitchen cabinet doors closed, his wife's actions roused his curiosity.

"What's the matter?" he asked, a grin tugging at the corners of his lips since he knew what she sought.

"Are all the chocolate bars gone? I could really go for one right about now."

Devon looked down at the candy bar on the table beside him and he fought that grin from becoming full-blown. In town, they'd purchased a couple of Hershey's for S'Mores and each had added one bar of their favorites, which turned out to be the same—Snickers. "I can't help it if you ate your candy bar. This Snickers is mine," he toyed with her. Then, he slid it closer to his laptop and watched her eyes widen.

Rylee slowly approached the table, an extra sashay in her walk. "How about sharing?"

Acting uninterested, he turned back to his computer screen. "Not on your life."

In one swift moment, Rylee closed in and snatched the bar, then raced to the front door.

Devon surged from his seat with laughter as he chased her outside.

She chose the car to circle around, laughing all the way. She faked left, then started right, then came back to the same spot when she realized he mimicked her movements. "You can have it back," she said through her merriment. "But only if you catch me." She taunted him by waving the candy bar in her hand.

Angel, seeing a game, bounced up and down, and then ran between the two, barking. Max was probably still curled up inside, uninterested in their shenanigans.

One thing Devon had been good at was running,

and he finally had a chance to use his speed. She had no hope of outrunning him, but what to do with her when he caught her? An idea popped into his head and his groin tightened as a huge grin formed. "Okay." He dug in and then sprinted around the side of the car.

She squealed and ran away, but it wasn't fast enough.

When he caught her, she was giggling like a little schoolgirl. Holding her back to his front, and with her feet off the ground, he spun them around, full-on belly laughing with her. When he stopped, a bit dizzy, he kept her aloft. "I think you've got something of mine."

She clutched the candy bar to her chest, holding on for dear life. He'd seen women this desperate for a chocolate fix, but they'd usually been pregnant.

Since trying to steal it failed, she attempted another route and proceeded to pout. "Won't you share some with me?" She turned to him and batted her eyelashes super-fast, amusement etched on her features.

"I'll tell you what," he growled in her ear. "I'll share…after."

Furrowing her brow, she asked, "After what?"

In a move he'd learned from Matt, he set her down and before she recovered, he spun her around and tossed her over his shoulder. Bouncing her to ensure she was secure, he grinned at her protests. When her laughter mellowed a bit, he slapped her on the ass and walked back into the cabin. "After."

Chapter Seventeen

Drawing her brow low, Rylee watched Devon. "Why are you bringing so much crap in your backpack? We're just going there and back. Good grief. Is that really a pump to purify water?"

"We should look authentic." He stuffed the pump and a first-aid kit in the small space available. They definitely looked the part in polypropylene and pile pants and shirts, and sturdy hiking boots. Almost chuckling aloud, he noted how her stuff looked worn, and his own looked as if it'd just been purchased. And, it had been. Hiking hadn't interested him before now. Rylee seemed to enjoy it though, so he'd have to get into it. "Besides, if we don't find anything, and it isn't raining, you and I are hiking, having a picnic, and exploring that cave you mentioned."

"And *if* we find something?"

Placing his hand on his hip like he'd seen her do to him, he assumed her frustrated pose and answered, "Then we hightail it back here, call Jesse along the way and find those girls."

"Ha-ha! I see what you did. I do not look like that."

Chuckling, Devon stepped to Rylee and took her hands in his, bringing them to his lips. He kissed each knuckle before releasing them and resuming his packing.

She picked up her juice glass and wiped down the

table from their breakfast. A flash of something—a vision of Rylee doing something similar flooded him. She was wearing a black dress and it was at a table in a restaurant or bar. Smiling, she lifted the glass and the dirty napkins from the table to a waiting waitress, then she turned that brilliant smile on him. His heart melted at the sight. As suddenly as it appeared, it vanished.

Vegas. There was no other explanation. He didn't want the vision to stop. There was so much more that he wanted to remember. Preferably all of it.

"Will it be safe to have a phone and still pretend to be lost?" Breaking him out of his thoughts, she sounded almost breathless.

Remembering why, he gave himself brownie points for her reaction and fought the tug at the corners of his lips. "We'll hide it before we go into the house."

"Are you worried they might search us?"

"It would be stupid not to be a little worried since somehow the owner knows Westbrook—good or bad." And, he knows me, which could also be good or bad. "If something happens—however we can—we get to the phone and call Jesse." A sliver of doubt crept its way into his mind, warning him he should call his brother now. Frustrated, he slapped it away. Christ, it was one man and no girls at the house. He had a pair of balls and his wife surely held her own since she'd been an FBI agent. Enough second-guessing himself, he nodded as if he'd resolved all the world's problems. "Did you give Angel and Max extra food?"

"Yes. We're lucky Angel doesn't wolf it down all in one bite. Do you think it necessary though?"

He shrugged and looked at the dog, wondering how old she was. Definitely not old enough that she'd slowed down as far as he could tell. "Probably not, but it can't hurt to be prepared for our getting lost or something."

After zipping his pack, Devon turned to his wife and raised his eyebrows. "Are you ready for this?" Christ knew he wasn't ready. Once again his thought shifted to Robert Carver. If he was there, alarm bells would raise with Rylee. She might think Devon had been keeping her away on purpose and trying to protect the man. However, now wasn't the time to discuss that relationship because if they didn't move, they'd never beat the rain that might come.

She huffed, pulling him back to his original question. "I'd be more ready if you'd allow me to carry my weapon inside."

"It's like the phone—a necessary precaution to stash them away from the house." Because he'd sure as hell have his there as well, and although he didn't normally carry one, his hand itched to have a weapon in it to protect Rylee. No matter the situation.

They departed and trekked through the woods in silence. The trip took longer since they'd swung around to come from a direction other than the rental. Devon and Rylee emerged from the trees with the horse corral between them and the house. He wiped at the sweat that beaded down his face. In her eagerness, she'd put him through a workout with the pace she'd set on the hike. As would any man, he'd refused to tell her to slow down. Instead, he fought to catch his breath when she wasn't looking.

The moleskin in his backpack called to him. They'd have to stop so he could remove his boots and apply some to his heels before they continued on their way. He'd have to concede that one to her since she'd foisted the healing product on him when he'd bought new boots in town.

Rylee stopped at the pen where two horses ambled toward her. The closest, a reddish-brown colored mare with white markings, halted in front of her and pushed her muzzle into Rylee's waiting hands. Stroking the animal, she spoke quietly, "I think we should wait here for a few minutes to see if the guy approaches us. Makes us seem less threatening."

Pride flooded in at her thinking. Devon would bet she'd been a damn good FBI agent. "That works." He dropped the backpack, wishing he'd listened to her and made it lighter. The second horse, a stallion, approached him, nudging at his chest. Devon reached out and stroked the horse's muzzle, and it pushed out a heavy breath that flared its nostrils.

He glanced at Rylee and caught her fighting to keep the hair the wind kept blowing out of her face. She pulled a stretchy thing from her wrist and tied her hair back in it. A laugh almost bubbled up from him because the hair around her face was too short to be contained and flew around. He turned his gaze upward and his gut did a summersault. The storm had rolled in faster than he'd anticipated while they'd been in the woods. The skies were nearly black and threatening to soak the inhabitants unlucky enough to be in their path as they breezed by. They needed to make this trip quick.

Watching the sky and knowing the picnic and exploring with his wife were not happening today, he almost missed the movement at the barn. Of course, his wife caught it first and she'd swatted at him before he fully caught the man's silhouette. "I see," he mumbled.

His pulse rate increased and his palms turned clammy at the fear of being identified and him not having prepared his wife. It'd been a stupid thing not to tell her on the hike over. Of course, being winded and talking were a hard mix. So, his excuse went.

Putting on what he hoped was a charming smile, he turned and his body relaxed a bit when the man before him wasn't Carver. "Hello," he said loudly. "My wife and I got lost and wonder if we can have some water and directions. We heard there's a great waterfall out this way, but we must've missed a turn." When he'd finished, the two men faced each other and Devon extended his hand. "Daryl Reynolds."

"And an indoor bathroom would be fabulous," Rylee piped in, as she came to his side, dancing around as if in urgent need of the facilities.

The burly man held Devon's hand and surveyed the two of them intently. So long, in fact, that Devon worried he'd deny them. They needed to get inside the house to move forward in one direction or the other. Finally, he let go of Devon's hand. "Nick is the name. Come to the house and I'll help you out."

They grabbed their packs and followed. "This is a nice place. You live out here by yourself?" Rylee asked conversationally.

Nick stuffed his hands in his front pants pockets. "Yep."

A man of many words. Great. How the hell would Devon keep him talking while Rylee searched? Time to test the waters. "How about them Broncos?"

The man nodded. "Great start to the season although they got robbed last week."

Devon smiled. He'd chosen the right topic and

team. Hell, it was a universal male conversation piece.

"Listen, you boys can discuss football later. I need a bathroom and I'm not peeing in the bushes again until I absolutely must."

Chuckling, Nick opened the front door and the outline of a handgun at the waistband under his shirt was evident. Cool air hit Devon's face as they followed the man inside the home. Keeping his head forward, Devon allowed his eyes to roam the area. Remembering what Jesse always asked for in surveillance, he looked for cameras, sensors, or anything that told him what type of security to expect in case they needed to return with the team. He'd expect some security from a former spook, but to have cameras in your own hallways wasn't a good sign. He hoped Rylee saw them before she went about exploring and equally hoped someone wasn't monitoring them in real-time.

"Down the hall"—Nick pointed—"third door on the right." He nodded to an open living area. "Wait in there and I'll grab you two bottles of water."

Devon and Rylee gave a knowing nod and went about their mission realizing time was critical. Dropping his pack inside the room, Devon made to bend down to pull something from it when he slipped a small listening device from his pocket to below the small table. He'd just planted a second one across the large room when Nick entered, two bottles of water in hand. "Where are you staying?"

"We rented a cabin about an hour from here. I think it's an hour. Hell, I'm so turned around right now." Devon accepted a bottle dripping in condensation. "We're not sure how to get to either the waterfall or where we're parked." Shrugging, he reached inside his pocket and pulled out a smashed compass. "It got stepped on and the needle bent. I straightened it, but it's not worth shit anymore." It had been Rylee's brilliant idea to doctor it up. She just kept earning more and more props on this mission of theirs. Christ, he hoped she didn't push it too far and go where she shouldn't. "What do you do?"

Nick narrowed his eyes at the abrupt change of topic. "Retired."

Hell, he had to go back to sports to keep him talking. "So, robbed, huh? I'm a Ravens fan and they played at the same time, so I missed the Broncos' game."

Nick dropped into one of the chairs. Devon followed suit. "Yeah, damn refs are crooked. They tossed flags on the Broncos all day long, but never on the Chargers. We lost by a field goal to them."

"Really?"

"Fucked up, that's what it was. We lost by three points. Three! And, if we'd had the field goal, we'd have tied and gone into overtime and crushed them, no matter the assholes ref'ing."

Pouring water down his gullet to keep from arguing with the asshole in front of him, Devon nodded as best he could. Robbed, my ass. The Broncos played a shitty game. It happened. One dealt with it and moved on, not blamed everyone else.

"Where's your woman? She's taking a long time."

"Oh." He cleared his throat and lowered his voice. "I think she really, really had to go. Sorry, dude." Where the hell had the word dude come from? He was not cut out for subterfuge, and she would have his ass if she found out he'd said that about her.

Laughing, Nick opened the bottled water he'd presumably brought for Rylee, stopping only long enough to drink. Wiping his face with his sleeve, he continued talking about the game as if they'd not spoken of anything else. Devon wanted to scream, but instead played the proper pal to commiserate the game loss with. There'd be no time for him to slip into the hallway and plant a bug so he hoped his wife did before she returned. Speaking of returning, he was getting worried about how long she'd taken.

When the man looked at the entryway and frowned, Devon attempted a redirect. "So, where is this beautiful waterfall we heard so much about? Please say we're close because I gotta tell you, my feet ain't made for this much hiking."

Turning back to him, the man took a moment and then laughed. "Well, buddy, I hate to tell you this, but you're a good two miles from it. You got good 'n turned around."

"Shit. She sure had her heart set on the waterfall. I'll tell you what, just tell me how to get back to the main road, and I'll let her think we're headed to her spot and act surprised when we wind up back at the car." He grinned with gusto, like he'd had a brilliant idea.

Nick chuckled. "You've got balls, man. Okay, it's not too difficult." He explained what Devon already knew, but to keep up pretenses, and add more time for Rylee, he asked questions and allowed himself to appear directionally challenged. When it seemed he'd have to go back to the Broncos, she magically appeared with a bright smile encompassing her face. Either she'd found something or she was a damn good actress.

"I'm so sorry. I actually dozed off on the toilet. So embarrassing." She tilted her head to Devon. "Is that water for me?"

"Shit. Sorry." Nick breezed past her.

Devon leaned close to her ear. "Don't say a word."

She nodded.

"Here." Nick returned extending a bottle of water. "I hooked your husband up with directions." He winked at Devon.

Quick on the uptake, she raised her brows at Devon.

"Let me grab my pack and we can get on our way."

They exited the house amidst small gusts of a chilly wind with a hint of rain in it. Time wasn't on their side. They would get wet. How stupid he'd been to think they could beat a storm.

Rylee leaned close to him. "Why are we going this way? Our phone and weapons are the other way."

Glancing over his shoulder to see Nick standing in the doorway, he nodded to the man and turned to his wife. "Because this is the way he told us to go. It would be mighty suspicious if we went in the opposite direction." Reaching out, he clasped her hand in his. "We'll just circle around and get them. But, first, I think we need shelter. Feel the dampness of the air?"

"The cave is closer than the cabin."

Protection was protection and a cave sounded awfully cozy. "Lead on."

As if by mutual agreement, they didn't speak of what either found, or didn't find, at Canyon Creek Ranch. Rylee bounced with energy, so he had an inkling of suspicion that she'd found something. How she kept it quiet after all her determination to search baffled him.

"Pick up the pace, the bottom is about to fall out. Grab some wood along the way and we'll make a fire. If we wait, we might only find wet pieces." Devon leaned down, almost toppling with the weight of his pack, and snagged a broken branch that appeared perfect for a small fire. Pity, he hadn't been a Boy Scout growing up, then he'd know what pieces were truly the best. Oh well, they'd have a fire—easy or not.

Chapter Eighteen

Robert Carver unbuttoned his light gray Armani suit jacket, grasped both lapels and then pulled it off his shoulders and down his arm before tossing it haphazardly on the back of a wine-colored leather chair. Walking to the plate-glass window in the room he'd designated as his office within his Manhattan home, he stared out over the clear sky, wondering when they'd have some rain to break their drought.

Pride swarmed him, from his thirty-fourth-floor space, at his grand life. A life not dependent on a ridiculous government salary or listening to someone in charge who had no clue. Now, he oversaw everything and had a small empire. Many years ago, the elder Westbrook—Keith—had shown him the easiest way to make money. The man would kill him if he knew that Robert and Dave had been lovers. His stomach clenched at the thought of Dave being murdered. They hadn't been in love, only lust, but the loss was still raw.

Hell, if the old man ever found out, he'd probably turn Robert over to the authorities. But, with Dave gone, it was too late for Keith to find out because Robert sure as hell wouldn't tell anyone.

There had been a benefit to having a relationship with Dave. Robert had jumped on Keith's share of the market in a matter of seconds after his arrest and used Dave, unwittingly, so his father would hand over everything the authorities hadn't confiscated without question or, most importantly, cost.

After he finished the current sale he had pending, he'd find the woman who got away. Rylee Hawkins. The benefactor who wanted her had offered double upon hearing she'd escaped them. Enough to make Robert almost default on other agreements, but no, he honored his word. A bitter grin grew on his face. Honor amongst criminals was true and alive.

The ringing of his cell phone interrupted his thoughts. Reaching for it from his pocket, he automatically drew himself up to his full five foot eleven inches—six foot with the lifts in his shoes. After seeing the number, he knew to expect bad news, and he hated bad news. Before he'd left the CIA, he'd set up a network that kept him knowledgeable about anything that mattered to him. He was always intent on getting information first. For some things, he had to rely on nonagency help, and that was where things usually went awry.

"Yeah," he said shortly.

"Um, boss, you told me to tell you if anyone ever came to the ranch. Well, a man and his wife did today. They were lost," the voice said nervously.

"What do you mean a man and his wife visited the ranch? How the fuck did they get lost around there? We're out in fucking nowhere land!" Robert bellowed to Nick through the phone.

He never should've left that idiot to oversee the ranch. Sure, he was excellent with the horses, but he was still an idiot. Having people inside one of his houses, without his approval, grated on his nerves and made him want to smash something. Right now, that something was Nick's head.

"Well, um, they were looking for the waterfall."

"The waterfall is miles away. Didn't you find that suspicious at all?"

"No. They were harmless enough and only stayed long enough for the woman to use the bathroom," Nick rushed to say.

Fuck! They'd been inside and she'd wandered the house. Robert pinched the bridge of his nose between his thumb and forefinger and took a calming breath. "What were their names?"

On the phone, thunder struck in the background and the sound of heavy rain reached Robert's ears. At least someone was getting wet.

"Um, the man was Daryl something. I didn't get his wife's name."

Who were these people? Were they really just lost hikers? "What did they look like?"

"The man was about six-one, good build, and dark hair."

That could be anyone. "Have you seen Chuck today?"

"He went back to town. Thought he'd seen that Rylee chick you were talking about."

His breath caught. No. It couldn't be that much of a coincidence. She wouldn't. Would she? "Tell me, Nick," he said slowly, "what did Daryl's wife look like?"

"Well, she was average height for a woman and had dark auburn hair." His gulp came through the receiver. "Her eyes were the color of whiskey. I know because they drew me in like she was a witch."

Witch. Stupid fucker.

"I have them…on surveillance…tape," Nick said.

"Snap me a shot of them and send it over." He waited, contemplating whom she could've brought with her.

His phone vibrated in his hand. Pulling it away from his ear, he clicked on messages and waited for the photo to load.

If it was Rylee—and something told him it would be—it appeared his prey had found herself a protector. Her coming to the house only meant one thing—she knew. Well, the girls were waiting in Belize, so he didn't have to worry about her finding anything. God, he hoped the house had been swept.

When the image fully loaded, his eyes widened. His grip on the phone tightened and his hand shook. *No! It can't be.* His heart raced as the blood boiled through his veins. It was Rylee Hawkins all right, but with her—

"Devon Hamilton," he whispered. He looked closer to make sure. *Holy fucking shit.* Anger surged through him. He fought to not toss his phone across the room and smash it against the wall.

This just got worse, and could not be a coincidence. He was one of the last men Robert wanted poking his nose around. Damned do-gooder. When the hell had he married? Were they truly married? He should've kept tabs on him, knowing he'd not give up on Greg.

He wouldn't put it past Devon to use his computer skills to spy on him. Word had gotten out about his success in that HIS group. Shit. He didn't feel like dealing with the whole lot of them.

"Hang on, Chuck's just pulled in," Nick said.

"Good, give him the phone when he walks in the door," Robert directed. He turned his hand up and curled in his fingers, observing the recent manicure's status to calm himself.

"Yeah," a gruff voice said impatiently.

Nick obviously hadn't told him who was on the phone or else something would need to be done about Chuck's attitude. "Your target was just at the house. They're on foot so they couldn't have gone far. She's with a man who needs to be eliminated. Find out which way they went and take care of it. After that, scour the tapes and find out what she saw. And, sweep the house in every room either of them were in. Chuck, control your brother to make the man's death look accidental. Then help Nick understand we don't let people inside the house." Hopefully, the idiot wouldn't break an arm because Nick needed them to care for the horses.

"It's pouring—"

"I don't give a shit. Find them!" He ended the call before any more shit could be spouted from the man. Dave had put up with way too much. Maybe Robert shouldn't have just accepted the employees of his at face value.

Although glad he had them today, this was Chuck and his brother Frank's time to show their worth. In this, he wouldn't tolerate failure.

Chapter Nineteen

Kate bit on her thumbnail, anxiously awaiting her husband's return. She hoped Brad would come with him as she'd asked. Staring out the window, cream-colored curtains pushed aside, she allowed her mind to drift. Waiting was a painful endeavor for her. Madison needed someone and her gut told her that Rylee and Devon did also, but she'd promised not to crash in on the couple. Madison was different, but that was for Brad to deal with. She grinned at the possibilities of how that scenario would play out.

When Jesse's SUV and Brad's truck came into view, she jumped back as if they'd caught her spying, and forced herself to wait for them to enter the home even though she wanted to rush outside and fling herself into her husband's arms.

As soon as they cleared the threshold, she shook her head at their black cargo pants and black T-shirts. No matter how many other colors of shirts she bought for Jesse, he always wore black on the job. Smiling, she didn't hold back her news. "Someone has to go to New York, ASAP," she said in greeting.

"Christ, can I at least kiss my wife first?" Jesse asked her while he and Brad both dropped black tactical backpacks from their shoulders.

"Not you." She then pointed at her brother-in-law. "Him."

As she'd expected, Brad exploded. "What the fuck? Why me?"

Smirking, she said, "Because my husband is not going." She crossed her arms over her chest, resolutely. Brad should be the one. She had a good feeling about him and Madison.

"Whoa, back up, sweetheart." Jesse leaned in and kissed her briefly on the lips. "I expect more of that later. Much more." He winked.

"Yeah, back up, sweetheart."

Jesse rounded on his brother. "You don't get to call my wife sweetheart."

Brad rolled his eyes and put a hand in front of him, palm out. "What-the-fuck-ever." He rotated the hand in a circle, which Kate took as move it along. "Just get on with why I have to go to New York. The last time I went, I almost landed in jail."

Jesse snorted. "That's because you got into a bar fight."

Shaking her head and ignoring what hailed to be a good story, she said, "Come on." Kate led the men to the spacious living room Jesse had designed so the family and team would have enough room. Sitting on a brown leather couch, she cleared her throat. "Madison, Rylee's sister, called about half an hour ago. She hasn't heard from Rylee in days and called me thinking I might have heard from her."

Running his fingers through his hair, Jesse sighed. Tiredness lined his face and her heart went out to him. He took on too much yet she couldn't get him to ease up on anything. "How does that constitute our running to New York? Did you tell Madison the cell service sucked in the mountains? That's what you told us." He shrugged and then leaned back, kicking his feet out in front of him and crossing them. "Give her a SAT phone number."

"It's not just that. What also made her call me is that a strange man approached her and asked for Rylee." She raised her eyebrows. "Since they're stepsisters and have different surnames, not many people know they're related, so it bothered her. Then, she's seen the man hanging around again, so she's a bit creeped out."

"What does she expect you to do?" Her husband appeared bored, but she could see that spark of concern in his eyes.

Beaming, she answered, "I'm glad you asked. She wants us to check on Rylee and make sure she's okay because she did call a SAT phone with no response. But"—she emphasized the word—"I want HIS to get rid of the man bothering her."

"Like kill him?" Brad asked incredulously. "You know we don't do that?" He snorted his disapproval. Boy, was he in for a shocker on this case. She wanted to rub her hands in glee.

"Of course I know. I want you to shoo him away."

Both men burst into laughter. At first, Kate had an incredulous retort on her lips. Then, she couldn't help a chuckle also at her choice of words.

Once done laughing, and she thought the men wiped at their eyes, Jesse took control. "All right. Brad, sorry, but pack up and make sure Madison isn't being targeted and"—his mouth fought a grin—"shoo away this man." Laughter only came from Jesse this time. Brad apparently didn't appreciate a shooing job. "That means if someone is looking for Rylee, there's plenty she's keeping secret. I take it you tried the SAT phone as well."

Barely holding onto her eagerness, Kate nodded slowly.

"Okay, sweetheart, pack—"

"Already done."

"In the half an hour since Madison called?" His brows knitted down in disbelief.

Her resulting answer was only a shrug.

"Hold the fuck up. Why do I have to go to New York? Why can't any of the other men go?"

Kate cleared her throat. "Because you're perfect for this assignment. Madison is every man's fantasy and I'm not sure the men could keep their focus. Besides, I thought you liked Madison Maxwell."

Brad surged to his feet. "Holy fuck! Her sister is Madison Maxwell? The supermodel Madison Maxwell?"

Covering her mouth to hide the giggle spurting forth, Kate could only nod in response. Hook, line, and sinker.

"I'm outta here." The door slammed shut within moments of Brad's hasty departure. She wondered if he needed anything in the backpack he'd brought into the house with him and forgotten to take as he'd left.

Jesse hooked his thumb to the front door and cocked an eyebrow. "Why not Matt? He's single. And, I might add, probably a safer bet. Plus, if you were so hell-bent on the man being single, we have a full team of them."

"Yeah, but did you notice he actually smiled and meant it?"

A smile crept across Jesse's face and his eyes

twinkled. "I did. You're a pretty smart woman. I knew I chose well. Now"—he stood and offered her his hand—"before we depart, I expect a true welcome."

Chapter Twenty

Darkness stretched before Devon and Rylee. Not something he expected in the afternoon except the storm had caught them. Lightning streaked across the sky, splitting into what looked like a hand reaching to the gods, but at least, it temporarily lit their path. Onward they raced, feet splashing in already forming puddles and through trees in an imaginary trail Rylee carved as she ran toward shelter. A booming thunder immediately rocked the ground they raced upon, making Devon worry about being in the trees with nature's wrath on top of them. When Rylee ducked into a barely noticeable cave, his relief was palpable until he was hit with a significant temperature drop.

Shivering, Rylee dropped her pack and firewood, then rubbed her hands up and down her arms. Devon heard her chatter.

With their clothes soaked through and the chill residing in the enclosure, lighting a fire took priority. Hopefully, the bits of wood they'd carried hadn't become too wet. They needed more though. He'd have to do something he didn't want to but had little choice in the matter. "I'll go back out and grab some wood that's not too wet while you start the fire." He dropped his backpack. "I'm sure there're some downed logs I can pull from beneath. There are matches in my pack." Remembering they were nearly on a drop off was critical while he wandered in the blinding rain. Stepping into oblivion was not something he wanted to do.

"No. I put some in the back the last time I came around before you showed up."

He raised his eyebrows at her.

She shrugged. "Just in case I needed a place to hide. I'll get it if you want to start the fire."

Pleased to not have to brave the storm again, he knelt and pulled the wood into a pile for a campfire, completely ignoring her first comment because it scared the crap out of him to think she felt that way. He'd have preferred to have stones around it, but the dust-covered, rocky ground should be good enough to keep it from spreading.

After the fire had come to life, he raised himself and his jaw dropped.

Stripping her shirt over her head, Rylee spoke through her chattering teeth, "We…need to…get out of…these wet…clothes," she finally forced out.

Not one to argue—at least not about that request— he began the same process. They danced around the crackling fire while pulling off their clothes to the sounds of the whipping winds, resounding thunder, and driving rain.

Christ, she was almost naked and his cock loved that fact as it jutted out toward her once he'd released it from his underwear. *Boy, you've got a mind of your own with that woman.*

Unable to move, he watched her pull the light green bra straps off her shoulders and reach back to unhook the contraption. Her breasts bounced free, and his mouth watered at the thought of tasting them.

Apparently not as distracted at their lack of clothing, she slipped her panties down her legs and spoke, "They were there. I just know it."

He yanked his head up to look in her face and growled in frustration. They? What the fuck was she talking about? Unbelievable that she expected him to discuss business while she stood with firelight gleaming off her naked flesh. He cleared his throat. "Proof?" was about all he could muster through his sex-fogged brain.

Leaning over, she pulled her hair to the side and twisted it, wringing out water. "Not exactly. But, it's set up for it. Don't you think so?"

Opening his mouth to speak, she continued before he could utter a reply.

"I found a room in the back that locked from the outside." She straightened and his gaze followed her hands as they raked through her glorious mane. "Plus, there was a chair outside it. Just like a jail."

Shaking his head to clear it, he didn't want to burst her bubble. She obviously felt she'd found something, but…. "Rylee, that doesn't mean the girls were there."

She put her hands on her hips, and he almost lost it when it pushed out her chest.

"Christ, woman, I can't talk about this shit when you're standing there naked." He leaned down and dug in his pack. Standing, he tossed her a small blanket. "I had this for the picnic. Wrap it around yourself, please."

Cocking her head a bit and raising a brow, she smiled coyly. "Oh, really. And look at you. All at attention."

Another growl emanated from deep within his chest and rumbled past his lips. "Cover up."

Laughing, she wrapped the blanket around as much

flesh as it would cover. "Better?" she asked him.

He nodded his answer. "Okay, did you plant the bugs?"

"I put them everywhere."

"Good. That'll give us something to listen to. Now, let's see if my program worked while we were in there." He squatted down and removed a device from his pants pocket, shook his head and put it back, and then dug in the other pocket until he retrieved his cell phone.

"What was that?" She pointed to his pants that he'd already deposited back on the ground and to, he presumed, the device he'd returned to a pocket.

"Personal locator beacon," he said absently while tapping on the phone screen. "The guy at the store recommended it if we planned to hike." Something beeped on his phone and excitement surged into him. "Got it!" He held up the phone for her to see.

Stepping closer, she asked, "Is that the WI-FI password you wanted?"

"Yes, and when we return, I plan to see if I can get into that monster surveillance system they have and watch what's in the tape storage bank."

"There was a second alarm keyboard for that room."

The entire thing twisted his guts. They might not have found the girls, but it was a good bet they—or someone else who needed help—had been there. That meant his old boss was up to his eyeballs in trouble. Because of who he was, it meant he probably had a good bit of help and definitely some skill at subterfuge.

"There were two other rooms that were locked. Based on the rooms I saw, I'm guessing it was the master suite and the office. I didn't want to take time to pick the locks."

Surprised, Devon opened his mouth to speak and then closed it. "You pick locks?" he finally asked, not sure he wanted to know the answer.

Rylee shrugged indifferently. "I had a stepdad who would lock me in my room, so I learned with little locks and then it became a challenge to do the house locks and then my stepdad's office locks." Glancing out at the raging storm, she shuddered. "I'm glad we left Angel and Max extra food."

Smiling, he nodded. "I am too." Because he planned to enjoy this little hideaway with his undressed wife.

"I hear tomorrow is your birthday," she said.

She'd obviously been talking with Kate. Curiosity rode him about their conversation, but he tamped it back. "It is."

"How old will you be?"

"Thirty-two."

Smiling, she opened the blanket and lay it beside the fire. "I'm cold." She tossed her hands on her hips and teased her lips with her teeth. His dick jerked as if she'd wrapped her mouth around it. "Want to warm me?"

Holy fucking shit. Praying no vicious animals would come to the cave, he smiled and approached her. "Christ, you're going to have me coming before we even start."

Standing in front of her, he gazed into her eyes and watched the light cast by the fire dance off them, gleaming as they slowly dilated to show her arousal. Another surge of desire shot through him. Placing a hand on each side of her face, he slowly lowered his lips to hers. So incredibly sweet.

He devoured her lips and the kisses became hotter and hotter, until she melted into him.

"My turn," she said in a hoarse whisper.

His breath caught at the implication and his dick jumped. "Don't think I'm going to argue."

With her hand on his chest, she guided him down on their sham of a blanket. At least his ass wouldn't be covered in dirt.

Her hand encircled his engorged length and began stroking up and down from root to head and back again.

He groaned at the pleasure that skittered through his veins. His heart nearly thrust from his chest when she lowered her head. Another groan escaped, one of pleasure and pain. She wasn't actually hurting him, but it hurt to hold back, and hold back what he needed to do. Hot and wet, her mouth mimicked the actions of her hand.

Reaching down, he guided her hair aside so he could watch her as she set a rhythm that would have buckled his knees had he been standing. Completeness filled him at the sight and the feel of her wrapped around him.

Tingling at the base of his spine sent passion like he'd never known before gripping him tightly. Without uttering a word, he reached down and hauled her up and on top of him with the hope he didn't come before he got a condom on.

Seeming to know his thoughts, she reached over and shuffled in his pants pockets, retrieving the foil packet. She opened it and sweat beaded on his forehead while she put it on him.

Checking her readiness, he slid a finger inside her and her pussy clenched around it. Damn, she was all hot, wet, and ready for him.

He had to be inside her, fast.

Leveraging her over him, he positioned himself for entry. "You're beautiful." He thrust up, sliding into her in one swift motion and he gritted his teeth to stave off his releasing too soon.

Moaning, Rylee rode him like a champion, moving up, down, circling, everything they both needed.

"I'm not gonna last long."

A smile and a pleasurable sigh left her. "I didn't think you would."

Pride in her work. He liked that. Hell, he liked everything about her. How the hell did he get so damn lucky? Best he not question it. She was his and that was all that mattered.

Her free breasts called to him, and he reached out and massaged them. Just enough for each of his hands. Anything more would have been a waste.

That was when she changed their rhythm, and he could tell she was getting close. With a growl, he increased the pressure of his thrusts. Between finger and thumb, he pinched her nipples. Immediately, she gasped, her head falling back.

Playing with her nipples, he rode with her while she circled. He needed her to stop doing it before he was a goner ahead of her.

Then, her pussy clamped on him and she slid up and down, crying out her orgasm, before her sated body began to slump.

Not wanting to flip her to the hard ground, he grasped her hips and slid her up and down on his cock with each heartbeat. It wasn't long before the pressure at the base of his spine rose its way through his balls, shooting out of his dick into the condom. The intensity that ripped through his body broke his away from time and place and left him in a mess of useless limbs.

Rylee collapsed on top of him, and he managed to wrap his arms around her. "That was amazing."

"Mm…hmm."

Chapter Twenty-One

Sated and relaxed, Devon stared at the fire, thinking about what had just occurred. Incredible fucking sex—outdoors. He wasn't a prude by any means, but he'd never just opened himself up that much. It was exhilarating.

"Tell me why you left the CIA," Rylee requested softly.

Turning to her, he realized that he wanted to tell her. Even though it meant admitting he knew Robert Carver. Hell, he'd have to chance it. He wouldn't keep secrets from her. Not any longer.

With Rylee sitting quietly beside him, comfort swam into his body in waves. He wanted to wrap her back in his arms, but instead, he leaned back against the cave wall, and began, "I was leaving the agency after a long day of sifting through computer data when Greg Donovan, an operative, approached me and asked for assistance. At first, I thought he might need me to research something for him, but he requested me to act as backup." Devon lifted one shoulder in a shrug. "I could have refused, but was told if I accepted, no one in the agency was to know. You see, an informant had contacted him for an immediate meeting and there were few people at the agency that late."

With his left hand, he ran it across the back of his neck. "I didn't understand why he'd need backup, but he explained that it was actually for the protection of this informant. He worried someone would get to Jackie."

"Jackie?" Rylee queried.

"Yeah—the informant's name. Whether it is the real one or an alias, I don't know. Anyhow, I agreed. When we reached Greg's car, he opened the trunk and extended a Glock to me. I took it, kind of excited about playing CIA spy."

Swallowing past the lump building in his throat, he continued reciting the events of that horrific evening, "The rain came down in sheets." He chuckled lightly. "Kind of like now." Taking a deep breath, his humor faded and he continued, "But, that didn't deter Greg from meeting this informant on the street. Heck, you could barely see the streetlights through the hazy rain. But, we waited."

Reliving the night so many years ago wasn't something he wanted to do, but he needed to share this with her, to make her understand she shouldn't be relying on him alone.

Mentally shaking himself, he focused on the story. "It slacked up a bit close to meeting time, and he had me move to the next corner so I could see but not hear or scare Jackie." Devon shook his head. "I didn't like it since he seemed anxious, but I obeyed. Truly, what did I know about how to handle covert operations? Greg was the trained one. He gave me some rules for the meeting: Don't get too close and don't harm his CI. Apparently, Jackie and the information were valuable."

His heartbeat sped up at the memory. "So, I waited and kept an eye out for any trouble. The streets were empty, so it wasn't a difficult assignment. When a petite figure with a hoodie approached Greg, I watched but kept my distance as directed."

Palms sweaty, he closed his eyes to regain his internal balance, visualizing Jackie's approach to Greg, dressed in gray with the hood covering Jackie's head. When he reopened them, Rylee watched him with concern lacing her expression. She slipped her hand into his as if realizing he needed the strength, offering Devon hers.

Bolstered by her action, he went on with the tale. "They appeared to argue and then Greg put his arms up...like when someone is held up at gunpoint." He demonstrated the movement, not letting go of her hand, and then shrugged while lowering them. "I couldn't wait. I rushed down the block and that's when I saw the knife in Jackie's hand. Not thinking, I pulled my weapon and screamed, 'Drop it,' or something like that."

Agony sliced through him. *If only I'd reacted sooner.* It hadn't mattered what he'd ordered me to do or not do. "They both turned to me, and I froze when I saw that Jackie was a young woman. My hands shook, but I knew what I'd have to do. However, Greg told me not to shoot, and he tried to disarm her while she'd been distracted by my appearance. So, I held my fire." Devon dropped Rylee's hand and jumped from his spot on the ground. Restless, he paced in front of Rylee while running his hand through his hair. "Christ, everything in me told me to shoot her, but my morals slammed forward reminding me she was a woman." Devon stopped and captured her gaze. "You see, we'd been raised to protect and value women."

A small smile split her face and a warmth breached

the self-loathing attempting to set in like it did every time he remembered that night.

The moment evaporated when reality crashed back in, his shoulders dropped and he resumed pacing. "Anyhow, I guess with the rain making her jacket slick, Greg lost hold of her arm, and she stabbed him in the abdomen before I realized he'd lost control. I shot and hit her in the side, but the damage was done to Greg." Dropping back on the ground with a thud, he scooted against the cave wall again and slouched, trying to fight the gnawing in his gut at his inadequacy. If only….

"Greg staggered to the ground with his hands clutching his gut, the blood thinned in the rain and ran rivulets through his hold." Leaning his head in his right hand, he sighed. "I'll never forget the sight."

An arm wrapped around his bicep and Rylee's other hand settled on his thigh. She helped ground and support him. The knowledge swept into his system, leaving a semblance of calm in its wake.

"What happened next?" she asked him.

He lifted his head. "I moved to them. I'd seen enough TV to know to kick away the knife by where Jackie lay unconscious, then I knelt beside Greg to check on him."

Deep breath in and slowly out. "I'm not a doctor, but I could tell he didn't look good." Reaching out and clasping her hand in his, he turned it so her palm faced up and he studied it as if reading her fortune or trying to distract himself from his remembrance. "When I told him that I'd get an ambulance there right away, he stopped me."

Weaving his fingers through hers, he placed their entwined palms in his lap. "My eyes probably widened to the size of saucers at his demand. He said I could call 911 from his phone, but I was to take everything on him and leave before anyone showed up. Then, I was to notify the CIA and tell them what happened."

Rylee inhaled sharply and he figured she had an inkling how this ended, so he ignored it and continued, "Unfortunately, he slipped into unconsciousness before he told me who I should contact at the agency or what number to use. Hell, I had no clue about the operatives."

Squeezing his hand, she nodded. "I understand. It was the same with other departments at the bureau."

Taking a deep breath and releasing it slowly, he eased some of his anxiety. "Well. I was unsure what to do, but knew, based on what Greg had briefed me on, keeping his identity secret was important, so I held my hand on the wound on his stomach and called 911."

"Oh, Devon," she whispered and leaned her head on his shoulder.

God, where had she been all his life? It didn't appear as daunting with her touching him, consoling him. Understanding him.

Needing to get the story out, he rushed the remainder. "I left Greg's side and checked on Jackie. I wasn't sure why she was unconscious. Maybe she hit her head when she fell. Her side was bleeding fairly badly, and I couldn't feel any pity for her. I knew Greg would probably die because of her. Then again, the fact that I might have killed her slammed into me, and I almost didn't leave the scene fast enough. When I heard sirens, I sprang into action and did as instructed, grabbing Greg's wallet, keys, and weapon. Then I walked away while calling my boss." He cleared his throat nervously. It was time to tell her. "Robert Carver."

"Carver?" Her head popped off his shoulder and her voice held the bewilderment he'd expected at this admission. Thank God it didn't contain anger.

"Yes, the same Robert Carver who owns the ranch house we searched."

Her grip tightened and he expected if he looked down that her knuckles would be white. Okay, maybe the anger hadn't been in her voice, but it appeared to have quickly followed her realization that Devon knew the man who might've kidnapped, and planned to sell, two girls.

"Be mad at me for not telling you later."

"Oh, I will be." She yanked her hand from his and crossed her arms in a huff. "First, I want to hear what this man did."

He picked up a twig, tossed it on the fire, and watched the sparks fly into the air and dissolve into nothing. "Carver told me that I'd done right to call him first. He informed me that everything would be taken care of with the utmost urgency. I mean, fuck, they had me leave a dying man by himself with the person who tried to kill him only feet away."

"Oh, Devon." Her arms unfolded and she turned toward him, her soft voice speaking to his soul.

He released a heavily burdened sigh. So much pain in his heart over the event… over Greg's death. There was the ever-present question of whether he could've saved the man.

"I take it there's more."

Glancing at Rylee, he chanced it and captured her hand, pressing the back of it to his lips. She offered no fight, but he chose to leave their clasped hands in her lap. That settled, he nodded. "I took Greg's car back to the office where Carver met me. I couldn't believe they'd allow Greg to be treated as a John Doe if he died. My boss told me not to worry that they took care of their own, though people didn't know about it."

People didn't know the half of it. The shit the CIA kept quiet because whoever was in charge at the time deemed it necessary was amazing. Like Greg's death.

"I take it Greg died."

"Yeah, he died. Jackie had disappeared before anyone arrived at the scene. I was a wreck. I'd been too weak to shoot and protect the man who'd asked for my help. And, when I did shoot, I thought I'd possibly killed a young woman."

The bandage had been ripped off with precision as he'd spoken his failure out loud to someone other than Carver. The fist that grappled with a tight hold on his soul—reminding him that because of him a man had died—loosened, and he breathed easier for the first time in four years. While a hold remained, something told him that Rylee was the balm to ease his burden...his pain...his sense of failure. With her, he believed the haunting at any time, day or night, would diminish. She was his salvation. No way would he let her go.

Devon knew she had to feel his trembling hand, but she kept quiet, holding it firmly. Since he didn't want to spill all of his epiphany to her, he spoke again, as if he hadn't stopped, "I spent countless hours searching for Jackie and wanted to tell everyone what happened, but Carver wouldn't allow it. He hadn't been happy about my accompanying Greg since that wasn't what I'd been hired or trained to do and almost angry that I'd spent my time trying to track down Jackie. That's also how he tried to console me—I hadn't been trained to be an operative."

He shook his head. "It didn't work. I couldn't stand the looks others at the agency gave me. Even though it had been kept secret that I'd been involved, it was obvious many knew it was my fault Greg had died. Never think you can keep secrets from spooks," he added with fake joviality.

She bounced her head a bit in obvious agreement to his joke. Then brushing it off, she asked, "How can you say it was your fault? He told you not to shoot."

"Even if he hadn't, I couldn't bring myself to pull the trigger on a young woman."

"Yet, you did."

He snatched his hand back and ran it through his hair in frustration. *Fuck.* She was supposed to be a damn balm. "Too damn late."

"Hmm. What happened with the CIA?"

"I couldn't let the situation go and eventually Carver helped me decide to leave the CIA since I couldn't deal with cover-ups. I wallowed in misery for a while until Jesse wanted to start up HIS. I needed something, but I couldn't allow anyone's protection to be in my hands. I'd proved how terrible an idea that was." He snorted.

Rylee turned and pointed her index finger at him. "Devon Hamilton, you followed orders. I don't mean this to sound harsh, but Greg is responsible for your not stopping the stabbing. You could've saved him if he hadn't directed you to hold your fire. I'm going to say this again. You followed orders."

"I don't know."

"Hadn't you been ready to fire when he told you not to?"

"Yes, but I hesitated when I actually saw Jackie."

She smacked his thigh. "Dammit, but you recovered. You would've done what was needed to save him. He didn't let you."

"You're saying that I should've shot anyway."
That was a fucked-up question, Hamilton.

Rylee responded before he could tell her to ignore it. "That's not what I'm saying. I'm saying you did as the leader of your mission told you. That's how it has to be. Think of what would happen if someone didn't listen to Jesse when he was leading a mission."

Clasping his right hand between the two of hers, she smiled. "I understand your strong feelings about your actions, as do most agents and officers after something happens in the line of duty, but I don't see how you can think it was your fault. First, you shouldn't have been there since you weren't trained for that job. Second, Greg never should've told you not to allow Jackie to come to any harm. And, finally, he shouldn't have stopped you from trying to save him."

Devon chuckled. "You make it sound so simple."

"It really is."

"Is this like the missing girls weren't your responsibility?"

She shook her head. "This is different. I haven't taken the blame for their being gone. I just won't allow them to fall through the cracks."

"But, don't you see, you can't rely on me if something ever goes wrong."

She leaned into him, her mouth closed, and whispered, "I'll take my chances." Then, she kissed him and he didn't care a bit about anything but taking her to bed. Or, in this case, to the blanket he'd thankfully packed for their picnic.

Chapter Twenty-Two

Confused by waking on a hard surface, Devon took a quick inventory of his surroundings without moving. Relieved at seeing Rylee lying on her side next to him, he sat and shivered from the chill still hanging in the air. Instead of covering himself, he pulled the blanket over as much of his sleeping wife as it would cover. Using his forefinger, he slid a bit of hair behind her ear and then traced down her jaw.

The resulting smile warmed him. But, he couldn't allow himself to be distracted. He had to hurry to collect their stashed items so they could get back to the animals. He snuck away from her and dressed quietly before taking his pack and leaving her to rest.

Pretty sure he'd get lost, he pulled the GPS from his backpack and marked the cave's location. Then, he pulled up where they'd stashed their weapons and phone, and headed off in the direction it indicated. He kept up a fast pace, cursing each branch that came into his path.

The night before, she'd listened to him and not judged. He'd opened his torn soul and she'd come in and stitched it up until it was almost as good as new. To have such love and tenderness all the time, almost overwhelmed him, but from her, he'd take it every day of the week.

To ease him, she'd simply said he wasn't at fault,

and explained it better than the only other person who knew—his bastard of an ex-boss.

Since discovering Carver was more than likely into something bad, he'd become a bastard. Devon hadn't been happy with him after the accident, but kept the respect of the supervisor-subordinate in his thoughts and actions. The gloves were off and the man would have a lot to answer for.

Shaking his head, Devon would never forgive himself for not taking the shot sooner, but he would accept that he'd done what he was supposed to and followed orders. He knew it was how some of his brothers felt when they'd left their job because of screwed-up orders. He could only hope, he, and them, didn't give out those types of orders themselves. Their next order though was to bring down Robert Carver if he was their man.

First, he and Rylee had to get off the mountain and back to headquarters. The team would be back and that would provide plenty of firepower to find Carver, and hopefully, the girls. Christ, part of him still couldn't wrap his head around the man selling young girls.

His research had told him his old boss had a lot more assets than one who'd been a civil servant, but he'd let it slide for further review. It was time for that review.

Thank the fuck Rylee hadn't held knowing the man against him.

He stopped as the handheld GPS pinged, then bent and pulled their items from inside a knothole in the tree. Putting them in plastic bags had been a smart idea on her part as the rain must've come in sideways at some point in time.

Everything secured in his backpack, he turned back to the cave and Rylee. He hoped she didn't wake up without him and worry. Pen and paper hadn't been something he'd added to his heavy pack. An oversight to correct if they did this again. He knew plenty of trails they could hike that wouldn't have them checking themselves for ticks afterward.

The thought of his hands gliding over her body sent a stab of heat to his dick. He groaned and picked up the pace. They wouldn't have time this morning, but he'd get his birthday sex before they left these fucking mountains.

Picturing Rylee in the throes of passion, set him to adjusting his thickening dick. He still didn't know how he came to meet or marry her, but he was sure glad he had. His step faltered and he came to a stop. Breathing heavily, he took a moment for the reality of it to sink in.

He'd heard love would bowl you over when it found you. He may not remember much of their night in Vegas, but it was becoming clearer why they had married so impulsively. He needed her to know he'd found that feeling. A smile grew on his face. If she hadn't, she would soon. He'd make sure of it.

****

The morning of Devon's birthday shined brightly into the cave. Rylee watched water dripping off the leaves on a branch nearby and dreaded the thought of trudging through wet bushes and mud puddles. Needing the distraction, she kept her thoughts on Devon.

She wished she'd had the chance to purchase him something nice, but she'd only recently heard from Kate. She'd find a way to make it up to him. A grin split her face and a deep-down happiness filled her.

She'd make it up to him in more ways than one.

Sexual escapades with Devon had been magnificent. Sex had never been this gratifying before. Devon had taken lovemaking to a new level. After rolling over to an empty spot beside her, she jumped to her feet in concern. Reaching for her dry clothing, reason told her that he probably only went outside to relieve himself. Though she felt jumpy and couldn't explain it. Maybe it was the excitement of where their relationship was heading. Maybe it was being able to celebrate Devon's birthday with him. Maybe it was that niggling fear of being found by Dave's goons.

The birthday boy walked into the cave wearing a huge smile and holding up their weapons and the SAT phone. The ones they'd forgone collecting the night before to remain dry.

She stopped stuffing her shirt in her pants and gave him her full attention. "Happy birthday, husband."

Closing the distance between them, he leaned forward and kissed her soundly. "Thank you, wife."

Grinning and resuming her dressing, Rylee finished tucking her shirt and zipped and buttoned her pants. "Thanks for getting those. We need to get back to Angel and Max though."

Devon leaned back against the cave wall. "I figured that, which is why I hurried to collect these."

Rylee paused a moment to take him in. He was so thoughtful. She couldn't find much better than him, and she didn't want to. Pleasure washed through her, sending her mind and heart reeling. She was falling in love with him.

Dressed, fire doused, and backpacks on, they emerged into the sunlight, ready to return to their cabin.

Devon turned to her and pulled her close, his lips almost touching her ear. The warm breath sent a shudder of delight through her, making her wish no animals depended upon them so they could roll back around on their pathetic excuse for a bed. "I love you," he whispered.

Her breath caught and her heart skipped a beat.

"Don't say anything," he continued. "Just let me kiss you."

Nodding was all she could muster until his lips touched hers and her arms wound around him. Pulled tight against him, she felt the movement of his cock against her abdomen. Exhilaration like no other surged through her veins as his lips devoured hers.

He reached out and cupped his hand over her cheek and a shiver stole through her body.

"Aww, how sweet," a voice broke in.

She and Devon tensed and their lips stopped moving. *Holy fucking shit.* Chuck had found them… in the woods. Devon pulled away and pushed Rylee behind him to protect her. Where the fuck were the weapons? *Son of a bitch.* They'd put them away in the packs.

This scene reminded her of how the man had snuck up on her and Brent. No way would she allow another man who loved her to be killed.

"Honey, you were promised to someone, and that benefactor is not happy about your getting away."

Rylee's heart pounded loudly against her chest. She could tell Devon tensed another notch, but he was smart enough not to ask her about it.

Devon held his hands out in the general surrender gesture. "Look, buddy, we don't want any trouble."

Another man—good old snub nose, Chuck's partner—stepped into the open. "Found 'em, huh?"

"That was a stupid fucking question, Frank," Chuck snapped.

Following Devon's lead, they began inching back away from the two men.

"Hey, they're trying to get away," Frank spurted.

A gun appeared in Chuck's hand and she and Devon halted. "Honey, come here and we won't kill your man."

Devon thrust his arm out to block her path. "She's not going anywhere with you."

"Big talk for a man without a gun." Chuck waved his to emphasize his point and Rylee nearly ducked, fearing the idiot might accidentally shoot. "Packs off."

Rylee dropped hers knowing escape would be easier without it. But, Devon waited. He and Chuck had some kind of standoff that took the goon waving his weapon again to get Devon to drop his backpack. Damn him, they didn't need to anger these two, not when they didn't have any weapons handy themselves.

"Again, over here or we kill him." He pointed the gun squarely on Devon's chest.

She couldn't allow them to harm Devon. If they took her, she had faith he'd find her and maybe the girls at the same time. He wouldn't agree with her choice, but she knew he'd do the same to protect her. With a churning stomach, she stepped away from him. "Let him go now and I'll come to you," she tried.

A maniacal laugh escaped the man. "Nice try. Come here." He waved that damn gun again.

She turned to Devon and saw one angry man. Surprised steam wasn't coming out his ears, she just shook her head when he mouthed, "No." He had to understand that she did this for him...to save him. "I trust you to rescue me," she whispered as loudly as she dared.

His head swiveled fast with his disagreement.

Don't let what happened with Greg cloud his judgment. He is capable of being a savior.

"Get the fuck over here," Chuck directed in a pissed-off tone.

Moving feet that felt like lead, she made her way to the man, glancing over her shoulder once to see Devon taking a step forward.

When she neared Chuck, he snaked his arm out and wrapped his large hand around her forearm, squeezed tight and pulled her in front of him, facing the approaching Devon. "Frank, you're up."

Frank cracked his knuckles and Rylee's stomach revolted. They'd lied. How could she have thought otherwise? "You said you wouldn't hurt him." Christ, Frank outweighed her husband by nearly sixty pounds, and those massive arms didn't bode well for anyone on the receiving end of his fist.

"No," Chuck said in a low voice filled with what? Joy? "I said we wouldn't kill him. Can't have him coming after us too quickly. Besides, you owe Frank since you had that ICE agent get in the car with you instead of getting the beating he'd earned for poking his nose around where it didn't belong."

She closed her eyes and her heart sank remembering Brent's death because she'd insisted he come along, and now Devon was about to be beaten up because of her. If she didn't doubt Chuck would pull the trigger, they'd have chanced it and ran. She'd have made sure of it, but she believed the man would shoot based on what she saw in his eyes. Dark. Soulless. Evil.

The sound of flesh being pounded had her heart bleeding rivets of red liquid and clogging all senses except pain and loss. Needing to see what happened to Devon, she opened her eyes to her husband doubled over from a punch to his midsection. Roaring, he came up with an uppercut to Frank's chin. *Yes! Fight back.*

After stumbling back, Frank roared his own war cry and tackled Devon. But, her husband got the upper hand. As they lay on the ground with Devon underneath, Devon's left arm crooked around Frank's neck, and his right fist repeatedly pounded the goon's kidney area.

Somehow, Frank head-butted Devon, stunning him long enough for the man to climb to his feet. He was spry for someone as large as he was. "Son of a bitch!" Frank roared.

"Just hold the fucker," Chuck ordered. "I'll shoot him."

"Not now. Won't someone hear?" Frank whined with blood dripping from his lip.

Devon pulled himself to his feet, but before he could move, Frank wrapped arms around him from behind. There they stood—her and Devon facing each other, but both being detained. His eyes were already showing signs of swelling from where Frank's forehead had hit him on the bridge of his nose.

"Let her go," Devon insisted.

"I think not. Someone has a lot of money on her. But," Chuck went on as if he'd only taken a long breath, "I think she'll bring more money on the open market."

Devon surged from his captor. He'd almost made it to them when Frank knocked him to the ground. The man wrapped his arms around her husband's waist and pulled him to his feet. Devon fought, twisting and punching, everything he could do to free himself. The blows all but glanced off the goon, as the man simply stepped back with the impact. It took a moment before she realized that in their struggles, they'd backed up near the ledge.

Rylee jerked, fear lacing through her veins and a surge of adrenaline rocked her. "Devon, watch out!" With her heart sunk like a rock to her gut, she watched, horrified and helpless, as he and his captor disappeared over the cliff's edge amidst screams. "Devon!" She wrenched her arm to escape her attacker, but his hold tightened. "You have to help him," she insisted, wriggling and kicking to free herself.

One of her wild kicks found purchase with Chuck's knee. When his grip loosened, she raced to the cliff's edge, sliding on her belly so she could look over without falling.

"Devon," she bellowed. There were several places where small amounts of rock jutted out and formed tiny ledges. Maybe, just maybe, he landed on one of them. Her head moved fast, following her rapid scan of the cliff wall below. "Devon!"

With no response and no sighting, a crushing blow took hold of her heart, driving it low in her belly. Neither Devon nor the brute were there. Tears sprang to life and she willed them away, not wanting the blurring of her vision. But they wouldn't leave. It was such a long fall, he couldn't survive. But, maybe—her heart told her—and she scanned again. *Nothing.*

"Lookie there, your man is gone. Guess that means it's time to go." He reached down and jerked Rylee up with force.

Tears made tracks down her face. "Don't you care about your guy? He could just be hurt. We should go check." *And do what exactly. Say good-bye? I can't do it.*

"Fuck him. He was my fucked-up stepbrother. I'm tired of looking out for him. No way they survived that. Let's get the hell out of these woods and Colorado."

They were leaving? No! That left no one to tell Jesse about his brother and help recover Devon's body. If that were possible.

Her posture snapped rigid and her mind cleared. This bastard was part of the reason she'd just become a widow. She'd make him pay.

Chapter Twenty-Three

Sweat ran down Devon's forehead and into his eyes, burning and blurring his vision, but he didn't move to wipe it away. His heart pounded nearly out of his chest at what had almost happened. He'd fallen off a cliff and almost died.

Yet, he'd landed on a ledge and somehow, he had no idea how, he'd had the presence of mind to roll into the cliff wall so he wouldn't be seen from above. He'd heard Rylee's desperate pleas, but he'd known calling out wasn't an option, fearing the other goon might shoot him and be done with it.

I trust you to rescue me, she'd said.

Dread washed over him as pain radiated through every muscle in his body. He did a quick assessment and the twinge in his left ankle captured his attention. It was painful and damned inconvenient, but not broken. His chest burned though. How many ribs had he broken?

Knowing Chuck had Rylee spurred him into action—pain and all. Why the fuck hadn't he called Jesse after he'd retrieved the phone instead of allowing his mind to be diverted with sensual thoughts of his lovely wife? He wanted to kick himself.

Easing to his hands and knees, he looked up at his obstacle. *Fuck. Me.* Over fifteen feet of wall loomed over him and it didn't appear to offer much in the way of something natural to hold on to. He dropped his head. He'd been rock climbing at an inside facility, but that was with harnesses and a good laugh if you missed. This was serious with deadly consequences. But, he had to try it, so he made it to his feet, leaning off his injured ankle as much as possible. Hobbling to the wall, he surveyed it and finding something that he hoped would work, fought the blackness at the outer edges of his eyes when he placed his full weight on his left foot and put his right foot on the wall.

With purposeful moves, he'd climbed three steps up before he ran into a solid, slick wall. Panic crept its way inside and his rational thought took a moment's vacation while he clawed at the wall, trying to find a way up it, to Rylee. Christ, that asshole had said they planned to sell her. He shifted, lost his hold, and slid down the mountain barely catching himself from toppling back over the ledge. "No!" he cried, no longer concerned he'd be heard. He was sure they were long gone.

Devon wiped his hand down his face, ignoring the tinge of dried blood in his hand, and refocused on the wall. If he shifted on the ledge, to an area about two feet deep, there appeared to be more options for grips. Taking a deep, fortifying breath, which burned across his ribcage, he slid sideways.

Inspiration struck. The personal locator beacon he'd brought with them. "Yes!" Reaching into his pants pocket, he pulled out the yellow piece of equipment, glad he'd sprung for the model with attached GPS so they'd know within 200 feet instead of three miles. He activated it and set it on the ledge like he'd been instructed.

He wouldn't just sit here and wait. He had to try to get out of his situation. Getting to Rylee—to save her—was foremost on his mind. Thinking of what they could do to her in his delay sent another rush of adrenaline crashing through his system.

Again he stepped up to find a foothold, then a hand one. With hands slick with perspiration, one slipped, jolting his senses to the severity of a mistake. His heart pounded at the desperate need to get up that wall. He was all she had and she counted on him to save her.

After a couple of deep breaths, he looked for his next handhold, unable to get the image of Rylee in the hands of that asshole out of his mind. She was a strong woman, but she didn't have a chance against a man that large and with a gun.

Straining and stretching to reach the next handhold, he missed and slid back down the wall. *No!* It'd been the closest place to grab hold but had been too far. There was no damn way up the wall! He'd have to wait for rescue. Time he didn't want to lose.

Pissed at his failure and the delay in saving Rylee, he pounded his fists against the wall in rage. Pain radiated through his head, originating at the spot where a rock had fallen and slammed into him. He reached his hand to the spot on his head, moaned at the painful touch, swayed, and dropped on his ass, temporarily disoriented. Fighting nausea and overwhelming dizziness, he leaned back against the cliff wall so he didn't accidentally slide over the ledge.

"Rylee," he whispered, his heart breaking at the thought that he might've lost her.

That was when another rock dropped, but after this one hit his head, he slumped to the side and fell into unconsciousness.

Chapter Twenty-Four

Robert Carver inhaled the succulent scent of bacon and whatever else the chef was preparing for breakfast. He hadn't had a guest in a long time, at least one who didn't stay overnight anyway. And the timing of the call couldn't have been more perfect.

"Mission accomplished," Chuck informed him, and sweeter words hadn't been heard in months.

"She's unharmed?" Examining his manicure—what he did to remain focused—he tamped down his excitement.

"Yeah. She's fine. I had to drug her because she fought like a woman possessed after the man she was with went over the cliff."

He considered the impact of that action. Not only had the FBI trained her, but also, she'd just watched her husband die, medicating her was probably the best thing for everyone. He'd dry her out in time for her new home. Decision made, he ordered, "Keep her out until you get her to Belize. Go to the private airport and I'll have a helicopter ready for you in two hours. You know the rest of the itinerary."

"You're gonna owe me more money. Frank died."

Disbelief at the audacity of this menial worker flashed. "I'm sorry to hear that, but we have an agreement, and I expect you to honor it."

"Then I'm not bringing the girl. I'll sell her

myself."

A heavy sigh escaped him. He hated being the bad guy sometimes. "No, you won't for two reasons. You don't have the contacts and I'll have you killed. Then I'll go after that sweet piece you meet up with at the motel once a week." At the hesitation on the other end of the line, Robert knew he'd hit a nerve. Little did Chuck know that his brother, Frank, had let that bit of information slip.

"All right. We'll be there."

"Good man. Two hours. Let me remind you that there is no sampling of the merchandise and there had best be zero marks on her. Do I make myself clear?"

The kitchen was quiet and he glanced at his watch. The meal would be right on schedule. One more minute here—

"It's clear."

He ended the call and turned to the woman sitting on his gray suede couch, a broad smile on his face. "Devon Hamilton is no more."

"I thought you liked him," she asked in that soft, sensual voice that made him almost forget his preference in partners.

Holding out a hand to her, he raised his brows in question. She accepted it and stood. "I did like him. However, I knew one day he'd be back. Too much of a fucking bleeding heart." They ventured to the dining room where a large table, seating twelve, held two place settings at one end. Walking to their chairs, he inspected the crisp white tablecloth for flaws. He tolerated no errors from others. Those who had survived one of his tirades knew that. This was the chef's job interview, so he should have heard that even presentation counted with him.

They settled into their seats and dug into the fare. Robert chewed methodically, enjoying the flavors as they burst on his tongue.

"Are we going to Belize?" his companion asked between bites.

He nodded. "Yes. I should've sent you already since I shipped several girls that way. I fly out in a few hours and expect you with me to take care of them like before."

"That doesn't give me time to pack."

"I'll buy you what you need when we're there. You'll need to buy clothes for the girls anyway." He found having a woman do the shopping for young girls was less conspicuous than an older gentleman doing it. This woman also kept the girls in line. He didn't even begin to examine how she could work for him with what he did, but she was his most trustworthy employee.

She shrugged. "Okay."

That resolved, they ate in silence. As soon as she laid down her napkin, someone appeared to remove the plates and they stood.

"Do you think Devon knew about me?" his companion asked.

"Doubtful or I think we'd have had more trouble." He smiled confidently "I don't think you have to hide anymore, Jackie."

Chapter Twenty-Five

Snatches of a rotating noise met Rylee's ears, but she couldn't fully wake up to explore its origin. Maybe the annoying sound would leave her be. *Wait, what's that jarring?* Her heart pounded rapidly against her breastbone, tapping out her confusion and fear. Were they...flying in a helicopter?

With extreme difficulty, she lifted her eyelids a fraction and saw the interior of the bird and Chuck beside whom she presumed was the pilot because she wouldn't believe Chuck could fly a damn thing. She slipped her lids closed again at the excruciating pain in her heart. If she was really with Chuck, it wasn't a nightmare and that meant Devon was really.... She gulped and, against her will, her eyes watered with unshed tears. She couldn't bring herself to even think the words.

They'd had so little time together, and every moment he'd made it count. He'd been patient with her every step of the way, even when she'd pushed back with her stupid reasons for them not being together.

His touch had done such wonderful things to her, and not just in a sexual way, although that way rocked. Everything about Devon made her feel alive and happier than she'd ever thought possible.

A tear slipped down past her temple. Her heart nearly burst from the pent-up agony welling there. He'd done everything right to make their marriage work, and she'd wasted so much time fighting it.

And then, he'd gone and done something even more special—he'd told her that he loved her. Why hadn't she given him the same precious gift? *Because it took losing him to realize what you'd been feeling was truly being in love.* No longer would she be able to tell him that she loved him. She would never recover what time they'd had in Vegas, but she'd never forget a moment of their time in the Colorado Mountains.

Floating on whatever had been injected into her system, she allowed herself to slip into blissful oblivion where her heart wasn't in bloody shreds, and she could dream Devon was alive and by her side.

****

Rylee's eyes fluttered open. A light smoky haze floated near her and swirled around when more joined it in a whoosh, making her wonder where she was this time. She sniffed and confirmed it was cigarette smoke. That meant Chuck must be around since his hands and clothing reeked of the scent when she'd been held up against him.

Groggily, the realization that she was flying on a plane, but not in the helicopter, hit her. She imagined since she was lying flat on her back and someone was smoking, that it wasn't a commercial flight and crew. In the bad guy business, when was it ever?

Her head throbbed with what she assumed was an aftereffect of the drug in her system. She was so pissed she wanted to spit, but her mouth was dryer than a desert. That fucking bastard had stuck a needle into her neck at the ranch.

While wanting to extract a pound of flesh as

revenge, she couldn't dwell upon it. Escape had to be her top priority. Escape and hopefully, along the way, find the girls. Chuck would probably spill the beans if she gave him enough lead rope, and she'd know everything necessary to bring in the cavalry. The biggest piece she needed was where they were headed.

First, she had to assess her full situation. Wiggling her hands to find them unbound, a soft moan built in her throat and slipped past her lips before she could halt it.

"Ah, you're awake," that fucking sinister voice she'd come to loathe said. "Let me put this on speaker."

Turning on her side, her brows knitted on their own accord. What kind of torture did he have in mind now? He'd already made sure she watched her husband die. Grief, deep and desolate, grabbed her and held on, squeezing, making her want to curl into a ball and wallow in the misery and loneliness. Tears pricked her eyes and threatened to escape. *No!* She strengthened her resolve, trying desperately to ignore her broken heart. *Right now, I have to escape.*

Closing her eyes and forming fists to control her inner turmoil, she breathed a sigh of relief when clarity rode back into her spirit. As much clarity as she could muster with remnants of the drug still in her system.

"Since we can't sell her, grab the sister," he said, looking directly at her. "This one owes us since her husband took Frank over the ledge."

A snort almost escaped. She thought he didn't care about Frank. *Whoa, wait a minute, sister? Did he mean… no! Not Maddie.*

"We got a problem there, boss. She's gone."

"Just grab her when she comes out of wherever

she's gone to, idiot." He placed a hand over the mouthpiece area and spoke to her, "You just can't get good help nowadays."

Somehow she imaged Carver, or whoever was in charge, said the same thing about him. She'd feed his ego later if that worked. News on Maddie was too important to interrupt.

"I mean gone, as in disappeared. All we know is that some muscle guy came in yesterday, told me to back the fuck off, and no one has seen her since."

"No one just fucking disappears!" he roared. "They're just holed up. Probably someone she's fucking."

"I don't think so. The concierge says she went on a trip."

Rylee slowly pulled herself to a sitting position, a monumental task considering the dizziness that assailed her. All the while she wore a wide smile on her face. Only one thing came to mind—HIS. In her heart, she knew Kate sent someone for her sister.

Shit! Max and Angel. Taking a breath, she relaxed that thought. If Kate knew they were missing, she had to have visited the cabin and therefore would've fed the animals.

"Find her," Chuck said in anger, then ended the call and took a long drag of a cigarette. "Your sister traveling somewhere?"

She snorted. Two could play twenty questions. She'd been trained to interrogate and could outmaneuver him all day long. "Where are we going?"

Narrowing his eyes, he took another hit of his cigarette. He nodded. "Okay, I give to you and you give to me."

Slowly, she dipped her head in agreement, knowing by his going first, he had no expectation she'd gain her freedom. "Okay, where are we going?"

"Belize." He shrugged. Pointing his finger at her, he asked the stupidest fucking question she'd ever heard, if he had any expectation of her answering truthfully. "Now, where is your sister?"

"How the fuck should I know?" She added to his ire by smiling as sweetly as she knew how. That hadn't been her plan, but she hadn't contained her anger at him for his part in her losing Devon.

"Why you little bitch!" He jumped from the seat and halted at the fast approach of a uniformed man. The flight attendant maybe? So, maybe they were on a charter flight and not the big boss's plane. That could work to her benefit. She wondered what he told them about her being unconscious.

"I told you, no smoking, sir."

"Fuck you," Chuck tossed out but crushed his cigarette in the saucer extended in the hand of the attendant. "Now, leave us alone."

The man, with incredibly green eyes, looked solemnly at her before returning to the front of the small jet, and discarded cigarette in hand.

"Who do you work for? Robert Carver?" she asked before he'd regained his footing.

His head whipped around to her. "Who told you?"

Yep, she was working with an idiot. She wiped the grit out of her eyes and covered a fake yawn. "I'm tired. Mind if I go back to sleep?"

An evil grin with a big splash of tobacco-stained teeth sat eerily on his face. "Oh, I've been told to watch out for any tricks from you. I don't know how you got away before, but you won't this time. You get the shot, right on schedule." He walked to the sideboard and picked up a needle, testing it.

Her breathing hitched and panic rushed in wave after wave, flooding her senses. Okay, not a complete idiot. Her mind screamed, *"No more drugs."* While she couldn't escape from the plane while it was in the air, she needed to be prepared when it landed. Scrambling to her feet, Rylee immediately reached out to steady herself while shaking her head to clear the fog that still resided from her last dose.

If she could make it, she'd hide in the bathroom the entire trip. Anything but having a shot, but her feet weren't cooperating. She'd played her card before her body was ready to be a part of the act.

"Bernard!" Chuck shouted.

Caught for a moment wondering who the hell this person was, she froze. A big mistake. While the flight attendant's eyes apologized, he grabbed her and held her tight for Chuck to inject her. All she could do was slowly shake her head in disbelief. It couldn't keep happening.

Shot administered, Bernard released her and she slid to the floor, her legs nothing but rubber. "No," she pleaded as the effects washed through her veins, making everything blur out of focus...her vision...her mind...and, ultimately, her world.

Chapter Twenty-Six

Agony wracked Devon's body from head to toe with every muscle aching deep down to the bone. He strained to open his eyes, trying to figure out where he was. When sunlight glinted through the tiny slits he'd created, he snapped them closed and moaned with the sharpness of the pain to his head from that brief burst of light. Reaching his hands up to hold his head, he sucked in a deep breath at the sharp twinge in his back when he shifted. What the hell had happened?

His heartbeat nearly stopped and his eyes flew open at the jolt of realization. *Rylee!* Good God, they had her. He had to save her.

Christ, how long had he been out? His head throbbed mercilessly. A rock. *That's right—*

"Hello down there."

He snapped his head up, crying out at the sharp pain. Someone was on the upper cliff ledge. Friend or foe? Hell, stupid ass, a foe wouldn't call out first. At least, probably not. Staggering to his feet, he took an experimental step and bit back the cry at the sharp twinge in his ankle. It wouldn't stop him. "Down here." He waved an arm so the head poked over the top of the cliff could see him.

"I'm with Rocky Mountain Rescue. Just hang tight while I tie a line."

Like he could do much fucking else. After his near-death experience and then braining himself, he would let the experts get him out of this. But when it came to Rylee, he wouldn't wait at the command center.

"I thought you guys worked in Boulder," he said as a chill crept into his bones.

The guy tossed a rope over the cliff, the end landing beside him. "We do. I was out here on vacation and heard the call come in and volunteered to assess for them."

Not really knowing the workings of these groups, or the area, Devon had to take his word that things were as should be.

"Name's Steven," he said. "Looks like you picked one hell of a spot to view the mountains."

Devon couldn't help but smile. "Yeah, and I'm done with it."

"Are you injured?" Steven narrowed his eyes. "Your face looks like it took one hell of a beating. Ain't my business how you got here." He shrugged. "I just need to know how we're going to get you out. Do we need a helo or can you climb? I'll help pull you up."

Shaking his head and holding back the wince at the pain, Devon said, "No helo. Help me up that wall and we're good." He didn't need a lift for a body probably just covered in black and blue bruising.

Steven surveyed him, appearing to want to do more, but eventually deciding to just help Devon up the wall.

He made the grueling walk upward with his savior pulling the rope, all the while fighting hard not to think of what would happen if his hands slipped.

Taking a deep breath of freedom at the cliff top, Devon's heart sped up with his need to chase after his wife. His patience wore thin at the constant chatter Steven kept up, and his slowly cleaning up his equipment. "Here's a bottle of water. I'm sure you're probably dehydrated."

Devon readily accepted the bottle and chugged it down.

"Do you need me to call someone? I've got a SAT phone here."

That reminded him and he scanned the area until his eyes lit on his backpack. "Nope." He pointed toward it by the bushes. "There's mine and I have one." Approaching Steven, he stuck out his hand. "Thanks, man. That was one hell of a thing you did for me."

The man's face reddened. "It's no big deal. Anything else? 'Cause if not, I'm off to rejoin my group."

Relieved he'd be alone in a moment, Devon didn't balk at the sharp pain when he shook his head for his answer.

On his own, Devon pulled the SAT phone from his pack and dialed Jesse. While waiting for an answer, he slung his backpack over his shoulder and turned in the direction of the cabin. Half walking, half stumbling, he cursed Jesse for not answering.

Tripping over a protruding tree root, he plummeted to the ground with a resounding thud as he hadn't reacted in time to catch himself. "Oomph." Sucking wind into his burning lungs and swallowing down the raging throb throughout his body, he wanted to remain in that spot and rest. But, he knew he couldn't. His stomach lurched at the thought that Chuck and company were probably gone, but he would still check.

"Where the fuck are you, Jesse? I can't believe I

was so stupid to think I could do this without the team," Devon chided himself.

"By the looks of you, I'd have to agree."

Devon groaned at his older brother. "How the hell do you do that? I didn't even hear you."

A cocky grin split Jesse's face. "It's a gift." He squatted beside Devon. "Want to tell me how bad it is?"

"Does it matter? I fell off a cliff and they've got my wife. We need to hurry." He made it to his knees before his brother put his hand on his shoulder in a staying motion.

"They've got Rylee," Jesse spoke, but not to Devon. So, he had others with him. Thank God.

"Not that I'm not glad to see you, especially since I just called, but why are you here?"

He shrugged but waved a finger back and forth in front of Devon's face. "You know the drill."

And he did, but even if he had a concussion, there was no way in hell that he'd be sitting this out. In fact, they'd taken too long already.

Matt slipped silently through the tree line. He loved how this family converged to help whoever was in need.

"We have to check the ranch and see if she's there," Devon stated as if the thought hadn't crossed anyone's mind. With a nod from Jesse, which was as good a thumbs-up as he'd get, he struggled to his feet prepared to hike to the Carver place, bad ankle and all.

"When we didn't hear from you"—Jesse answered a question miles away from Devon's current train of thought—"we decided to visit. With no one at the cabin, Matt and I took to the trails, while AJ, Jake, and Ken went to the ranch you had mapped out on the kitchen table. I thought they might find out why you were interested in the place. Give them a bit more time."

Grasping the men's locations, Devon turned to Jesse. "Where's Brad?"

A chuckle erupted from his brothers. "He's with Rylee's sister."

He sighed in relief that HIS had thought to reach out to her, just in case. Another thought crossed his mind. "Is Kate here?" Fuck. Rylee was a good friend of hers, and she wouldn't take the news of her abduction well.

"Yeah, she said she had to come because of a dog, but we found a gray ball of fur next to it." Jesse wiggled his eyebrows. "We weren't expecting you two to have children in such a short time." His smile fell and his playfulness vanished. "She's coordinating transport for them to Baltimore."

"Thank you." Devon closed his eyes for a moment, relieved to know their pets were safe. Worry that the cabin might've been invaded and the animals harmed or his equipment broken or stolen, had eaten at him. Looking at Jesse, he opened his mouth and stopped what he'd been about to say.

His brothers stood frozen with their hands on their weapons on their side. A twig snapped and Devon tensed with his heart thudding painfully against his chest. Funny, for a man who'd never wanted to carry a weapon, after being tossed off a cliff and having one's wife kidnapped to be sold into sexual slavery, makes one redirect priorities, and one of his new priorities was a fucking weapon.

"Dammit, AJ. You have to learn to be quieter,"

Jesse chastised as AJ appeared in their path.

"Fuck you. We're here alone. It's vacant. Looks as if they left in a hurry," the youngest Hamilton brother said.

Devon would not allow even a sliver of defeat to wash into his mind. They'd find them if it was the last thing he ever did.

"Ken and Jake stayed back to see if they could find anything that would lead us to her." AJ walked to Devon. "We'll get her back."

An overwhelming feeling of love from his brothers flooded him, causing mist to form over his eyes and choke him up. Not wanting to appear a pussy, he suffered through the pain of a brief jerk of his head in acknowledgment.

They trudged to the cabin with a brother on each side of Devon, in case he needed their support, and Matt in front in case of trouble. "So you saw my old boss is who we're searching for?" They'd said they'd looked through his and Rylee's notes at the cabin and had the foresight to search Carver's home for them.

Jesse shook his head. "Didn't realize he was your old boss."

"He is and he's into some fucked-up shit."

"You can fill us in now."

Devon relayed all he and Rylee had learned about Carver and what he might be into. They were certain but lacked proof. The man who'd taken Rylee never said he worked for Carver, so Devon prayed HIS wasn't wasting their time chasing him because that was who they'd begin with in the search for his wife.

When they entered the rental, Kate clucked like a mother hen after hearing the news. After demanding she be part of the team to rescue Rylee, she insisted on doctoring his cuts even though he, just as stubbornly, insisted he needed to get on his computer. They compromised and he told AJ where he'd hidden it so he could have it ready for when Nurse Kate released him.

When Jake and Ken returned, they were empty-handed. "They may as well have burned the place," Ken Patrick, the HIS field team leader had explained. "There is nothing personal there."

AJ rushed into the large room with a bag of chips in one hand and a laptop bag in the other, which he held up with a beaming smile, unaware of the devastating news that had just been delivered. "Got it!" He deposited the laptop on the table and whistled. "Man, this is a fucked-up way to spend your birthday." Shaking his head, he ripped open the bag of chips and stood helplessly as they flew everywhere.

A light chuckle knocked around the room, a welcome levity, before the attention focused back on Devon.

"Yay. Happy fucking birthday to me," Devon grumbled.

"Birthday or not, think you can stop letting your brother's wife coddle you and get those magic fingers to working?" Matt asked with a bit of humor laced in his serious tone.

Jake crossed his arms across his chest. "Are we bringing Arthur in?"

"No," Devon ground out with more anger than he'd expected. Like hell he'd involve the FBI in anything unless he absolutely had to. Their recent experiences with them hadn't been great, and he wouldn't risk their fucking up with Rylee's life at stake. "At least, not now."

The men nodded, apparently all in agreement.

"Why don't you three grab some air while Dev works?" Jesse asked the men.

After they exited the cabin amidst jests at AJ for eating more food, the eldest Hamilton brother turned to him, but Kate piped up from the kitchen. "You can have your boy time, but I will wrap those ribs and that ankle, Devon, before the day is through." She hummed and busied herself making a meal for the group.

Jesse turned back to him, smirking, but sobered his face quickly. "You up for this?"

"My memory is back." His entire Vegas trip flashed fresh in his mind and his heart swelled with excitement at its return and the events that had occurred on that trip.

"So that jump off a cliff did you some good?"

"I love her, Jesse."

A broad smile grew on his brother's face. "I kind of figured that was the case if you'd married her— drunk or not."

No, he hadn't been drunk. He'd fallen hopelessly in love with her at first sight—something he thought was imagined for romantics. He hadn't thought she'd been drunk either, but a stab of worry broke in without warning. She couldn't remember. Had she been drunk and not meant to marry him? No. He wouldn't believe that. She'd been just as in love with him as he'd been with her.

And, she needed him more than ever.

Chapter Twenty-Seven

After nearly half an hour of frustration at Robert's cabin, Devon exclaimed, "I'm in!"

Kate, who'd insisted they search the place again when he told the team they *were* breaking back in, hovered over him in the office while he searched the computer that housed the home's security footage. Hoping against hope that Carver had left the program defaults in place so footage of Rylee would still be saved, Devon rewound until he found her. He had no idea what he was looking for in the footage, but he'd refused to leave until he saw that she'd been okay. The bugs they'd planted had been found, so there was no audio.

"Here we go." Anger infused in him and he wanted to bellow at the top of his lungs as he watched Rylee being led down the hallway by Nick and the brute who'd taken her from him. Her red-rimmed eyes constantly scanned the area but never looked directly at the cameras she knew to be there. That caught his attention and he straightened. She would, of course, be seeking an escape, but he'd think she'd have given him a look or a sign through the camera since she had to have known he'd tap into it to find her.

He groaned inwardly and his heart bled for her. She didn't expect him to check the tapes. Christ, she thought him fucking dead. Imagining how she felt was impossible.

Just losing her this short time made him feel like his heart had been ripped from his chest and shoved down his throat. So, she may not have been thinking fully about rescue. But, he had to believe she'd trust that HIS would look for her. Kate and Jesse wouldn't forget her.

Even dealing with what she thought had occurred, and her fate sketchy, she appeared to be full of fire. He still didn't understand it, but it didn't matter as long as she liked to say it. As for her fire, he couldn't decide what had lit her fuse the hottest, but whatever it had been, it'd been strong enough that two big men had to bind her wrists. His anger notched up. Those sons of bitches would pay.

Kate pointed to the screen. "What's she doing with her hands?"

He zoomed in on the footage and focused on what he thought had been Rylee flexing her fists in anger or to keep the circulation moving from her the cable ties encircling her wrists. "Is that sign language?"

"Yes!" Kate answered. "It looks like she's spelling something, but I'm not certain."

It explained why she hadn't looked at the cameras. She hadn't wanted to draw attention to herself. "Matt," he shouted with force, "get in here, ASAP." Devon had memorized the alphabet in sign language when he was a child, but he wouldn't leave that old, rusty knowledge to this important message when he had a former SEAL around. Hell, he didn't know if they learned it as SEALs, he just knew Matt was nearly fluent in sign language.

Devon didn't have to turn to know the remaining

cabin's occupants had crushed up behind him in the small room, peering over his shoulder. The sudden weight of their dominant presence and the warm air from their breaths reached him and he wanted to jump out of the way and send them all out to find Rylee.

"A...I..." Matt translated aloud. "R...P...O...."

"Airport." Devon slapped the desktop with his pronouncement.

"R...T," Matt finished. "Then it repeats."

"But we knew she was going to—" Kate began.

"Son of a motherfucking bitch!" Devon shouted and surged from his chair, running a hand through his hair and barely avoiding the men behind him. He wanted to lunge at the man on the screen. That Chuck bastard had injected her with something before they reached the front door and she'd collapsed not long after. Different types of drugs they could've used flashed across his memory, but sodium pentothal came to mind first. No matter what they used, he prayed it wasn't something dangerous, or they didn't overdose and kill her because sodium pentothal was also used in euthanasia.

Then, the man moved. *Dammit.* That bastard carried her like one would carry a lover to bed. Rage vented out every one of Devon's pores and his pulse pounded at a merciless rhythm. No one handled his wife's body like that except him.

They fucking thought they would sell her. Just wait until the goddamn HIS found the bastards. Every single one of them would regret selling or buying human beings.

"Get everyone ready to mobilize," Jesse instructed and their brothers moved away, pulling sat phones from the pockets of their cargo pants. He turned to Devon. "We're going home."

"Jesse—"

As if sensing his question, he held up a hand to forestall Devon's words. "We're going to find her, but unless you know where to fly, we may as well be where all our support and equipment are located. Should you figure out where they went while we're in flight, I promise to God that we'll divert for her." Slapping a hand on Devon's shoulder, he grabbed and squeezed tight. "We'll find those girls too. Maybe not at the same time, but we'll find them."

"I've never felt so fucking helpless in my life. I pulled all I could find on Carver." He snapped his fingers. Now he was thinking straight. "Manhattan. He has a suite there. I doubt he'd chance taking her there, but we need to check it out."

Jesse smiled with pride. "Now that's more like it. We'll do Manhattan. Do you think you can handle it?"

"Give me a weapon, but don't stand in my way if they've hurt her."

"That's not—"

"Jesse," Ken, a former army ranger who worked with Jesse, said as he stuck his head in the doorway, "company's coming."

Devon hurried toward the door, but Jesse put out an arm to stop him. "You"—he pointed with the other hand—"get everything together on Carver and be ready to brief the team when we hit the air. We'll handle this."

"What if it's Carver?"

Jesse's expression displayed his doubt. "Do you really think it is?"

His shoulders slumped. "No."

"Good. Get it ready." He turned and strode from the room.

Caught between wanting to be involved in this interrogation and getting the material together, he opted for the one where the team relied upon him. He counted on them to question whomever it was for Rylee's sake. That was how the team worked.

Dipping into the FBI server longer than he should, Devon couldn't get out. It was a goldmine on Carver. Why hadn't he checked it before? The man had accumulated a small fortune that sat in US banks, and they had leads on several overseas accounts of his.

He'd been doing this for a while, but only made it big time when Keith Westbrook went to jail. By Devon's guess, he picked up the other criminal's buyers and tactics. But, what struck him was the property list. While there were several, the one in Belize is where his gut told him she'd been brought.

Jesse burst in the door.

"Belize," they said simultaneously.

"Nick, the caretaker, was our company. We just had a nice chat with him." Jesse smirked. Devon doubted nice had been in the cards. "According to him, Rylee was to be treated with care on her trip."

Plopping an elbow on the desktop, Devon dropped his chin in his hand. "Yeah, but what about when she gets there?"

"She waits for us. The two girls are there as well. Plus another two or three. Nick was vague on those details."

"I'd like to have a word with Nick," he bit out angrily.

"No." Jesse's cell phone rang. "Hamilton." His eyes narrowed on Devon and Devon's insides crawled. What the fuck now? "I see. I'll take care of it." He ended the call but blasted at Devon, "Get the fuck off the FBI server. Christ, you're already screwing up."

Jumping at the rebuke and that he had, in fact, not logged out of the FBI's database, he assumed an apologetic expression and executed the required keystrokes to clear him. "Arthur?" he asked quietly.

"Yeah. And, don't give me any shit about him. Jason has us going to church since his birth parents used to take him. He insists I forgive, so I have." He waved a hand as if shooing a fly. "No, I didn't forget, but I will grant forgiveness. Now, pack up and let's get the hell out of here." Spinning on his heel, he bellowed, "Well, boys, looks like we're headed to Belize," as he exited the room.

Chapter Twenty-Eight

A female voice reached Rylee through the thick fog swirling in her mind. Chuck had drugged her once more before they'd landed in Belize.

"Chandra, can you hear me?"

There was that voice again, but it was clearer this time. Who was Chandra? Maybe she'd found where the girls were. Something niggled at the back of her mind. What was it? Oh, she'd used Chandra when she'd been on her last op. The girls would know that name. Had she found them? She fought to open her eyes or speak to ask the question, but her attempt failed.

A hand shook her. Wanting to reach up and swat it away, her mind focused but her body didn't react to her demand for movement. Her world became fuzzy again. She knew she was drifting away, but couldn't fight it much longer. Yet, she had to because she needed to get them out of there.

"Wake up!" The voice was more insistent.

The hovering darkness ratcheted up its effort to drag her under its spell. Hearing that name again, one more attempt at pulling herself from the depths, but the fight to remain alert left her and she slipped into blessed darkness.

****

RYLEE woke and her senses went on alert before she opened her eyes. An odd feeling of clarity filled her mind, and then Devon's image flooded her thoughts. That sick feeling in her stomach hadn't left her and she couldn't attribute it to the drugs. It was the loss of her husband.

For the briefest of moments, she wished the nausea wasn't from grief but from the possibility of life. Such a precious gift was a dream, even though she knew the chances were slim to none. Yet, she held onto the idea for just a little longer, hoping that their last time together hadn't been as safe as they'd intended.

But, he'd always be with her. His life had been cut short way too soon. If only after she'd returned from her op, she'd sought him out as he'd requested—

A movement to her right jarred her mind back to her present situation. Realizing she lay on her back on top of a lumpy mattress, reminded her they'd arrived in Belize. She wished she had an idea of how long she'd been here. She inhaled and almost gagged. Whatever room she'd been put in smelled of urine and feces as if a toilet had long ago overflowed.

"I think she's waking up again," a soft female voice said from her left.

The girls. Her eyes flew open as several young women gathered around, staring down at her, making her want to feel all over to ensure she was dressed. The dim lighting in the room forewarned her not to expect windows. "Wa—" Her voice broke. "Water," she croaked out.

A redheaded teenager scurried away, and Rylee took that opportunity to attempt to sit.

"Here." Misty grabbed a pillow off the small cot beside them and put the two pillows beneath Rylee's head.

Although dizzy, it was nothing compared to what she'd suffered already.

The girl returned with a bottle of water. "Here."

She accepted the bottle, leaned on an elbow, twisted the cap and surveyed her fellow abductees while swallowing down as much as she could in one gulp. Taking in the room, she wanted to scream. It was a big square with no windows, six cots crammed close together, and not a fucking thing else except a door. And, it didn't look like a cheap door. Sighing in relief at a bit of hydration, she capped the bottle. "Misty. Mandy. I'm so glad I found you."

"Chandra, what are you doing here?"

Oh. There was a lot to explain. "Um, my name's not Chandra. It's Rylee. I was undercover with the FBI when I met you."

"You're FBI?" a teenage girl with long blonde hair that nearly reached her butt asked with wide eyes.

Shaking her head, she quickly recognized it as a mistake. Her head wasn't that clear. "Not anymore."

"Then, what are you doing here? Do you know what they plan to do with us? They told us they were selling us." Mandy shuddered.

"No one is getting sold," Rylee said firmly. How she planned to prevent that, she wasn't quite sure. Her hope was Kate and Jesse figured it all out from what they'd left in the cabin and sent someone for her. But, she couldn't wait around and see. "Why don't you tell me who all is here?"

Misty pointed at each girl as she introduced them. "That's Holly O'Halloran."

Red hair. Green eyes.

"That's Natalie Thatcher."

Blonde hair. Blue eyes.

"And, that's Gina Keller."

Black hair. Chocolate eyes.

And the twins had strawberry-blonde hair with violet eyes. Without asking, she'd guess they ranged from about twelve to fifteen years of age. Quite the collection. *Dirty fucking bastard.* Speaking of dirty, the girls' clothes could use a cleaning, and by the odor of them, so could they. "Why does it smell like—"

"Shit?" Natalie cut her off with a sweet voice and a hint of a southern drawl. "Because they make us use a bucket and only take it out once a day. Or every two days, depending on the guard."

Levering herself up so she could swing her legs over the side of the bed, Rylee kept with her information gathering, but she asked her next question hesitantly so as not to upset the girls. "How long have you been here?"

"We've been here the longest," Mandy said and rushed to her side, reaching out arms to assist. "Since that night they took us from the other house."

Her feet finally planted, she placed her hand on the bed for support, and with Mandy grasping her forearm, she stood. Then, she swayed and fell back to the bed. "Dammit," she said under her breath. *You can do this. Remember, every moment counts. Who knows if they'll drug you again before....*

There was no time to sit and revel in the success of finding the girls because they were in a precarious situation. She'd overheard talk on the plane that buyers were on their way to the location. To include some asshole named Hogan, who thought he could own her. *Fuck that!*

"Okay, girls, remember I was with the FBI?"

"Yeah, but you're not now. How does that help us?" Holly needed to dial down her attitude.

"Because I have training. We're going to find a way out of here."

Not surprisingly, Holly rolled her eyes. "Can't be done."

"I want to know everything. So"—Rylee looked around the group and her gaze stopped on one girl— "Misty, how often does anyone come in here?"

The girl twirled a finger in her hair. "Three times a day. To feed us."

At least it was three. But, she guessed the amount of food was substantially lacking. "Okay, Mandy, how many different men have you seen?"

"Two," she piped up, almost cheerful to be called upon.

Nodding, she thought. "Natalie," she said, wanting to include them all, "when they open the door, do you see anyone besides the person bringing in the food?"

She shook her head. "No, and Walt is pretty clumsy juggling it all."

"Walt?"

"Oh yeah. Walt and Ricardo. That's the names they gave us when we pestered them."

Interesting that the men would allow a familiarity with the girls. That could work to their benefit.

"Of course," Holly began snidely, "it took both of them to carry you in."

"Well," she said, biting her tongue, "that's good to know they might be together. How long before they bring our next meal?"

Half of the girls shrugged, and Rylee could

sympathize since she saw they weren't wearing watches. Hell, they might not even be fed on a regular schedule. Since they were such a prize, she thought Robert would run a tighter ship. Then again, she never understood the demented mind.

Natalie, the eldest by the looks of her, answered, "Maybe an hour."

Her heartbeat sped up in anticipation. She had an hour to prepare them for their escape.

Chapter Twenty-Nine

When they reached Baltimore, the remaining men of HIS were present and loaded. Beside them stood crates of what Devon knew to be their weapons stash. The men weren't fucking around. Ken did a great job pulling the team of law enforcement and military men together. And, one woman when you counted Kate.

He figured they didn't know Rylee, except maybe the ones who'd once been FBI, and they probably didn't know he and Rylee were married. Still, they'd come off their break to do this, and he knew they'd give their lives if necessary to save his wife. Hell, they'd lost one HIS member saving Amber. *We miss you, Les.* These men knew the risks and took them without fail. He couldn't be prouder to have them as part of the team.

They taxied to the hangar near the men and after they halted and the plane powered down, Jesse spoke with the pilot about flight plans and other shit Devon didn't care about. A flash to his right caught his attention and he watched a refueling truck hauling ass to meet them. Damn, how did Jesse do it? Shrugging, he met the men as they began to board.

A tall blond stepped onboard. "Trent?" he said in disbelief. "What are you doing here?"

The blue-eyed man, who the men had termed "God's gift to women" and was half-brother to the

Hamiltons, smiled. "I'm here for family." He reached out his hand and shook Devon's. Giving him a hug of any sort, even the manly slap on the back, was out of the question. The man was recovering from multiple skin graft surgeries on the back of his body. "Don't read anything into it," he rushed to add. "I'm out of here afterward. But, for now, let's bring your wife home."

So they knew he'd married her. Kate. He shook his head. The woman couldn't keep her mouth shut to save her life. Good, he wouldn't have to explain why he'd kept it a secret.

Trent stalked past him to allow the remaining men—Steve, Rob, Danny, Kevin, Jamaal, Joe, Mike, Neftali, and the two men they'd recently hired—to enter, carrying various items. No one spoke, only small head nods and fist bumps with AJ were used to communicate.

Jesse strolled back to the crowded cabin and everyone's eyes darted to him. "We're going to have an extra passenger with us today, and I don't want to hear shit about who it is."

A few low groans were heard because even though they didn't know whom yet, that speech meant the men wouldn't like their guest.

He continued, "I want our asses covered there. Believe me, getting approval—"

"Fuck approval," Devon spat out. They were already wasting fucking time. Everyone was on board, which meant he was ready to go get his wife.

Jesse narrowed his eyes at him, challenging him to say more. "As I was saying, we wouldn't be the first chosen to go in on this, but I finagled the job, which means you'll get paid and we have the right US backing should the shit hit the fan. Which," he scanned the group, "won't happen."

A sick feeling formed in Devon's stomach while the men hoorayed. Somehow, he knew who their guest would be. If allowing Arthur to fly with them, and cozying up to him, was needed to rescue Rylee, he'd be first in line, even though he'd hate every minute of it.

Ducking his head, Jesse looked out a plane window. "Here he is."

Devon craned his neck and sure enough, a black Town Car drove close to the plane and Arthur Hall, Deputy Director of the FBI, stepped out in his snappy suit with a briefcase and navy duffel bag.

A thought suddenly occurred to him. How many fucking people did they have on the plane? "Uh, Jesse," he said hesitantly, "where the hell are we going to put everyone?"

His brother hoisted a thumb over his shoulder. "Jump seats."

Meeting the man at the door, Jesse shook his hand. "Thanks for helping us on this."

Devon frowned. Shouldn't that be what the FBI said and not his brother? That forgiveness shit had gone to Jesse's head.

"Believe me, I want this bastard." Arthur scanned the plane, his gaze resting on Devon. "It's not just Rylee we think he has."

The plane began to power its engines and Ken went to the door to pull up the stairs and close it.

"Ladies and gentlemen, please prepare for departure," a voice said through the speakers.

"Everybody grab a seat so we can get our asses to

Belize." Jesse moved to the cockpit with Steve following him, while everyone searched for lap belts and buckled himself or herself in safely.

The plane lifted smoothly from the ground and in no time, they were informed that they were free to move about the cabin. Devon had no idea where the hell they would go. There was barely enough room for legs and feet while seated. It was definitely lucky Jesse hadn't picked the smaller plane he sometimes commandeered for missions. They'd have never fit.

Jesse entered the cabin. "Get comfortable. We have about seven hours of flight time."

Normally the men would've been digging in their packs for headphones or phones or books, but today they waited. That was because typically they were already briefed by the time they hit the air. Today was different, and it sizzled in the air.

Jesse slid into the seat facing Devon. He reached over and pulled out a fold-up table from the cabin wall and spread it between them.

Arthur, sitting beside him, slapped his briefcase on top and opened it, then reached in and pulled out a folder about an inch thick.

Fuck. Now he was glad Jesse had pulled in Arthur because Devon's research was pathetic compared to that. He hadn't found that much in the FBI system.

"Okay, boys, it goes without saying this is confidential information." Arthur bolstered his voice loud enough for the entire cabin to hear. "After Robert Carver left the CIA, he took the wrong path. Probably before, but we couldn't find anything for certain." He set the file on the table but didn't open it.

Devon's pulse kicked up a notch. Had that been

why he'd refused to publicly acknowledge Greg's death, or had it truly been part of the spook creed?

With a hand on the file, like he was swearing in at court, Arthur continued, "He started kidnapping girls and selling them right away."

"We know that," Devon growled. He couldn't believe that tone had come from him, but he wanted something new, something they could use.

Arthur appraised him, nodded for whatever reason, and moved on to his recitation. "Anyhow, he did it one at a time, because he didn't have the right contacts or setup. But, he continued to build from it until next thing we knew, he was buddy-buddy with Dave Westbrook."

Devon's mind began to spin at Dave's name being thrown into the mix. Chuck had said something about her getting away before. She'd never told him that Dave had taken her to be sold. Her always looking over her shoulder made more sense, but at the time that was the last thing he'd have considered. When he found her, he wasn't sure whether he'd hug her or put her over his knee for keeping that secret from him. Never would he have allowed her to go to Carver's house if he'd known that. *And that's exactly why she didn't tell me.*

"Papa Westbrook didn't give him up. Swore he hadn't had anything to do with him. Which could've been true, but Carver sure used the opportunity to grow his business. We're wondering if he had Dave killed, but that's just speculation. There's no reason for it since our source said they were working together."

A light bulb moment flashed. "Was this source Brent Fuller?"

Raising his eyebrows, Arthur slowly nodded. "It was. We think they found out about him and that's why he was killed."

"Uh, did anyone tell you that Rylee had been in the limo when it all happened?" Devon asked.

Arthur's head swiveled to Jesse and he spoke through a clenched jaw. "No."

"At this moment, that doesn't matter." Jesse leaned forward with his forearms on the table and his hands clasped in front of him. "What matters is getting Rylee—and any other girls—out of there. Now"—he inclined his head to the forgotten folder—"what else have you got for us?"

Index finger flipping the top edge of the folder, Arthur stared at Jesse.

Christ, this couldn't come down to a pissing match. "Look, how many girls do you think he has?" Devon asked to break the uncomfortable silence.

Their guest inhaled deeply once, then answered flatly, "Five."

Curses filled the plane.

"Okay, so we have possibly six females to extricate. You told me you have a layout of the property," Jesse said to Arthur.

The folder was finally opened and aerial surveillance photos slid across the table. "It's a 300-acre teak plantation."

"Teak?" Trent asked from over Devon's shoulder.

Arthur shrugged. "It also has smaller parts within of mahogany, Spanish cedar and other local hardwoods. Approximately forty acres have cacao. About a hundred and fifty are untouched."

The photos were passed over Jesse's shoulder to the men for their review. "What about water access?"

"The Machaca Creek is the best you'll get."

Matt looked up from the paper in his hand, which turned out to be a map Devon hadn't realized had been distributed. "Is this a wildlife sanctuary near it?"

"Yes." Arthur exhaled heavily as if a huge burden was about to be released and Devon feared it to be true. "There's no government support on this."

"What fucking bullshit is that? I thought you cleared this," Devon belted to Jesse.

"Calm the fuck down, Dev. He means Belize government." The eldest Hamilton brother turned to Arthur. "At least that had best be what he meant."

Arthur nodded.

Devon turned to Rob. "Did you bring all of my equipment?" He didn't have a go-bag ready like the other men since he didn't usually travel with them preferring to be behind his computer.

"Everything we could lift."

With the bulging muscles on some of the men, that could mean with their strength they'd even packed the mainframe that was bolted to the ground. His hands itched to dig into his goodies, but he fought it and remained where he was. "As soon as we get there, I'll get to scanning. Get me close enough and I can probably get into their surveillance and see what we're up against."

Arthur cleared his throat.

Devon turned to him. "What?"

"There may not be time. We got wind that a known buyer arrived this morning. Because of that, we're assuming the girls are there. It is possible that Carver moved them, though."

If the table hadn't been in the way, he'd have surged to his feet. "What. The. Fuck, Arthur? Maybe you like fucking the Hamilton family over on a regular basis, but you knew five"—he splayed his fingers out—"girls were there and did nothing. Nothing!" he ranted without restraint. "Now, because you let that asshole Carver just do his thing, he has my wife." He thrust his thumb to his chest. "My wife."

His chest heaved, and he wanted to throttle the man. *Possibly not there?* He couldn't handle that thought. She had to be there. The cabin was eerily silent. He didn't give a fuck because he knew they agreed with him, except it wasn't their wife about to be sold. It sickened him to think of how many females had passed through Carver's hands, while the government had done nothing.

"Devon," Arthur said calmly, "I'm sorry about things with AJ and Jake. I can't fix them nor can I fix the fact Carver is free. Don't let it cloud your judgment today. I think the world of Rylee. We're going to fix this and bring her home."

It was as if every person on the plane held his or her breath awaiting Devon's response. He inhaled deeply, held it, and then slowly released it. Calm began to infuse itself through his muscles. Instead of issuing a rebuttal, he turned to Jesse. "I'm fine." About as fine as he could be in the situation, but he wouldn't screw up. Rylee had reminded him that following orders was required. He wasn't in charge and considering his bouncing emotions, that was probably a good thing.

"Okay, tell me what you got from the pictures and let's get our plan together." Jesse nodded and smiled at him. That show of confidence, because that was his brother's "I trust you" face, soothed the fraying around his nerves. "And this time, Dev will be beside us in the field."

I'm coming, Rylee. Hang in there for me.

Chapter Thirty

The clicking of the lock on the door rang loudly in the room, bouncing from barren wall to barren wall. Rylee and the girls had found nothing they could use to fight with. If only they'd been strong enough to break apart one of the beds, they'd have had something to use as a weapon. Instead, they only had the force of them combined.

Rylee's plan was when the guard came in carrying a tray of food, she would jump on his back, and when he dropped the tray to grab for her, two girls would run forward with a sheet and trip him. While down, Rylee would then restrain him using strips of the sheets from their beds. She didn't mention that it wouldn't be that simple and there'd probably be fighting in there. She thought it best to not worry the girls.

It wasn't a grand plan or even very well thought out, but they didn't have time to make up some masterful strategy that required more than they had at hand.

Nervous energy pulsed around the room. A light flamed in the girls' eyes that spoke of the craving for their upcoming freedom. They'd wanted to be a part of the takedown.

Rylee tried not to fidget too badly. She didn't want the girls to get injured, but she couldn't bring down a man as big as they described by herself. Hence starting her attack from behind. Of course, by the time they were done describing the men, their guards were ten feet tall and broad as a barn. Being taught to take down a man as an agent had been standard, but she'd never mastered one significantly larger than her without a weapon of some sort. Hell, she'd even take a fork. Inspiration struck. She'd have one of the girls grab one from the tray and toss it to her. Risky because she'd have her focus off the man. To escape, she'd give it her best shot with whatever happened.

"To your cots," a deep voice boomed in broken English. Based on the girls' description that had to be Ricardo.

They were supposed to stand at their cots when someone entered with the food. Like hell.

A man poked his dark head in the room, and slid inside, empty-handed. From behind the door, Rylee stepped forward and to her horror, another man slipped in behind the first. She froze. *Fuck! I can't take two at once without a weapon. And they are broad as barns.*

The first man turned to her and narrowed his eyes. Displeasure at her not being by her cot written solidly across his features. "You're awake," the man she suspected was Walt said. "Good. The boss wants to see you."

That was unexpected since none of the other girls had met Robert. Then again, the man had been stateside until, she guessed, recently. Unless there was another boss. That got her blood boiling. One sicko was more than enough.

Looking at the girls and nodding, she played the submissive because she didn't want them to inject her with anything again. "Lead on."

Walt nodded toward the empty door and she followed Ricardo out the portal. Noticing the outline of a weapon at his lower back, she considered whether she could grab it fast enough. If he carried, that meant Walt carried. Was she quick enough? The door slamming startled her and she watched the lock keeping the girls away from freedom being engaged.

Rylee constantly scanned and took inventory of everything around her. The house was decorated quite richly apart from the room she'd been held prisoner. Carver must like nice things and needed to sell girls to get them.

Down one hallway, a right turn and she'd yet to see a doorway to freedom. When they turned yet again, she kept her bearings so she and the girls wouldn't get lost. There was the problem of what to do once they were free. She'd seen no more evidence of guards, but she found it hard to believe there wouldn't be any. They were bound to be outside.

Once again, she considered her opportunity to snatch the weapon when Ricardo stopped and turned to a set of double doors. She almost plowed into him before she halted her steps. Walt opened one of the doors, and he waved an arm telling her to enter. Good, no goons were going with her. Maybe she could take Carver, and then what? There were still these two men to take care of.

The room she entered stunned her. She'd never have expected such opulence in Belize. Decorated as a parlor of sorts, the golden walls and large floor-to-ceiling windows brightened the room. Even the heavy burgundy and cream curtains at the windows and double patio doors didn't take away from the light feeling. Had it been another time, she'd have wanted to curl up on the light burgundy suede chaise lounge.

In one of the Louis XIII chairs, sat a young woman who raked her eyes over Rylee as if sizing her up. Well, two could play that game. Rylee raised her brow and looked the woman over slowly. When she raised her eyes back to the woman, she snorted to show she didn't feel threatened.

"Rylee Hawkins. Or should I say Hamilton." The man's smooth voice came from her left. "Or was that a ruse to get into my house?"

She turned. Standing in front of a gigantic picture of an artist's work that looked familiar, but couldn't focus the brain cells on remembering, stood a man with his hands in the pockets of khaki slacks, wearing a white, short-sleeved button-down shirt. Tilting her head, she ignored his question and commented, "Robert Carver, I presume."

His laughter grated on her every nerve, making her prefer fingernails scratching across a chalkboard. Pulling a hand from his pockets, he waved her to the seating area. She acquiesced and sat in the second Louis XIII chair.

All she could think to do was gain information for the FBI when this was over. It might not matter, but she had to do something. However, if the two left her alone, she would pick up one of the candlesticks, which probably cost a small fortune, and take on Walt and Ricardo. Maybe she could sneak something out with her. She scanned the tops of the tables and cabinets in the room.

"I'd like you to meet my associate. She's here to see to your"—his mouth twisted into a vile grin—

"comfort. Jackie, this is Rylee Hamilton."

Her stomach somersaulted. Jackie? The Jackie? *Son of a fucking bitch.* That only made matters worse. It amped up her grief, the pain so raw she expected to see her heart bleeding on the floor. It also revved up her anger. His fucking employee killed Devon.

"Are you the Jackie who killed CIA operative Greg Donovan?" Her calm voice belied the turmoil within her.

The woman smiled proudly. "You've heard of me."

Heard and want to run a fucking fireplace poker through your black heart, she thought. "Devon mentioned you," she said instead, nonchalantly.

That agitated Carver. "What"—the man said as he picked imaginary lint from his shirt—"exactly did he tell you?"

"I'm hungry. Do you have any food?" Rylee asked just to piss him off.

He narrowed his eyes, then looked at Jackie and nodded for her to leave, presumably to get food.

As if on cue, her stomach rumbled. She could use a bite, not knowing when she'd last eaten.

Once the door closed on the woman, he turned back to her. "What did he tell you?"

"Everything." Sitting straight, she crossed her legs and assumed a casual pose. "Why did you have Greg killed?" It was a shot in the dark, but why the hell not?

Carver cocked his head and surprise washed across his face. Walking near her, he assumed the seat Jackie had vacated. "He knew?"

"Yes," she lied.

The man scrutinized her. "I don't believe you. Otherwise, he wouldn't have let it go."

"Did Greg figure out what you were doing?" *Don't let him sidetrack you, Rylee. Stay focused and get the evidence. A confession works. For Devon.*

"You know, it was dumb luck Devon went with Greg that night. Greg was supposed to be alone." He sighed as if it pained him to regale her with the story. "Greg found out about my—what's the right word?—branching off before I left the agency. He just needed proof. Jackie offered that. He'd just not done enough investigation to know she worked for me."

"So you had Jackie kill him."

"What did Devon Hamilton know?" he asked, sidestepping her question.

"Oh," she said flippantly as her defensive mechanism against the agony of thinking of his passing and the fact they were there was her fault. She'd pushed to search and she'd not told him she was being hunted. Although she didn't know that... for sure. "Do you mean like you selling girls into sexual slavery to the highest bidder?" She raised her eyebrows. "Yeah. He knew that." And to rub salt in the wound, she couldn't stop. "And, he told his brothers, so your ass is cooked. In fact"—she looked at her watch and then back at him—"I'd expect them any minute."

Carver's head swiveled to glance around the room as if HIS would jump out from behind the furniture. Then he roared with laughter and slapped a hand on his thigh.

That didn't work as she'd planned. She'd wanted him on edge. "Did you have Dave killed?"

He sobered and actually looked a bit sad. "No. That was retaliation from Louis Blakney, one of his buyers, for his father ratting the man out. But, Chuck did tell me how you were there. We didn't share that bit of information with anyone."

Jackie took that moment to return with a plate of cheese and fruit and handed it to Rylee. She accepted and began nibbling, all the while praying the food wasn't laced with anything.

"After she gets her fill," Robert said to Jackie, "get her in a bath and ready. Hogan is here."

Rylee clasped onto the name Hogan and mulled it over in her mind to see if she recognized it. When she didn't, her heart plummeted to her stomach, and it roiled at the invasion. How would she help the girls escape now?

****

Rylee's mind spun with possibilities of escape. The challenge lay in getting the girls out as well. If the buyers weren't due in, she could get out and bring back help. With their time constraint, she couldn't chance it though. She might not make it back in time. She also couldn't chance some asshole trying to carry her away. Like this Hogan.

Glancing down at her foot, she noticed one of her hiking boots was untied. She also noticed her thoughts were slowing. That was when she realized they had drugged her. Her heart stuttered. She shouldn't have accepted the food, but she'd felt weak and knew the fuel would be needed. Besides, it was hard to drug fruit and cheese. Okay, given the world they lived in, not so hard.

Her footsteps in the hallway felt sluggish and heavy. Stopping to tie her shoe, she placed her hand on the wall to steady herself. Looking up into Jackie's smiling eyes, she considered trying to rip the woman's throat out.

"Problem?" the bitch cooed.

It had to have been in the water. Jackie had opened it in front of her, or so she'd pretended. She hadn't tasted anything though. "What'd you give me? GHB?"

Surprise lit the woman's eyes. "Ah, I'd been told you were smart. Come on, let's go." She grabbed Rylee's forearm and tugged her down the hallway. Jackie was damned strong for someone smaller than her.

The pulling continued until Rylee tumbled into a luxuriously decorated bedroom decorated with cream silks over a large canopy bed. Her captor didn't allow her to stop and gather her wits, or tie her shoe, she dragged her into a bathroom that was larger than the two in her apartment combined.

When Jackie did release her and walked to the huge tub, Rylee stepped backward to test her strength and her captor's reflexes.

"I do toss knives very well, so don't try me. My father will be disappointed if his merchandise is damaged."

That stopped Rylee short. Her father? "Who's your father?"

Removing her hand from beneath the running water, she stood and faced Rylee fully. "Hogan. My father." She sniffed as if detecting a foul odor. "I don't know why he chose you though."

She didn't either. There was no telling what Keith Westbrook had said to pay her back for helping ruin him. A sudden need to sit fell upon her and she collapsed to the ground.

Heaving a heavy sigh, Jackie shook her head. "I

told that bastard it was too much. I should've known when it worked too quickly."

She wanted to get up, wanted to move, but her body wasn't reacting to her commands. Devon would've told her to fight it and she tried, but she wasn't strong enough. Feeling like nothing more than a puppet, she allowed Jackie to undress her and then help her up and into the steaming water.

Wet warmth infused her and a shudder racked her body. A delightful shudder, and it made her sick. In her mind, she knew she shouldn't be here, that she should move, but…it felt so…good. Moaning, she leaned her head back and accepted the comfort of the bubble bath.

Dozing off, her mind warned her to remain alert and look for opportunities. It just told her too late.

When she woke, her heart leapt into her throat.

A man stood in the bathroom doorway, in a casual pose, but rubbing his crotch through his slacks.

Out of reflex, her hands flew to her breasts where most of the bubbles had evaporated. "Who… who are you?" Her eyes flew around the room, frantically searching for a weapon and finding none. There had to be something in one of the drawers.

"I'm Hogan."

The man, with his slightly graying dark hair and lean build, didn't jog her memory of any faces she'd seen. Searching the contours of his face to see if it sparked any recognition, she decided that he could be considered handsome. If unaware of his sickness.

"Doll, you were supposed to be ready for me."

Rylee narrowed her eyes, which should've been spitting fire. "Only one person gets away with calling me Doll, and it's not you."

With his lips twitching suspiciously, Hogan advanced toward her. Rylee couldn't heed her impulse to fight or flee so she shrank back from his angry eyes. "Don't push me," he said in a low, throaty rumble. "Doll." He spun on his heel as the bottom dropped out of her gut. "Jackie!" he bellowed.

Rylee couldn't see him any longer or make out what was being said. What she did notice was that she was coming to herself, not fully, but a little would have to be enough. Hearing a door slam, she expected to see Jackie in the next minute.

The woman did not disappoint. "Get the fuck up." She held out a large cream-colored towel.

To her relief, she found she could push herself to a standing position. It took some work, but she was on her feet again. Before accepting the towel, she stepped out of the tub onto a plush rug. Drying her body, slowly to delay, she tested her strength by twisting the towel into a tight rope. Pulse pounding, but feeling confident enough, she called on Jackie, who was rinsing out the tub. "Can you help me? I'm just so weak."

"Oh my God. How pathetic," the woman ranted but stepped closer.

Before she could retrieve the towel, Rylee swung it to loop around Jackie's neck, slipped behind her, and crossed the ends to pull tight until the woman choked.

Jackie went up on her toes and grasped at the towel. Rylee tightened her hold and crossed the ends more. The next thing Rylee knew, Jackie must've reached down because a blade sliced across her forearm.

"Ow," Rylee cried and loosened her grip enough that Jackie got free. Fuck. Rylee's heart pounded and her limbs trembled more than she wanted. She was at a disadvantage. How could she have forgotten about the knife? *Because my mind is fucked up with drugs.*

"You bitch!" Jackie heaved deep breaths, gulping loudly.

Rylee took the chance and sped to the vanity, flinging open drawers, searching for anything she could use as a weapon. She completely ignored the blood running down her arm. Drawer one. Nothing. Her courage sank a notch. Drawer two. Nothing. It dropped to her midsection. Drawer three. Absofuckinglutely nothing. Her stomach absorbed the drop of courage within her.

Jackie approached her slowly and Rylee grabbed the only thing she could find that was useful—a towel. She twisted it up fast, hoping to use it to help deflect any blows while she skirted around to the door. If only her body kept pace, she'd make it to the door.

The first strike happened and she interfered enough that Jackie pulled back. They circled each other, her eyes never leaving Jackie's to ensure she didn't miss what her eyes projected. Another lunge and Rylee stumbled back, a pain in her right side. She looked down and saw blood cascading down her side.

A noise rang through the halls. *Oh no! Hogan's on his way back. This is it. I can't do anymore. I've failed.*

Chapter Thirty-One

Occupying a breakroom in a hangar, the HIS men, somehow, made do with the limited space. At least with Mike and Rob standing guard, there were two less bodies crammed into the room. Beggars couldn't be choosers. They didn't want to advertise their presence with Arthur, so they'd remained where the plane had taxied except when two of his brothers and Devon had driven close enough to Carver's plantation for him to scan and find the security footage of Robert's house. Devon hadn't been able to stay in long enough to rewind so he got what they needed and returned.

He'd wanted to go in right then but calmer heads prevailed. He hadn't seen Rylee or the girls. For some reason, Devon had expected a camera in the room with them. Probably an oversight because a sick fuck who sold females would probably get his jollies watching them too. Then again, if his preference had been men, maybe not.

They'd pieced together the house from the footage. It was obvious which room the girls were kept because a very bored guard either paced or stood in front of the door. Finding that door was where Devon would be. Jesse had approved his being with the group who split off in that section of the large house.

"Make sure you spray good, boys. I don't want any of you to get Malaria." Jesse handed a bottle of insect repellent to Devon and walked away.

"I know you started the pills, men," Ken said. "But, take the precaution. Besides, who wants to itch like fuck when we're out at this hellhole?"

"Beautiful hellhole," Jamaal, a team member, piped in, then fist bumped with Neftali, one of their sharpshooters, who nodded.

"Well then, when through ridding the place of scum, take a fucking vacation here." Ken turned and walked to Jesse. The two spoke in low tones and many eyes watched them.

It'd never bothered Devon before when they'd done that because he knew his place on a mission. This time, it rankled the hell out of him, but he wouldn't say it in front of the men. With his brothers and sister as partners, they played as equals out in the field, but always, Jesse was boss. It had to be that way, or it'd get awfully confusing because his family didn't always agree. His older brother ordered, and Ken made it happen.

Matt slid closer to him. "Are you ready for this? You know we'll get her out of there."

Frustration slammed into Devon. He couldn't fault Matt because all his brothers had asked him the same thing. "She's my wife. I'm going."

The calmness in Matt was sometimes eerie. One wouldn't have thought him a former SEAL. The profile he fit was closer to peacemaker. Yeah, he'd be one hell of a negotiator because nothing seemed to ruffle him. Yet, Devon hadn't seen him actually on a mission either. And, this particular one—where women had the potential to be repeatedly raped if they failed—would be a true test to them all, but especially to Matt.

"Good." He held his hand out and Devon knew what he wanted. Again, his brothers, even Trent, had all stopped and double-checked his weapons. How easily they forgot that he went to the range with them on a regular basis. Because it wasn't worth arguing about, he handed first his AR-15 and then his Glock over for inspection.

Apparently satisfied, Matt nodded, slapped him on the shoulder, and left with, "We *will* get her out of there."

"Saddle up, boys and girl, it's time to go," Jesse said.

A queer feeling formed in Devon's stomach, and his pulse raced. Not quite nerves or fear. Anxious was how he found himself.

Crowded into three vans, they careened down the road toward Carver's place. To avoid detection, they would infiltrate through part of the jungle. After Neftali and Jesse, their sharpshooters, took out the outside guards. Some part of him wanted to scream that they just drive up and ring the doorbell, then take everyone by force, but that could get them or the girls killed. It always seemed so cut and dry behind his computer.

A sickening sensation slid through him. These men depended on him. What if he hesitated like before? He couldn't live with one of their deaths on his conscience. Greg's was more than enough. *I know, wife, I did what I was told.* A smile slipped on his face, and he almost burst out laughing at himself for responding to Rylee.

"What's the smile for?" Kate asked.

For some unknown reason, that made him laugh out loud and all heads turned to him. They probably thought he'd lost it, and he didn't care. Having a surge of joy flow through his veins leveled him. It brought him back from thinking he wasn't enough.

His laughter was short-lived. The van stopped and his muscles tensed. Jesse and Neftali exited and slipped into the jungle.

The rest of the men exited and were on instant alert. Actually, as far as Devon could tell, they'd been on alert since he'd seen them back in Baltimore.

With a few hand signals from Ken, they disappeared into the jungle at various points, rifles at the ready. Devon assumed his position between AJ and Trent, who'd been assigned to babysit him as far as he could tell, and pushed his way through. With each step, his blood flowed faster and faster until when they stopped, he thought his veins might burst.

The area to the house was an open field, where armed guards patrolled. Suddenly four pops sounded, rifles with silencers, and the four guards dropped. The sharpshooters were fucking awesome.

Through his earpiece, which he'd almost forgotten he had because the men were so quiet, Jesse commanded them to converge on the house. Again, with his small group, they raced across the field, his blood pounding loudly in his ears. They were the second group entering the house. The first was to locate Carver. He was to find Rylee. Silently they made their way down the hallways they'd mapped out. When they reached where they'd make the final turn and run into a guard, AJ signalled them to halt.

Leaning back against the wall, Devon gave a silent prayer that he'd be able to do what it took to save his wife and the girls.

AJ nodded at Trent and the two turned in the

hallway, weapons pointed, with AJ screaming, "Get down, motherfucker!"

More shouting and then he heard two shots. His heart skipped a beat and he turned the corner to see his brothers over a prone man with blood seeping onto his shirt. It took several deep breaths for him to relax from worrying about his brothers.

"The fucker reached to his back." AJ kicked a handgun aside, then nodded again at Trent.

During that time, Steve and Danny arrived. The group set up surrounding the door while Danny had their six.

Coming up beside him, AJ spoke quietly, "I know you want to go first, but be smart and stay behind me this one time."

With his pulse racing and adrenaline surging to his heart, Devon didn't think he could wait that long, even behind one person, but his mind remained clear and he knew when to follow. His brother had been trained in this. There was no way he'd chance putting Rylee or those girls at risk.

He gave a short nod in agreement.

They turned back to the heavy door. After removing keys from the downed guard's pocket, Trent passed them forward to Steve who inserted them in the lock, but waited to turn the key.

The men slung their rifles over their shoulders and unholstered Glocks so Devon did the same. He preferred the handgun anyway. If the women weren't alone, he'd have to use his weapon. His hand shook. *Breathe. I can do this.*

AJ nodded and Steve unlocked the door. Then, his brother counted to three with a flash of fingers. Devon took a deep breath and held it to calm his nerves, but his heart still pounded rapidly, beating hard against his chest. Surprisingly, his hands were steady. *I'm coming, Rylee.*

Steve stood with them, weapons ready, covering the door to the room now absent a guard. Trent and Danny had pulled the man out of the way and watched the hallway. Devon wondered for a moment if the girls heard the shots. Using silencers didn't mean silent. Rylee would know what the sound was though.

When AJ extended three fingers, Steve jerked open the door and AJ eased in, weapon pointed.

Devon entered next and stopped in shock. A dark-haired girl was on AJ's back and two strawberry-blonde girls, twins, tripped him with a white sheet. When he fell, amidst extreme profanity Megan would kill him for, he spun and caught the girl on his back, initially pointing his weapon at her. When he realized it was a kid, still trying to corral him, he grabbed her wrists with one large hand and yelled, "Stop it!"

While Devon fought laughter, watching that hilarious scene, the other room occupants noticed him. His gut clenched. None of which were his wife.

"There's another one, girls. Get him," a red-haired girl charged.

To forestall them, he raised his hands palms toward them in surrender with his Glock slipping to his thumb, away from them. "We're here to rescue you. Where's my wife? Where's Rylee?"

While he spoke, the girls had gravitated closer to each other and further from him. They whispered and one of the twins stepped in front of the group. "Are you really Devon?" she asked softly.

He nodded and smiled. "Yes."

"Rylee said you died."

Rocks tumbled in his gut. How he wished he'd been able to give her some sign he'd been alive. There was no telling the grief she'd been enduring.

"I survived and I'm here to get her. And all of you," he added before looking at AJ, still sprawled on the floor, straddled by the girl. Devon looked over his shoulder to see Steve and Danny wearing shit-eating grins. Thank God, Trent covered their asses because their attention had been derailed.

Glancing back at his brother, he shook his head. Poor AJ. He just couldn't catch a break with these guys. They were always on his ass about something. This would be the big story on the flight home. A chuckle slipped out against his will. It was fucking funny. "AJ, get the hell up." He turned back to the girls. "Where *is* Rylee?"

"They took her hours ago, and she never came back," the girl climbing off his brother said.

Had they sold her already? Were they raping her? Torturing her? Pain stabbed at him as if his heart had been ripped from his chest in a brutal assault. Devon couldn't be too late. *Couldn't.*

Chapter Thirty-Two

Devon's heart nearly stopped. "Where?" he barked out as he holstered his weapon. The poor girls, who'd appeared defiant in their attempt to escape, now looked scared shitless. He hadn't meant to make them jump, but dammit, he wanted his wife. Right the fuck now.

"Th-they—" one of the twins stammered with a quivering lip. A gulp slipped down her throat.

"They took her to see the boss," a red-haired girl said matter-of-factly.

"Fuck!" he roared and spun in a circle tossing his arms up. "Fucking Carver." God, he wanted to punch something, and he'd never been violent. It was why he'd joined the agency instead of a gun-toting job like his brothers. Something behind a computer and without a weapon. This situation sorely tested that restraint.

Taking a deep breath to bring down the hostility within, he focused. Finding Rylee was all that mattered; it was the key to soothing his soul. Jesse's team was in the main area of the house where they'd expected to find Carver. Devon hadn't heard his team check in. Then again, they hadn't checked in either.

Devon's heart pounded soundly against his breastbone, as if seeking an escape to the turmoil. Enough was enough. No more following the fucking leader. This was *his* wife. That made this *his* mission. Bucking up and snapping his body straight, he turned to

AJ with steel in his resolve. "You and Trent are with me." His thumb pointed toward his chest to ensure there was no confusion. Then, Devon spun and hustled out of the room at what he could've sworn, had he taken longer to observe, was a grin from his baby brother.

Outside the room, he halted and hailed Jesse over the comms. "We've got the girls. Rylee's with Carver. Do you have her?" he said in clipped tones, ready to race to his wife's side. Yet, something held him back. Something that told him not to leave the area. Maybe it was mission planning. Maybe it was something else. He couldn't describe it, but he obeyed that overwhelming urge and waited for a response.

In his mind, it took hours for that answer, even though it was spoken in his ear almost instantaneously. "We've got Carver and she's not here," Jesse said.

"Ask him where the fuck she is." Devon's hands clenched at his sides, and he could sense his anger rushing into reason as his pulse increased and adrenaline infused him.

"Can't do it. Matt introduced his fist to the man's face, and he's taking a nap."

Devon's stomach plummeted to his feet. Wanting to rant at Matt for making this harder on them, he held back because he didn't have time. Squeezing his eyes shut, a shot of despair lanced his heart. He'd never forgive himself if they'd sold her that afternoon while the men had waited. His head snapped up. No way would he allow those emotions to run through him. "Okay," Devon said to his two brothers in the hallway. "We still need to check each room on this wing."

At the other end of the hall, Neftali and Jamaal, from Jesse's team, appeared. They nodded and went to the first door, and Matt and Kate came around the corner next and went to the second. They had six rooms to check and Jesse had just made it faster. *Thank you, big brother.*

Like the others, they could've done the job in twos, but no one questioned his wanting his brothers to have his back. Besides, they'd both worked with Rylee and didn't like the situation any more than he did.

"On me." He led them to a door. While not the nearest, something drew him there. Did he imagine the noise? Listening intently, it didn't reappear. It didn't matter. Devon had chosen and he'd stick to this door.

Nodding, they removed handguns, and he took a deep breath. Once they were set, AJ opened the door and Devon led them in, weapon sweeping the room from left to right for any threat. An empty bedroom. That feeling of despair tried to peek its ugly head into him again, but he set his jaw and squashed it.

Hearing a noise in an adjoining room, they silently continued until they entered the brightly lit room, Devon stopped dead in his tracks at a sight that almost drove him to his knees.

To his horror, none other than Jackie stood behind a kneeling Rylee, bloody and naked, and his blood ran cold. With her hands twisted in Rylee's hair, Jackie tugged and his wife's head leaned back exposing her neck to the shiny knife Jackie held there.

This time he allowed his rage to soak in, but held a firm control of it. He couldn't allow this to happen again. Counting on the men had their aim on Jackie, he allowed his gaze to meet his wife's.

"Devon." Rylee's disbelief swam in her voice and features, and a tear slipped down her cheek. She tried to move toward him, but was held in place. "You're alive."

Something inside him almost broke at her emotions. If that bastard let anyone touch her, he'd kill him. "I am," he said calmly. "And, I'm here to take you home." He'd love nothing more than to banter with her, and soothe her physical and emotional ailments, but a little bitch needed to be taken care of first.

"Hello, Devon," Jackie said.

Turning his attention upward, Devon narrowed his eyes at his wife's threat. "Jackie," he bit out. Only the top of his wife's head if his aim wasn't true. Why couldn't the woman be taller? He sensed his brothers behind him. And while he wanted to make them leave and not look at his wife's unclothed body, he needed them there. If nothing more than moral support. He *would* get Rylee out of this.

The woman tightened her grip on Rylee's hair, and her eyes darted between the men.

"Let her go." Devon's hands felt clammy on the weapon and a slight tremble appeared. He willed it away, but it remained. At least it didn't get worse as his nervousness amped up.

"Are you willing to risk my hand not slipping if you were to shoot me? How about instead"—she licked her lips and his stomach revolted—"I get a ticket outta here. I can give you names and whatever you need to put Carver behind bars."

"Shoot her, Devon. Don't trust her." Rylee's words may have been strong, but there'd been fear laced in them that maybe only he could hear. Did she fear his failure? He couldn't have that.

Jackie jerked Rylee's head back and his wife's

eyes gleamed with fury. "Shut up," Jackie said.

The tremble on his Glock disappeared and his aim, he knew, held true.

"I can take her," Trent said.

"Me, too," AJ added.

Relief flooded him just as it bolstered him. Rage like he'd never known flowed through his veins. "Why should I trust you? Last time you offered information, you murdered a CIA operative." Devon's finger lightly touched the trigger. Just one movement from Jackie was all he needed.

"Carver ordered me to do it." The little bitch's flippancy grated on his strained nerves.

"Release Rylee and we'll bring you in. In fact, you can talk with the FBI deputy director." Let Arthur deal with the fucking shit.

"Liar." A small bead of blood formed on Rylee's neck when Jackie's knife pushed against her throat.

That slight movement of her hand was all it took. Devon pulled the trigger. Jackie gasped and her eyes bulged before she crumpled to the floor. He then slid across the floor on his knees to his wife. "Rylee."

Lifting her into his arms, he barked out orders to the men. While awake, all her fire was gone and a grogginess had overtaken her. He stood and laid her on the bed in the adjoining room and either AJ or Trent, hell, he didn't care who, handed him a blanket to cover her. It didn't take long for the light-colored blanket to have streaks of blood from her two wounds.

Touching her face ever so lightly, he whispered her name. Her eyes fluttered open and she smiled at him. Devon stood, ready to call for Matt.

"I'm here," Matt bounded into the door. While not

a medic, Matt's SEAL training set him up as the closest thing they had to one. They really needed to hire a real medic though. It wasn't fair to his brother since his training only went so far.

Glancing at the door, he saw most of the team congregating.

Matt worked as gently as possible with her naked body covered.

Devon watched like a hawk to make sure of it. He should've shooed the men out, but knew they were only concerned about her condition. Running his fingers through his hair in frustration and worry, he watched Matt wipe away blood and probe. "How is she?"

"Patience, I just got here." Matt checked her eyes and asked her how she felt. She told him she was nauseous. Then, she rolled on her side and threw up all over a silky-looking bedcover.

Standing, Matt smiled. "I think she'll be fine. The gash on her stomach could use a couple of stitches, but she can wait for those. I'll bind it good enough for now. Give me about five more minutes and we'll be ready to go. Are you planning to carry her the entire way?"

"Yeah," he said incredulously. As if he'd let another man handle her.

"Walk," Rylee said weakly.

Rushing to kneel beside the bed, Devon held her hand between both of his. "Rylee, we may have to hurry out of here."

"Please. I need to walk out of this hellhole," she pleaded.

Devon looked at Matt, who nodded, and then back at his wife. "Okay. You can walk, but if you get tired or start bleeding, I'm carrying you."

Her free hand cupped his cheek, and he leaned into the softness. Immediately, all felt right in his world.

"I love you, Devon."

His world achieved perfection. Hearing the words was as sweet as he thought it would be. "I love you, too."

"Great, everybody fucking loves everybody," Trent said from the doorway. "Can we get this show on the road before the locals move the fuck in?"

With that, Matt took care of Rylee, then Kate helped her dress. And on her two feet, they walked out of Carver's and into waiting vans. Although he guessed Rylee could make it, when she stumbled at the front door, he hoisted her into his arms and carried her to their transport.

Sitting with Rylee across his lap, Devon only half listened to the chatter over the comm system. His focus was on her. She was becoming more lucid.

"The girls?" she asked with her hands wrapped in his T-shirt.

"We got them. Arthur acquired a second plane so we can take them home."

"I want to be with them."

"Hang the fuck on!" Mike, their driver, shouted.

Devon tensed, as did his wife. She slipped off his lap to the seat next to him that'd been left vacant. Fumbling a bit, she connected her seat belt.

"What's going on?" she whispered.

"I don't know yet." Focusing on the comm, he heard what they'd been trying to avoid. "Fuck," he said. "Belize authorities are chasing us."

The van swerved into the opposite lane to pass a car and swerved back to avoid an oncoming vehicle.

"I take it we're not stopping."

Reaching down, Devon clasped her hand in his, felt the tremble in hers, and held it tight. Rylee drugged, even if she was coming down from the effects, wasn't the tough and strong woman he'd fallen in love with. Oh, he still loved this one, but his woman would be ready to kick some butt, not sit here with a tremble, even as slight as it was.

Another swerve and he reached to the ceiling to hold himself in place. They had three vans that needed to outrun the locals. Arthur was supposed to have cleared the way as best he could, but they knew the government didn't approve. Hell, they might not even be real police. HIS wouldn't be finding out.

"Dragonfly," Jesse stated firmly in Devon's earpiece. Drivers were to proceed to their alternate route.

Gunfire erupted and the van careened to the right, and he slid into his wife on the left. Straightening, but keeping his head down, Devon asked, "Are you okay?"

Maybe the jostling was clearing her mind, because the eyes that looked back at him appeared clean and focused. "Fine. Is there a plan?"

Here they were running for what could truly be their lives, and like an idiot, he laughed, a big, deep and come up happy laugh. Thankfully no one either took notice or said a thing about it. Maybe they thought he'd lost it. Maybe he had. All he knew was he had Rylee by his side, and that was all that mattered. "With Jesse, there's always a plan and a backup plan and another backup plan."

"Listen up. Steve lost our tail so we'll clear the airport for you. Don't engage unless you absolutely have to. And, don't...dilly-dally." Jesse must be watching his language since he had the girls with him because Devon expected something coarser from him in that directive.

With one hand on the seat in front of him, he slipped his other out of Rylee's and wound it around her shoulders, then pulled her snug up against him. Kissing the top of her head, he said, "I love you."

"I love you, too."

A smile embedded itself and he couldn't imagine it would ever go away.

"We've got a bit of space, sit up at your own risk," Mike advised.

Brave, but not stupid, everyone slowly rose and peered over their shoulders to double-check Mike's bit of space.

After much bouncing and jerking back and forth in the van, Mike warned them that they were approaching the airport. The unbuckling of Rylee's seatbelt—as he imagined she was the only one who wore one—and the clicking of clips being released and reinserted in rifles filled the silence. When Mike slammed on the brakes, the door was slung open and Devon grasped Rylee's hand following AJ out. His job was to get Rylee there, not worry about anything else, so they raced to the plane, and with its engines ready, amidst gunfire, but from what he could tell, it was only from their men to the vehicle that had chased them.

Pushing her in front of him, he hustled her up the stairs, keeping himself plastered behind her in case their pursuers engaged and a bullet happened to make it their way.

Flinging herself into a seat on board the aircraft,

Rylee bent over, working to catch her breath, and Devon sat next to her and breathed a sigh of utter relief.

His wife was safe.

Epilogue

A couple of months had passed, and Devon and Rylee were enjoying married life and living together. Except for her habit of ironing his jeans and the sheets. She believed everything should be pressed and that drove him nuts.

Knowing how close he came to losing her still had the power to bring him to his knees. With her now a member of HIS, he imagined he'd hyperventilate many times while she was out with the team. While Devon had had his fun playing rescuer, behind the computer was where he was comfortable. It was where the team needed him.

Glancing around the room once more to make sure it was ready, he approached the bed and spread out the rose petals more. Chilling was non-alcoholic cider instead of champagne. They'd both decided they didn't care for another alcoholic drink, and he didn't see this occasion being any different since the first time they'd been together was the catalyst in that agreement.

He swiped the key card off the table, shoved his wallet and phone in his pockets, and exited the room. The great thing about the high-roller room was there were separate elevators for their floor and two others. Less wait time.

On the main floor, the noise was almost overpowering, but he did his best to ignore it and sought his brother. Devon found him at the bar in the middle of the activity of slot machines. Before approaching, he watched Matt for a few moments. Hell, another wedding for him. Another reminder of what he'd lost.

With a friendly slap on the shoulder, he slid onto the barstool beside his brother. He hailed the masculine bartender. "Bottle of water."

With a harrumph, the man turned to, hopefully, fill Devon's order.

"I hope you're not going to drink that," Matt said.

The unhappy employee returned, twisted the top off a bottle of water, and slapped it in front of Devon, and turned away.

He shrugged. "Not on your life. Has the bartender gone anywhere?"

Bringing a beer bottle to his lips, Matt shook his head and then appeared to take a drink, but Devon knew he'd only done it for show. Scratching at the label wrapped around the neck of the plastic bottle, he approached the touchy topic he'd wanted to discuss. "I can check in on her again if you want."

Matt hesitated, rolling the beer bottle between his hands. "No. I said the last time would be it. I meant it."

Devon sighed, a wash of sadness for his brother slipping through. "You really should go see her."

"And do what? She left, remember? She blamed me and left."

It always came back to that, and if the shoe were on the other foot, he wasn't sure what he'd do. All he knew was that Matt had loved Caitlyn enough that they'd planned to marry. He couldn't imagine ever giving up on Rylee. So how could Matt give up on

Caitlyn? "You know she didn't mean it."

"Yes, she did."

"What about her dad? You two were close. Go visit him." Maybe then the two would run into each other even though she'd moved away.

Shifting in his seat, Matt cleared his throat. "I saw him when we were in Oxford. He invited me to come back. Promised she wouldn't be there."

Big ass first step chancing that visit. Maybe there was hope for Matt after all. "Are you going?"

"I don't know. It's a lot to deal with." The beer bottle spun in his hands again, and liquid sloshed over the top giving away Matt's ruse at drinking. He stilled the bottle and began to wipe up the mess. "It was my fault."

"Matt, you know better. You can't guarantee you'd have been able to prevent it."

"At least I could've tried." He stood, something akin to resignation on his face. "I thought we were here to get this asshole and then get you married. Or married again." He nodded behind Devon who turned and saw two uniformed officers walking toward them.

Allowing for the brisk change of topic, he smiled and stood. "That we are."

"Hey, buddy," he called to the bartender. "Can you come here a minute?"

The man looked nervously over Devon's shoulder but approached. "What can I get ya?"

"You can get around here so these nice officers can arrest you for drugging women." Devon was sickened at what the man had done—he'd drug women and then his friend lured them away where they had parties with the unsuspecting women later. Rylee had been a mark for the two of them. After they'd married, Devon and Rylee had stopped in this bar. She'd ordered the drinks while he'd gone to the restroom. He was certain that was why she felt out of sorts when they'd returned to the room. Somehow, he believed it was also responsible for her losing the entire evening because she'd been lucid while they'd enjoyed the strip—eating, gambling, wandering the streets, falling in love, and getting married.

He wanted to launch himself at the man for even thinking of hurting his wife.

"I don't know what you're talking about, man."

"Don't even try to play innocent. Your buddy is already in custody, and he likes to talk."

Fear laced the man's eyes and he darted them around the men.

The officers stepped forward and Devon and Matt handed them their bottles. They had no idea if the man would drug men, but they weren't taking a chance. Then, they turned away, ready for the rest of the day.

With Rylee having no memory of their first wedding and their friends having missed it, they were getting married again.

"We'd best hurry. Brad and Madison might end up strangling each other."

Devon snorted. Truer words had never been spoken. He wouldn't tell a soul he'd seen Madison leave Brad's room that morning. They appeared to have a love-hate relationship.

The two brothers wove their way around gaming tables and slot machines until they stepped out on the Las Vegas Strip. He'd thought his wife would've chosen a traditional wedding, but, in her odd sense of humor, she said they needed to go back to where they'd started. So, they swarmed the same chapel he and Rylee had married in the first time—Graceland Wedding Chapel.

He inventoried the guests—Jesse and Kate, AJ and Megan with little Alex, Jake and Em, Brad, Matt, Madison, and most of the men on the team. A slight frown appeared. If only Trent could've been here. He'd taken off right after they'd returned with Rylee. Helping family on the mission wasn't the same as accepting that his parents had lied to him all his life, nor that he'd almost died doing his job. Devon would have to keep an eye on him and when it was time, they'd bring him back into the fold.

The organ began to play and everyone settled, eyes on the doorway in the rear of the room. In she walked, and his eyes almost popped out of his head. Stunning was the first word that came to mind. He'd never seen Rylee really dressed up, and in an ivory lace dress that reached about midcalf, she made a fetching picture.

When she reached him, he couldn't resist and pulled her in for a kiss. They finally broke apart when their official imparted, "We're not at that part yet."

Laughter bubbled up out of the two of them at their Elvis impersonator's accent. It would be a wedding neither would forget.

A word about the author...

Sheila Kell writes about the romantic men who leave women's hearts pounding with a happily ever after built on memorable, adrenaline-pumping stories. Her debut novel, His Desire (HIS Series #1), launched as an Amazon #1 romantic suspense bestseller, later winning the Readers' Favorite award for best romantic suspense novel.

As a Southern girl who has left behind her days with the U.S. Air Force, and as a University Vice President, she can usually be found in South Mississippi, where she lives with her cats and all the strays that magically find her front door. When she isn't writing, she has her nose in a good book, is dealing with the woodland critters who enjoy her back porch, or is wishing she had a genie to do her bidding.

Ways to connect
SheilaKell.com
facebook.com/sheilakellbooks
goodreads.com/sheilakellbook
bookbub.com/authors/sheila-kell

I'd love to hear directly from you, too. Please feel free to email me at sheila@sheilakell.com.

Don't miss out on new releases, exclusive excerpts and giveaways!

Join my newsletter:
www.SheilaKell.com/subscribe

www.ingramcontent.com/pod-product-compliance
Lightning Source LLC
Chambersburg PA
CBHW052003020726
47501CB00004B/985

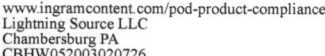